HERCULES

THE LEGENDARY JOURNEYS ™

The Official Companion

by

ROBERT WEISBROT

D1445606

A DOUBLEDAY BOOK

For Brad Carpenter
— R . W .

A Doubleday Book

Published by
Bantam Doubleday Dell Publishing Group, Inc.
1540 Broadway
New York, New York 10036

Library of Congress Cataloging-in-Publication Data
Weisbrot, Robert.
    Hercules, the legendary journeys : the official companion / by Robert
Weisbrot.
        p.   cm.
    Summary: A companion volume to the television series about Hercules,
featuring interviews with the stars, producers, and behind-the-scenes wizards, an
episode guide, and information about the myths behind the show.
    ISBN 0-385-32569-X
    1. Hercules, the legendary journeys (Television program)—Juvenile literature.
[1. Hercules, the legendary journeys (Television program)]   I. Title.
PN1992.77.H44W45   1998
791.45′72—dc21   97-40806
                                                                           CIP
                                                                           AC

The text of this book is set in 10.25-point Janson Text.

Book design by Semadar Megged

Manufactured in the United States of America

February 1998

10   9   8   7   6   5   4   3   2   1

Acknowledgments

I experienced the power of Hercules nearly two years ago. I was writing a book on the Cuban missile crisis—the "Thirteen Days" when America and Russia nearly went to war. But at the same time I was becoming immersed in a unique TV series marked by epic adventure, sly humor, stunning production, and a hero whose appeal lay in his vulnerability as well as his fabled physique. Suddenly I realized that the Twelve Labors were even more compelling to me than the Thirteen Days. This book on *Hercules: The Legendary Journeys* is the result.

In writing this book, I was privileged to have the cooperation of producers, cast, and crew members, whom I found as remarkable for their kindness as for their artistic talent. I am especially indebted to executive producer Rob Tapert, who allowed me the fullest access to all aspects of production and the fullest freedom in writing about him and the series. His unfailing generosity has been deeply gratifying, both personally and professionally.

Kevin Sorbo took time, amid an extremely demanding schedule, to afford me numerous interviews, always with grace and good humor. His warm assistance proved invaluable and delightful. Michael Hurst, the first person I interviewed in Auckland, provided a wonderfully invigorating start to my New Zealand stay and extended every possible courtesy throughout my project.

This book greatly benefited from interviews with Peter Bell, Robert Bielak, Tim Boggs, Marisa Borchers, Jerry Patrick Brown, Bruce Campbell, Sam Clark, Andrew Dettman, Ngila Dickson, David Eick, Dan Filie, Liz Friedman, Robert Gillies, Galyn Gorg, Eric Gruendemann, Tracy Hampton, Charlie Haskell, Liddy Holloway, Beth Hymson-Ayer, Bernie Joyce, Tawny Kitaen, Lucy Lawless, Joseph Lo Duca, George Lyle, John Mahaffie, Ned Nalle, Renee O'Connor, Kevin O'Neill, Sam Raimi, Claire Richardson, Diana Rowan, Josh Schneider, John Schulian, Chloe Smith, Kevin Smith, Rob Tapert, Jeffrey Thomas, Erik Thomson, Robert Trebor, Daniel Truly, Alexandra Tydings, and Christian Williams. I am indebted, too, to Joseph Anderson for typing accurate transcripts of several dozen interviews, without which I would still be preparing notes for the book.

Eric Gruendemann, already balancing myriad tasks of production, warmly expedited my work in New Zealand. Claire Richardson acted as a guardian angel on set; Jane Lindsay arranged with notable efficiency for housing and contacts with cast members; Joanna Henaghan helped me orient before and during my stay; and Tim Stewart facilitated my travels and my contacts with Kevin Sorbo.

This book is at once shorter and stronger thanks to my editor, Fiona Simpson, who offered many valuable ideas and reviewed my manuscript with an enviable gift for grammatical precision. In addition, her early enthusiasm for the series was crucial in moving the project forward. So was the readiness of Nancy Cushing-Jones, president of Universal Studios Publishing Rights, to extend an opportunity to me despite my inexperience in this genre. Cindy Chang, senior director of Universal Studios Publishing Rights, expertly coordinated my efforts with those of Universal, Doubleday, and Renaissance Pictures, and helped speed my progress. I would also like to thank Sue Binder, Jeff Cruce, Stephanie Meyer, and Crystal Anne Taylor for their thoughtful assistance.

Finally, I wish to express a personal word of appreciation to my wife, Andrea, for her keen critical eye, her creative suggestions, and her loving support in welcoming Hercules into our lives; to my parents, for their constant encouragement and help; to John Schulian, for his warm interest in my work; and to Brad Carpenter, whose kindness has been an inspiration.

Contents

HERCULES

THE LEGEND BEGINS

Old myths never die or even fade away. Thousands of years after the ancient Greeks first told the epic tales of Mount Olympus, we still delight in their heroes, gods, and adventures. But we tell these stories now, on shows like *Hercules: The Legendary Journeys*, in ways that speak to our own age, our own hopes and desires.

Hercules was the greatest of all Greek heroes. He embodied virtues the ancients most admired: strength, courage, and devotion to the greater good. The son of Zeus, king of the gods, and Alcmene, a beautiful mortal woman, Hercules was forced by Zeus' jealous wife, the goddess Hera, to battle giants, tame ferocious beasts, and hunt treasures at the world's edge—and beyond. Yet no labor could withstand his club, his arrows, and above all, his fierce will. Hailed as the mightiest man ever to walk the earth, Hercules proved he could outwit as well as overpower enemies, whether human or divine. His deeds inspired dreams of glory and the faith that people could face seemingly impossible challenges—and overcome them all.

Down through the ages the name Hercules has stood for invincible valor. Hercules' triumphs set the standard by which other heroes are measured. Today our craving for heroes is as great as ever, but the demand is not easily met. So it is no surprise that television should go back through the mists of time and legend to find Hercules, an ancient hero for a new day. Starting as the hero of five action-packed TV movies in 1994, Hercules quickly became a legendary hit and, ultimately, the star of a syndicated TV series. Combining action, adventure, great characters, humor, and a little romance, the series debuted to high ratings and even critical praise.

In June 1995 an article in *Newsweek* praised, albeit sheepishly, the Hercules phenomenon. "The first surprising thing," it noted, "is that it isn't dubbed. It's not some strutting body-builder in a toga battling crude special effects on an Italian back lot. This is an all-American Hercules . . . with big-screen production values and a knowing '90s sensibility."

"Even more shocking," *Newsweek* admitted, "is that [the show] 'Hercules' is actually good." For this the magazine tipped its helmet first to Kevin Sorbo's "supremely relaxed" portrayal, his "azure eyes hinting at a brain and a sly sense of humor." It also credited Sam Raimi's talent for "genre pop," though in fact Rob Tapert, Raimi's less heralded partner, had chiefly given *Hercules* its vision and vitality. *Newsweek* stood on firmer ground, though, when it proclaimed the surging popularity of TV's updated mythic hero: "Move over, Steve Reeves, for a '90s 'Hercules.' "

The Action Pack

The journey Hercules took to become the mightiest action figure on television ranks as one of his longest and least reported labors. It began in late 1992, shortly after Ned Nalle, then executive vice president for Universal Television, met with the powerful Tribune Stations, which controlled twenty percent of the syndicated television market, and asked, "What are you guys missing?" Their reply: "Sports and action movies." Sports posed a problem for Universal, because the company had no experience broadcasting athletic events. But action movies sounded promising. Independent stations that had once played action flicks at eight o'clock on weeknights were losing them to cable TV. Here was a void that Universal, with its record of landmark action productions like *Miami Vice* and *Crime Story*, was well qualified to fill. The question was, who would be television's new heroes?

Nalle and Dan Filie, the senior vice president for drama development, decided to create a movie "wheel" featuring different action characters on alternate weeks. Their idea recalled the glory days of the NBC Sunday night "Mystery Movie," which during the 1970s rotated hits like *McCloud*, with Dennis Weaver as a New Mexico policeman transplanted to New York City, *McMillan and Wife*, starring Rock Hudson as a police commissioner and family man, and *Columbo*, with Peter Falk as the sly, rumpled detective. Now the movie wheel would turn again, but this time action, not suspense, would pull it to ratings success.

Nalle and Filie assembled a team of exceptional stature to create potential "spokes" in this new movie wheel, dubbed the "Action Pack." They invited Hal Needham, director of two hugely successful "good old boy" chase flicks, *Smokey and the Bandit* I and II, to do *Bandit* III, IV, and more, only now for the small screen. William Shatner, a television icon basking in the glow of six high-grossing *Star Trek* movies, was then pitching a new sci-fi project to the networks, *Tek War*; Filie brought him on board as well. He also enlisted Rob Cohen, who had just directed an imaginative film biography, *Dragon: The Bruce Lee Story*, to shoot *Vanishing Son*, the adventures of an Asian American martial artist falsely accused of killing two federal agents. Before coming to Universal, Filie had developed a script for ABC with filmmaker George Gallo called *Midnight Run*, and he now recruited Gallo to direct the syndicated TV version. John Landis, whose movie credits ranged from the John Belushi–Dan Aykroyd comedy *The Blues Brothers* to a segment of *The Twilight Zone* movie and whose TV credits include *Dream On*, also signed on, to film *Fast Lane*. Filie might well have rested content with having lured five major film talents to his TV movie mix, an extraordinary achievement, but he felt the need to add one more genre—"sword and sandal."

"The title that we were kicking around was *Conan* or *Hercules*," Filie recalls. Everyone thought it might be a good addition "just to differentiate" one genre from the others. "No one was really excited about it," though, "because we didn't know what the take was." But at this early planning stage, what mattered was simply to present an array of projects from which the syndicated station groups might choose a couple, "and we'd make a whole bunch of those individual titles. Originally we were going to call [these projects] 'the Magnificent Seven,' only we ended up with six."

To round out this remarkable roster of producers and directors, Filie called on two innovative young filmmakers, Sam Raimi and Rob Tapert, to bring Conan or Hercules to life for several television movies. Friends since their days at Michigan State University, where Tapert roomed with Raimi's older brother Ivan, the two had first collaborated as undergraduates on an hour-long Super-8 movie, *The Happy Valley Kid*, which became a campus sensation. By January 1979 Raimi, a sophomore, and Tapert, just several months from graduation, felt ready for bigger projects, and dropped out of college to write, direct, and produce a horror movie. They soon discovered that attempting this without money or prior feature-film credits could make for a real-life horror story.

Just after resolving to pour all their time and money into filmmaking, Raimi and Tapert were evicted from their apartment when neighbors complained of the noise from their artistic endeavors. They persevered to make a Super-8 short subject to lure investors and raised $100,000 to finance four months of round-the-clock filming, but ran out of money midway through their movie. Brushing off these disasters as short-term nuisances, they completed their film in 1981, handling ever more tasks themselves as the crew dwindled during the last five weeks of production to the star, the sound man, and the cook. Finding a distributor added more than another year's frantic effort. But in 1983 *The Evil Dead* at last began to haunt theatergoers across the country, and brought Raimi and Tapert a cult following among horror fans, critics, and fellow moviemakers.

A supernatural thriller, *The Evil Dead* winked at audiences while jolting them. The acclaim for its mix of humor and horror generated two sequels, *Evil Dead 2* (1987) and *Army of Darkness* (1993), more violent but also more polished than the original. With Raimi directing, Tapert producing for "Renaissance Pictures," and Raimi's high school friend Bruce Campbell playing a reluctant hero beset by spirits out for blood (and souls), the films dazzled viewers with unusual camera angles, fast-paced editing, and gripping effects on a budget as bare-bones as the movies' deadly skeletons. Among the ardent admirers of Raimi and Tapert's offbeat cinematic style were Universal's Ned Nalle and Dan Filie.

Shortly after *Army of Darkness* finished shooting, Filie called Tapert and David Eick, head of TV Development for Renaissance Pictures, and asked, "Do you guys want to do *Hercules* or *Conan*?" But they were then in New Orleans producing a Jean-Claude Van Damme adventure, *Hard Target*. Eick shrugged off the offer: "You should talk to Sam, I don't know, we're kind of busy." Filie next repeated the offer to Raimi, but he

Legendary Facts

Bruce Campbell now appears frequently on *Hercules: The Legendary Journeys* as Autolycus, the Prince of Thieves.

was in North Carolina helping direct *The Hudsucker Proxy*, and hesitated: "Oh, I don't know. What kind of commitment do you need, sir?" (Raimi's male friends as well as first-time callers are greeted as "sir.") Filie urged, "Give me three weeks. Because in three weeks, we'll have either sold it, in which case we can switch you with somebody else, or they won't like it and you'll be off the hook." Raimi came on board, in effect lending his name as a master stylist to help Filie pitch his "action movie wheel" to syndicators.

To sell the "Magnificent Six" Filie prepared a presentation tape that featured the directors each speaking briefly about their projects, intercut with clips from their movies. Hal Needham's segment, Filie recalled, "had a whole bunch of [*Smokey and the*] *Bandit* and *Cannonball Run* stuff, for *Midnight Run* we showed clips of the original movie, for William Shatner we cheated, I think we showed scenes from *Blade Runner* just to give a sci-fi feel, it wasn't for broadcast, so . . . for *Fast Lane*, we showed clips from *Blues Brothers* and chase scenes from some Landis films, and for *Vanishing Son*, we took pieces of *Dragon: The Bruce Lee Story*. For *Hercules*, we cobbled together bits of *Conan*, *Army of Darkness*, and other things. The only thing we had was Sam on-screen, going, "Get ready for action, get ready for adventure, get ready for *Hercules*!"

Early in 1993 Nalle and Filie presented their "Action Pack" tape to the heads of two syndication station groups. At first glance they had little to show: Not a scene from the proposed movies had actually been shot, or cast; and some projects, including *Hercules*, lacked even a clear plan, let alone a script or two. But in Hollywood, deals have been made out of less. Nalle and Filie had brought to this meeting two irresistible assets: an idea perfectly pitched to stations desperate for a steady supply of action, and six prospective directors with box office clout; in Filie's words, "This was an impressive group of guys."

The meeting exceeded both of their hopes. Rather than picking a couple of items from the six-course menu, the syndicated station groups bought them all. And *Hercules*, originally a curiosity included for variety and the thump of that powerful eight-letter name, was suddenly a full-fledged member of Universal's Action Pack.

But just what kind of hero would Hercules be? Beyond the obvious aspect of his great power, no one really knew. Until now, it hadn't much mattered. The only feat of strength Universal had counted on from Hercules was to help lift the movie wheel. No one cared whether the strongman could actually carry several made-for-television movies. Suddenly, though, Universal faced an urgent and taxing question: How could an ancient Greek character win over modern audiences accustomed to high-speed chases, high-fashion locales, and high-powered shoot-outs?

Legendary Facts

Hercules was almost *Conan the Barbarian*! Raimi and Tapert originally thought they'd rather do Conan, but a question about who owned the rights to the character led them back to *Hercules*.

The Five Labors of Hercules:

LAUNCHING THE TV MOVIES

By the time Filie cleared the last hurdles to production by selling the Action Pack to independent stations nationwide, Sam Raimi was preparing to direct an offbeat Western, *The Quick and the Dead*, with Sharon Stone doing a Clint Eastwood turn as a mysterious gunfighter out for revenge. But fortunately for Filie, "Rob Tapert started to get the itch to make *Hercules*. He'd taken the 'Nestea Plunge' into the myths, started to feel hooked on the idea of retelling them . . . and he was seeing the possibilities. And he worked out a kind of take on it based on the *Army of Darkness* tape."

Raimi and Tapert quickly realized that the original Greek myths would not work for television: They were too tragic and shocking to lure a mass audience. Yes, Hercules had exciting adventures: He killed a rampaging lion by choking it to death, subdued a giant bull, brought back the hellhound Cerberus from the underworld, held the earth on his back until the Titan Atlas could return with several prized golden apples, slew the poisonous Stymphalian birds, and, with each new labor, made the world safe for Greek civilization. Yet there was also a darker side to Hercules, as with all Greek heroes.

The Hercules of the ancient tales was not only strong but headstrong: Badgered as a teenager by his music teacher for being clumsy and slow, the enraged Hercules raised his stringed instrument and crushed his teacher's

Legendary Facts

The twelve labors of Hercules were:

1. Kill the Nemean lion.
2. Kill the Hydra (a nine-headed monster).
3. Capture a stag with golden horns without harming it.
4. Capture a giant boar.
5. Clean the Augean stables.
6. Kill the Stymphalian birds.
7. Go to Crete and capture a savage bull.
8. Capture the man-eating mares of Thrace.
9. Bring back the girdle of Hippolyta, Queen of the Amazons.
10. Bring back the cattle of Geryon (a monster with three bodies).
11. Bring back the Golden Apples of the Hesperides.
12. Bring Cerberus, the three-headed, dog up from Hades.

skull with it. Years later Hercules appeared finally to have mastered his emotions, becoming a devoted husband and father. But his vindictive stepmother, the goddess Hera, sent him into a fit of madness, during which he killed his wife and three children. He performed his twelve famous labors to atone for these crimes. Such horrific deeds fit the ancient Greek view of a world marked by mindless violence as well as courage, and by terrible human weakness as well as great strength and moral purpose. But this bleak vision would scarcely appeal to modern audiences raised on upright heroes and happy endings. Raimi and Tapert turned next for inspiration to the wave of Italian movies during the 1950s and 1960s that exalted Hercules and other ancient heroes.

The Italian "sword and sandal" pictures solved the commercial problems of selling Greek tragedy by simply omitting it. Instead they offered action and spectacle in abundance, and brightened the myths, often beyond recognition, by making the heroes unfailingly good and the endings invariably happy. Still, Hercules did not catch on as a movie character in America until rescued by a former salesman-turned-shopkeeper-turned restaurant owner-turned-driving instructor-turned-small-time movie distributor, Joseph E. Levine—one of the canniest cultural merchants of modern times.

In 1958 Levine learned of a low-budget Italian flick, *Hercules*, starring Steve Reeves. Already passed over by American distributors, the film transfixed Levine with its commercial possibilities. "It had action and sex, a near shipwreck, gorgeous women on an island, and a guy tearing a goddamn building apart," he summed up its selling points, then noted its one convincing special effect: "And where did you ever see a guy with a body like Reeves has?" Levine might have added that Reeves also had a magnificent voice—though only on loan. When Levine bought the picture for a rock-bottom $120,000, he dubbed in English dialogue, even for Reeves, who, he rightly surmised, "ain't gonna win no Oscar this year."

The solemn epic tone of this low-budget flick might invite ridicule, but Reeves' appearance inspired wonder. When he raised his arms to the gods, viewers forgot about the cheap sets, the poorly synched dubbing, even the gods themselves, and simply riveted their gaze on the actor's sparkling blue eyes and awesome physique. *Hercules* might not impress as art, but audiences were dazzled by Reeves and nodded in agreement: Here *was* Hercules.

While Reeves was the focus of all eyes, he owed much of his soaring fame to the marketing genius of the movie's feisty distributor.

Legendary Facts

Steve Reeves, the original Hercules, was Mr. Universe in 1950.

"If this picture had a star," Levine said, "it'd be a flop. Nobody could imagine that even Clark Gable or Victor Mature could do such things. But they never heard of Reeves—a year ago he couldn't have got arrested—so they'll believe anything he does." To further help people believe, Levine organized a promotional campaign as mighty as any of the Twelve Labors (and costing eight times Levine's purchase of the film): He sponsored Hercules comics, "Herculean Hamburgers," and Test-Your-Strength machines placed in key cities, making a contribution to charity every time a local muscleman rang the bell. In a savvy act of restraint, he did all this without the aid of his leading man. "I don't want Steve over here for the buildup," Levine explained. "With clothes on, he ain't Hercules."

Critics rushed to pan *Hercules*. They called it "one of the funniest pictures to reach U.S. screens in years—although the humor is not deliberate." *Time* magazine conceded that "Reeves's acting is considerably more expressive than King Kong's" and noted his ambition to star in a Western, "apparently unaware that he is making nothing but Westerns already." Acknowledging the countless movie sequels, remakes, and familiar variations that the movie spawned, the *New York Times* some years later crowned *Hercules* "the original mistake."

But *Hercules* brushed aside its detractors. It opened in 145 neighborhood theaters and made $900,000 in its first week. Soon Levine had 600 Eastmancolor prints ready to show, the largest order Pathé Labs had ever filled. *Hercules* packed 135 theaters in New York City alone. Reeves became for a time the biggest box-office attraction in the world, shooting another dozen Italian movie spectacles over the next decade, including *Hercules Unchained*. A publicist explained, "We had a few labors left over."

Although *Hercules* had triumphed at the box office, time proved the genre mortal. It did not help that lesser American musclemen followed Reeves to Rome, in hopes of becoming the next Hercules, Samson, or any of a couple of dozen other mythic heroes of antiquity. With rare exceptions these fledgling actors stood out mainly for their rippling muscles and blank expressions, making the charismatic Reeves appear, by comparison, the Laurence Olivier of Italian spectacles. Long before a chariot-riding injury led Reeves to retire to a Montana ranch in 1970, the genre was fading fast, though the Italian movie mills continued to grind out variations like *Hercules and the Moon Men* and *Hercules and the Vampires*. The sword-and-sandal epics, which had survived laughter and ridicule, succumbed to sheer boredom, as audiences worldwide discovered a new, more sophisticated cinematic hero, complete with beautiful women and stunning production values. Hercules had become an early victim of James Bond's license to kill.

After spending many hours sampling Italian versions of the Hercules story, Raimi and Tapert agreed, "This isn't gonna work." Just as they had found the ancient myths too grisly and depressing for American viewers, they considered the movie versions too stilted to serve as a model for the new Hercules. They warmed instead to a suggestion by Dan Filie, after he attended a cast-and-crew screening of *Army of Darkness*, that they do *Hercules* in the same irreverent style: Hercules would be "somebody who didn't sound like an old-style Greek thing. Instead he would have a contemporary sense of humor."

Two other executives became increasingly involved in the brainstorming sessions. Twenty-four-year-old David Eick had already helped Raimi and Tapert establish a TV division for their company, Renaissance Pictures, and Filie now tapped him to expedite production on *Hercules*. Among those Eick approached to become head writer for the four TV movies was Christian Williams, a writer-producer at Universal who impressed Eick as "charming, very smart, preppy—different from those in the Renaissance operation, but they can get along with anyone." Williams was also versed in the Greek myths, and delighted at the chance to give them new life. "Let me at this project!" he told Eick.

Raimi, Tapert, Williams, and Eick developed their take on a Hercules who would be as modern as he was mighty. They agreed that for the movies to appeal to American viewers, Hercules himself should be an

Legendary Facts
The new Hercules was born over dinner at Musso & Frank, a well-known Hollywood restaurant.

American, at least in spirit. Other rules quickly fell into place. One was "No togas." Another was "No Parthenons, no Acropolis, no chariots." The show must not appear set in Greece but rather in some fresh mythic universe; the aim was to escape the sword-and-sandal look.

The producers also decided to avoid period dialogue. In both big-budget spectaculars like *King of Kings* and off-the-rack spectacles like *Hercules Unchained*, even the lowliest peasant would speak in high-flown phrases. At times this style achieved eloquence, as in the award-winning Hollywood epic *Ben Hur*; more often it appeared laughably stiff and pompous. Raimi and Tapert were emphatic that their Hercules should speak in believable ways; the dialogue should be casual and contemporary, though without too much slang.

Nor would the Greek gods intrude too often in this human drama. Raimi especially thought it would be great if they could get away with making four movies without ever personifying the gods. They finally decided to admit one god only, Zeus, the truant parent of Hercules who wants reconciliation with the son who has always sought his approval. And to afford Hercules a formidable opponent, they would also keep the mythological backdrop of the goddess Hera's despising and plotting against her stepson.

Williams presented a particularly vivid road map for the character of Hercules, offering his angle on a hero that people would care about: "As in the myths, Hercules is given tasks to do. So we have a story—the strongest man in the world has challenges. It is

a picaresque tale, a fellow on the road having adventures." Williams saw a man whose heroism came not just from his physical power but from his striving for greatness despite great vulnerability and pain: "His stepmother hates him because she associates him with Zeus' unfaithfulness. Zeus likes him. In today's world everybody comes from a broken home. His father loves him, his stepmother hates him. Zeus is this irresponsible wanderer who isn't much help to Hercules."

Williams explained just which American Hercules would be: "He is Joe Montana," former star quarterback of the San Francisco Forty Niners and Kansas City Chiefs, "a completely American persona." Montana—that is, the *mythic* Joe Montana, whom Williams freely imagined—"sums up the American man better than Clint Eastwood because of his vulnerability. He is rich, good-looking, talented, but he doesn't know whether it will continue. One broken bone and it's all over. Montana is tremendously powerful, but he doesn't know whether he is mortal or not. He can lose everything.

"He is good-looking. He was the Big Man on Campus. Yet when he throws a pass he never knows whether a linebacker could break through the line, break his leg, and end his career. He could lose love, status, money, his future [on one play]. But he is destined to be an NFL quarterback. He has a gift from God, and his gift is his destiny. It is the same with Hercules."

Williams drafted a memo incorporating these ideas, and it became the prototype for creating the character of Hercules and his universe. For his part in shaping the early direction of the movies, Williams received equal billing with Raimi and Tapert as executive producer. At first Raimi had offered a title just below that in rank, coexecutive producer, which still marked a clear step above the usual honorific for a TV movie writer, supervising producer. But as David Eick recalled, Williams pressed for equality, in a humorous and disarming way, explaining, "My mother in New Jersey expects to see my name on-screen as an executive producer." In the interest of harmony, and perhaps motherhood, Raimi and Tapert went along.

Encouraged by Universal, the *Hercules* producers made it their goal to write for "the eight o'clock show," but *not* write it *down* to the time period. Thinking back to a popular and wickedly clever cartoon from the 1960s, Filie says of their approach to *Hercules*, "It's the *Rocky and Bullwinkle* standard: Write the dialogue for the adults, and then the visuals are for the kids. So the kids are going to watch because it's fun and it's action, and the adults are going to get all these jokes and references that are going to sail right over the kids' heads. Because the tradition is at eight o'clock you watch something that's pretty stupid. [But] when I was a kid, I used to watch stuff that was, I think, for adults, like *The Man from U.N.C.L.E.*

People forget that kids would rather imagine the adult world than be in a kid world."

Originally Universal conceived of *Hercules* as a few motion pictures—big pictures, which meant finding a big-name performer for the title role. So the company offered millions of dollars to lure Dolph Lundgren, a tall, blond, muscular actor who first won attention as the nearly superhuman Russian boxer Ivan Drago in *Rocky IV*. Lundgren was more a glowering presence than an actor, but for movies that traded in bullets and punches more than words, this served to make him a box-office draw. But Lundgren backed away from the role of Hercules.

Without a name star, Filie, Tapert, Williams, Eick, and a new casting director for Universal, Nancy Perkins, settled on creating one. The preliminary auditions liberally featured musclemen, athletes, and martial artists. But Filie recalls, "When you read the script, it was as if it had been written for James Garner," an actor who could project an easygoing sense of humor and fun. "It quickly became apparent at the readings that every time we got somebody who was an athlete first and an actor second, the scene just sat there, it wasn't good." Around the fifth person to audition was a thirty-four-year-old Minnesotan with glasses, short hair, and a modest demeanor, named Kevin Sorbo. When he read, the casting session unexpectedly came alive.

Sorbo was an avid athlete, a big man, but not nearly so muscular as many of his competitors for the role. But to everyone at the session, that was fine, for they were looking for someone accessible. Here was "a guy you wanted to hang out with," says Filie, "you know, he wasn't obsessed with his body, he was a regular guy, a good guy."

Unfortunately for Sorbo, the first time was not the charm. Nor the second, third, fourth, or fifth time. "We put Kevin through the tortures of the damned," Rob Tapert says of Sorbo's casting ordeal. The problem, as those involved in the casting were quick to point out, was not with Sorbo but rather their own uncertainty in charting a Hercules so different from anything seen before. Sorbo himself became dispirited by the repeated casting calls, and doubted whether the role was worth such suspense, prolonged over a half dozen auditions—half as many labors as

> **Legendary Facts**
>
> Kevin Sorbo almost ended up chasing aliens instead of monsters. Sorbo auditioned for a part in *The X-Files*.

those of Hercules himself. But by his sixth reading, everyone in the room felt sure that Sorbo's ability to convey humor, charm, and a strong presence without pretense perfectly suited their image of Hercules—a Hercules for the 1990s.

> **Legendary Facts**
>
> The role of Zeus has always attracted legendary stars. For the *Hercules* movies, Anthony Quinn played the role, while Disney's Zeus was voiced by the well-known actor Rip Torn, and in *Clash of the Titans*, the legendary actor Sir Laurence Olivier filled the throne.

Zeus, king of the gods and the father of Hercules, posed a special casting challenge. Even in a small role the actor would have to project surpassing power and stature. Tapert and Williams rounded up the usual suspects for larger-than-life roles, starting with Charlton Heston. Having portrayed vaunted heroes from Moses to John the Baptist to Spain's warrior-saint El Cid, Heston, nearly seventy, already carried such Olympian stature with moviegoers as to assure instant credibility as Zeus. Indeed, for an actor who had provided the voice of God in the film *The Ten Commandments*, Zeus would actually be a step down rather than a stretch. But Heston passed on the role.

Filie then suggested Anthony Quinn, another great film presence since the 1950s, who signed on to play Zeus for five *Hercules* movies. Quinn was a movie legend who imbued the whole project with respectability. "If you said Anthony Quinn's in this," Filie reasoned, "all of a sudden you know this is not some cheap movie, but a picture that's going to have some quality to it."

Choosing an alternative mythic universe to Greece was a pressing but elusive goal for the producers, for no one could say just what this universe was like, or what production site could convey its epic aura. Rob Tapert's aide Eric Gruendemann had already scouted "the usual low-budget production centers"— Florida, North Carolina, Portland, Seattle,

Toronto, Vancouver. Whatever their charms, none impressed him as a fitting home for the son of Zeus. With filming to start in November, Tapert considered Australia, South Africa, and other locations in the Southern Hemisphere, where daylight hours would be longer. Then by chance he ran into an old acquaintance, Courtney Conti, who was about to shoot a children's film, *Mrs. Piggle Wiggle's Theater*, in New Zealand, and who praised the country as an undiscovered production treasure. Tapert was intrigued, and soon Gruendemann, Chris Williams, and David Eick were each taking the twelve-and-a-half-hour excursion from Los Angeles to New Zealand to scout locations.

Gruendemann needed little encouragement to embark on this South Pacific adventure. Nearly a month before signing on to help produce *Hercules*, he had caught a series that *Good Morning America* did on Australia and New Zealand, and "fell in love" with New Zealand courtesy of ABC's footage. Also, as the producer charged with stretching the modest budgets, Gruendemann brightened at the currency exchange rate that brought a full New Zealand dollar for 53 American cents. True, the movie industry in Auckland, New Zealand's largest city, was in every sense a long way from Hollywood. It took Gruendemann two weeks to check out people who could tell him how to film down there, because New Zealand did not even have a film office. But on seeing the country up close, all doubts dissolved amid the spectacular greenery, beaches, seas, and mountains.

The variety of scenic backdrops in New Zealand was important to Gruendemann, because it could help portray Hercules convincingly as "a lone wanderer. He goes from place to place helping people, and we needed to be able to show many different environments. We were looking for dramatic waterfalls, snow-capped peaks, and arid deserts, the whole megillah. I spent six or seven days [in New Zealand] and realized [there] was more here than I had even imagined."

Australia, once a leading candidate to host the *Hercules* telefeatures, slipped quietly off everyone's list. "It would have been more expensive to shoot in Australia," Gruendemann explains, "and it was not quite as diverse. Within two or three hours of Auckland, we can do so many different kinds of looks. With Australia we probably couldn't have the grandeur we have here or the real primordial, lush look we can get right in Auckland."

On returning to California, Gruendemann showed Rob Tapert and Sam Raimi two hundred pictures he had shot down there. He assured them, "We can get just the look we want in New Zealand. Plus the monetary factors, the exchange rates, will work for us." It helped, too, that New Zealand was experiencing a film renaissance. The award-winning movie *The Piano* had just been completed, and *Heavenly Creatures* and the gritty *Once Were Warriors* were about to shoot. And "this was a *slow* period for New Zealand," Gruendemann observes, "the dead of winter." The country offered "a great creative base" for filmmakers. Raimi and Tapert agreed to make the 6500-mile leap of faith from Hollywood to Auckland.

At first Tapert played with different formulas for using New Zealand. "Should it be a coproduction?" he wondered. This would allow much or most of the filming to be done in America, while filming in New Zealand only for selected "location scenes." But "we just decided to do this the way we would a feature film. We'd just go down there. Eric [Gruendemann] and I knew there would be many exterior shots, and we needed eleven to twelve hours of daylight. New Zealand was also cheaper than shooting in America. The determining factor in going to New Zealand is it just looked different. It really looked pastoral, primitive in a funny way, but inviting. So it really looked great on film."

Tapert realized he was breaking totally with the look of fantasy and sword-and-sandal films that offered scenic reminders of Greece or the Middle East. But he sensed this might be all to the good: "You know what's funny, and it's a weird thing: The desert doesn't look that great on film. Even Athens, you look at the old [Ray] Harryhausen pictures [like *Jason and the Argonauts*]. It looks kind of dry, dusty brown, sometimes blue skies, but they blow out." In effect Tapert resolved to film a world the ancient Greeks themselves might have embraced, had they only had the chance to leave their rocky isles for an Elysian paradise.

The decision to film entirely in the South Pacific did not bring Universal cheers. David Eick recalls being stunned by the news: "When Rob [Tapert] first brought this up I thought he was out of his mind." The distance from Los Angeles was great, the time difference "not just hours, but nearly a day apart." But Eick realized that "except for *Murder, She Wrote*, nothing is shot on studio back lots anymore." Later, musing on the look of the films and the speed of the filmmaking, Eick said, "It turned out to be a *great* decision."

Hercules and the
Amazon Women

7he first of five telefeatures, *Hercules and the Amazon Women*, began shooting in the fall of 1993. It established Hercules as a hero in the Western-movie mold, who wore his legendary reputation lightly and fought only as a last resort. The movie also set a pattern of combining several of Hercules' labors into a single story that would give a modern twist to the ancient tales.

The Amazons of Greek myth were a nation of women warriors, famed with the bow and fierce in hand-to-hand combat. They spurned everything that Greek men expected their women to be: quiet, submissive, rooted in the home and marketplace, and, of course, devoted to their husbands and families. The Amazons instead lived apart from men, though physical desire and the need to perpetuate their kingdom led them to seduce men, whom they then deserted or, as some legends related, killed. Amazons lovingly raised the daughters who sprang from these brief unions, but left the infant sons on riverbanks as useless. And they trained relentlessly for war.

To the men of Greece the Amazons embodied a nightmare of women's pride spinning out of control. Who better, then, to tame this menace than the world's strongest man? The ninth labor of Hercules, to bring back the girdle of Hippolyta, the Amazon queen, posed just this test.

The ancient myths soften briefly in relating the warmth that Hippolyta felt toward Hercules. She admired his legendary bravery, and gladly gave him the girdle, a golden belt fashioned for her by the god of war himself. Aboard Hercules' ship these two warriors regaled each other with stories of their adventures. But the goddess Hera, unwilling to let her stepson depart in peace, spread rumors among the Amazons that their queen had been captured, and incited them to storm the ship. Believing himself betrayed, Hercules lashed out at Hippolyta, who fell dead at his feet. Dozens of Amazons charged him, sword in hand, only to be killed by blows of his fists or club. At daybreak, recognizing Hera's hand in Hippolyta's death and mourning her loss, Hercules sailed back to Greece with the queen's girdle, a shimmering prize of an accidental war.

This version of the myth was too dark for a television movie. The death of the heroine at the hands of the hero, the triumph of fear and suspicion over friendship, and the literal battle of the sexes were simply not promising themes for two hours of family viewing. *Hercules and the Amazon Women* instead plays variations on the myth that the ancient Greeks could scarcely have imagined.

The film tells two related stories about Hercules: his quest to save villagers from dread "beasts," as they call the Amazons, and his love for Hippolyta. Early on, Hercules reveals the values of his roguish father, Zeus, as he tells a recently betrothed friend, Iolaus, that yes, women are beautiful and useful for cooking, cleaning, and sewing, but why settle down with just one? When Iolaus replies, "Someday, Hercules, you're going to meet a woman unlike any other," one who will change his mind about both women and love, Hercules merely smiles and says, "Me? Never."

Hercules and Iolaus are suddenly encircled by Amazon warriors springing from the trees and wearing masks of birds, deer, and other animals. Iolaus is stabbed, and dies in the arms of his grieving friend, who is led away, bound and gagged, to the palace of Queen Hippolyta. She tells her exultant subjects, "This is Hercules, champion of men. He's the best the enemy has to offer, and you've put him in chains. Be proud!" The hostility between Hercules and Hippolyta crackles throughout this encounter; but there is fascination, too, that neither has planned on.

"You came to destroy us!" Hippolyta accuses Hercules, who answers, "We were sent to destroy a vicious beast—we didn't know the beast was you." Hippolyta yanks her prisoner's head back as if to open his eyes to a hard truth: "Just because we're not the kind of women *you* would like us to be, make no mistake, these are women: women who will not be controlled by men, not beaten down, not bought or sold like

oxen. Men will never dominate *these* women." "We don't dominate you," Hercules insists, "we protect you, because you're weaker." "Weaker?" Hippolyta inquires mockingly, as she looks down at her bound and kneeling guest.

Dismissing her guards, Hippolyta holds out a sacred candle that shows Hercules his past, beginning when he is a newborn whom Zeus holds joyfully and instructs, "Son, women are the sweetest journey you will take in life. But don't take just one, take many." Hercules next watches himself as a teenager practicing for war with other boys while a trainer shouts, "Emotions are for girls; you must learn to be like stone." And he sees young Iolaus eagerly speak of fighting and dying together in battle. Hippolyta asks Hercules sorrowfully, "What have men ever brought into the world except death and destruction?"

The experience of reliving his past moves Hercules to ask, "What if I change?" Hippolyta shakes her head at this: "You *can't* change, you're a *man*." "If I learned to be the way I am," Hercules persists, "I can learn another way." But Hippolyta suddenly fears her own growing affection for him, and abruptly leaves. In prison Hercules hears the amused voice of his father, Zeus, saying that surely no jail can hold the world's strongest man. Hercules admits that curiosity about Hippolyta holds him. "Just think back upon all the things I've taught you about women," urges Zeus, king of gods and philanderers. "I have been," Hercules muses. "I'm thinking maybe you were wrong."

Hercules realizes that to accomplish his original mission of saving the villagers—all of them male—from the Amazon "beasts," he must first get them to respect women. When the Amazons attack the village, the villagers amaze them with a newfound attention to their feelings and wishes. Barriers that had stood between Amazons and men for generations are dissolved. And Hercules and Hippolyta acknowledge their own love.

As in the ancient myths, Hercules has reckoned without the malice of Hera. Enraged that Hippolyta would forsake her man-hating ways for Hercules, Hera takes control of her body and orders the Amazons to "kill every living thing" in the village, down to the last boy. Under Hera's spell Hippolyta cuts the throat of the head villager and then attacks Hercules, who defeats her but cannot bring himself to kill her. "I won't allow both of you to live," Hera's spirit rages. But Hercules refuses to fight, saying of Hippolyta, "I couldn't bear the thought of living without her." The possessed queen taunts him, "Then live without her," and, lured on by Hera, plunges down a waterfall to her death on the rocks below.

Hercules implores his father to use the sacred candle to turn back time and restore the lives of Hippolyta, Iolaus, and the slain villager. Zeus waves away the request, exclaiming, "It's not the way it works! If you only knew how *complicated* it gets with the stars, the planets, not to mention the other gods. They would go *insane* if I started messing around with things. Son, you can't imagine. Have you any idea how angry *Hera* would be—I couldn't go back home!" "You never do, anyway," Hercules points out. Zeus laughs, then looks lovingly on his son and blows on the candle. The whole adventure is undone, and Hercules finds himself back at dinner with Iolaus and his bride-to-be.

Hercules' mother, Alcmene, watches Iolaus and his betrothed, rejoices at how much they "belong together," and asks, "Hercules, do you think there's a woman out there who can make you that happy?" As Hippolyta's face, gazing into the distance, appears superimposed on-screen, Hercules smiles with just a hint of sadness, and says softly, "She's out there somewhere."

Although turning back time appeared to be the work of Zeus, it owed even more to Rob Tapert, who had to override the strong objections of his head writer, Chris Williams. Tapert recalls, "Chris and I got into a very bitter argument—and I got into this same argument with the studio . . . about a gag that we did in the *Amazon Women*: spinning the globe around and turning time back." Williams claimed this would cheat the audience by denying the reality of all that had gone before. It also would mean restructuring the story and changing the ending. Tapert explained that Iolaus simply could not be sacrificed: "You know, it's Hercules' buddy, every hero needs his buddy." Tapert added that in contrast to Williams' version, reversing time "allows us to kill Hippolyta," echoing the tragic aspect of the Greek myth.

Williams refused to yield, and Tapert finally broke the deadlock with an end run around his head writer: "I did something that's not couth. I didn't have Chris implement those changes. I used two other guys [Andy Dettmann and Dan Truly], who were writing one of my best scripts. So I was going out of the pecking order. . . ."

The rewritten fourth act gives the movie its strongest dramatic moments. The heartfelt words between Hercules and Zeus over turning back time reveal a love that decades of parental neglect could never destroy. The final act also shocks viewers with the loss of Hippolyta, who even after coming back to life remains beyond Hercules' reach. He is left to yearn for a woman "unlike any other" whom he can have only as a memory.

The need for an actress to give Hippolyta strength, fire, and charm worthy of Hercules led the producers in unexpected directions. Their search came down to three women who each looked more likely to wear a pageant crown than wield a sword. Two were extraordinary beauties with only modest acting experience. Vanessa Angel, a thirty-one-year-old blonde of British descent, would go on to star in a hit comedy series, *Weird Science*, as the dream creation of two teenage computer geniuses. The British model Elizabeth Hurley was a twenty-eight-year-old brunette best known from the pages of *Vogue*, *Glamour*, and other magazines. Half a foot shorter than either Angel or Hurley was Roma Downey, twenty-nine, an Irish actress with a heavy brogue, best known for her starring turn in a TV miniseries as the demure and urbane Jackie Kennedy. On paper Downey seemed the least plausible candidate to play an Amazon warrior. Yet something about her inspired Rob Tapert to believe she could make the dramatic shift from First Lady to Amazon queen.

"Everyone had their opinions," Tapert says of the spirited discussions over which actress should play Hippolyta. "But Roma Downey, at five-foot-two, even though she didn't look like an Amazon, had a presence . . . a way she carried herself." Tapert chose her and never wavered, even as doubts arose about Downey's ability to handle the movie's demanding action scenes. "We sent her out to Doug Wong [a martial arts expert in Los Angeles] to do a small amount of training. Wong told us, 'You guys are in trouble if you expect her to do anything very physical.'" But Tapert shrugs away the whole issue:

"You know what gave me faith [in casting her]? . . . I had just done a

[Jean-Claude] Van Damme movie, *Hard Target*—and he does so few of his stunts now, so little of his own fighting. We can find ways to cover it, with a good stunt double and a wig." Wigs were indeed in ample supply during Downey's fighting and riding scenes. But her performance—sensitive, poignant, and charismatic—made it all worthwhile.

Debuting in April 1994 on hundreds of syndicated stations, *Hercules and the Amazon Women* startled television executives by earning high ratings and appealing to men and women, young and old. Viewers could enjoy the movie as a throwback to vintage spectaculars, as a love story, or as a lighthearted adventure. The action scenes are free of blood but exciting: several inventive fights, mixing trademark Western punches with hints of Eastern martial arts movies, show to advantage both Sorbo's athleticism and the New Zealand stunt team's rough-and-ready daring. And for American audiences saturated by California and New York locales, New Zealand's dense forests and unfamiliar beauty add an alluring mystery to this mythic tale.

Special effects also help transport viewers to a world of ancient wonders. Early in the movie Hercules comforts a crying girl, who suddenly transforms into a tentacled lizard wrapping itself around him. As in

the myth of his battle with a nine-headed sea serpent called the Hydra, each time Hercules beheads the creature, two new heads immediately sprout in its place; only by burning the stumps with the help of Iolaus does Hercules finally destroy the monster.

Creating such effects on a modest budget under time pressure struck Tapert as the most difficult aspect of producing the Hercules movies apart from crafting the stories. Timesaving computer-generated effects were just coming on the horizon but too late for this and later telefeatures. Instead Tapert's talented effects artists, headed by Kevin O'Neill, relied on stop-action puppetry and other painstaking techniques to conjure the Hydra and kindred illusions.

Hercules and the Amazon Women benefits especially from uncanny casting, beginning with the title character. In his debut outing as Hercules, Kevin Sorbo anchors the film's distinctive style with a winning blend of intelligence, humor, and vulnerability to complement his muscular frame and his character's Olympian aura. And Sorbo enjoys ample, often memorable support. In several brief but buoyant scenes, Anthony Quinn imbues Zeus not only with authority but also with boundless zest: He is Zorba the Greek god. One of New Zealand's foremost Shakespearean actors and directors, Michael Hurst, brings to the role of Iolaus an edgy love of adventure that goes well beyond the usual amiable qualities expected of the hero's best friend. And Roma Downey is luminous as Hippolyta, projecting a royal stature far beyond her tiny frame.

Underlying the success of *Amazon Women* is the producers' willingness to go where no myth has gone before: to take Hercules out of ancient Greece not only geographically but culturally. Relations between men and women may be as uncertain and problematic today as in the days of Homer, but they have surely changed in myriad ways.

Legendary Facts

In *Hercules and the Amazon Women*, the Amazon second-in-command was played by Lucy Lawless, who may be better known to fans as *Xena: Warrior Princess*.

The Greeks could envision nothing better for Hercules and Hippolyta, the world's foremost male and female warriors, than violent tragedy. As recently as 1959, the movie *Hercules*, with Steve Reeves, showed that time had softened but not greatly revised this scenario: Hercules still strides among the Amazons as an intimidating physical presence from whom they run shrieking; and while he is no longer so lacking in chivalry as to kill these women en masse, he drugs their wine before they can attack his men, then sails away forever. By contrast, the evolutionary march to Kevin Sorbo's hero is a steep climb indeed.

Hercules and the Amazon Women weaves a feminist parable into a tale of the world's greatest male adventurer. Hercules begins his labors as an inspiring but still incomplete defender of justice, until love leads him to shed his prejudices toward women and accept their rights and worth as full human beings. This message of course treads lightly behind an emphasis on action: Within a two-hour span Hercules decapitates and torches the Hydra, battles (unarmed) the entire Amazon army, battles Hippolyta, and reverses time. Along the way, he proves a hero whose inner journey can touch our own.

Hercules and the Lost Kingdom

A little-known myth tells how Hercules, on his return from the land of the Amazons, stopped at the great port of Troy in Asia Minor (modern Turkey). There he saw a young woman named Hesione chained to a rock on the shore. Hesione was the daughter of the Trojan king, who hoped this desperate sacrifice to the sea god Poseidon would rid his city of a sea monster that was devouring townspeople and destroying their lands. Hercules rescued Hesione, then killed the sea monster from inside its belly after it had swallowed him. But when the king afterward broke an oath to reward this heroic deed, Hercules returned with an army, slew the king, and conquered Troy. This tale, in kinder, gentler form, inspired the second telefeature, *Hercules and the Lost Kingdom*.

Troy is the "lost kingdom" of this film, Hera having enveloped the city in a mist after sending her "blue cult" of hooded warriors to drive out the inhabitants and depose their king. A hundred exiles from Troy search for Hercules to plead for his help, but Hera kills all but one before they can reach him. The lone survivor barely manages to tell Hercules of his city's hardships before dying in his arms and crumbling to dust. With pity for the Trojans and revulsion toward Hera's cruelty, Hercules sets off on a labor that will stretch even his powers: to save a city no one can find, from a curse sent by a god.

Hercules spies his father, Zeus, who had earlier joined a cheering crowd as his son knocked out a rampaging twenty-foot giant with his own club. Once again, father and son try in vain to find common ground:

Zeus: You were great with that giant!

Hercules: *Forget* the giant! How do I find Troy?

Zeus: Hercules, *don't* get involved.

Hercules: Involved? Hera killed that messenger in my arms.

Zeus (exasperated at his son's taking this to heart): She does *strange things*—she's *queen of the gods!*

Hercules: And you're supposed to be king.

Zeus (sternly): Who says I'm not? . . .

Hercules: So you're not going to help me—*again.*

Zeus: How can I explain? (agonizing) I *can't.*

Hercules: Fine. Thanks, father. (He turns away.)

Zeus: Hey, wait a second, wait a second. I probably shouldn't tell you this, but you must find the *one true* compass. It points directly to Troy. Queen Omphale had it last. (Thunder crashes around them, a warning from Hera.) I can't tell you any more. You'll have to find it yourself.

Hercules (hopefully): Why don't you come with me?

Zeus: Oh—if I were only a thousand years younger. (He shakes his head wistfully.) And *single.*

Hercules heads for the kingdom of Queen Omphale to obtain the compass that will guide him to Troy. His path brings him upon a group of people, chanting as they prepare to sacrifice a young woman, so that a water god will bring rain for their crops. She is Deianeira. Hercules brushes past an indignant priest, saying, "Human sacrifices don't work," and rescues young Deianeira despite her protests that he is "interrupting a religious ceremony." But Hercules, having seen the gods of Olympus up close, is not impressed by talk of blind worship:

Deianeira: You have no right to interfere with my destiny with the gods.

Hercules: Take my word for it, the gods don't care about your destiny.

Deianeira: And who are you that you know so much?

Hercules: I'm Hercules.

Deianeira: Your parents named you after *Hercules*? Hah—what a laugh!

Hercules admonishes the entire group, "Forget the gods. You can get along without them. If it doesn't rain"—here he picks up a bucket and hands it to the priest—"*irrigate.*"

Deianeira decides the gods must have sent Hercules to save her for a different fate, and travels with him. Her origins are unknown even to her: At first she boasts that her father was a handsome king who had to send her away in troubled times, but when Hercules remarks that this is a well-known fairy tale, she confesses, "Orphans need fairy tales too." They arrive in Lydia, the land of Queen Omphale, just as a slave auction is beginning. To gain entry into the palace, Hercules agrees to sell his labor for one day, and although bidding is fierce, the queen herself orders that this stranger be brought to her. Luxury surrounds them, and when Omphale asks her guest, "Are you comfortable?" he admits, "Too comfortable." Although she hopes to keep him forever by her side, Hercules explains that he must urgently journey to Troy. Omphale gives Hercules her magic compass and bids him a sad farewell.

> ### Legendary Facts
> According to Greek myth, Deianeira was the name of Hercules' second wife.

The brief time in Lydia is not without adventure. Hercules rescues a slave named Waylin from bullies in a tavern, hurling several through the walls to make his point clear. Waylin is a puzzlement to Hercules and Deianeira, for he seems delighted to be a slave, for the "financial security," and proud to be "the best slave I can be." Later he escapes from the palace but only to offer himself as a slave to Hercules. Unable

to make Waylin value freedom, Hercules reluctantly gives him a single command: Return to Queen Omphale and serve her for the rest of his life.

As Hercules and Deianeira walk along the shore, a sinister priest of the blue cult proclaims, "Rise, blue serpent, and do the work that Hera asks of you." A towering sea lizard crashes through the surface of the wa-

2 7

ter and extends its long neck toward Deianeira. Hercules rushes to cover her and the two are swallowed together, hurtling on a water-filled ride down the creature's throat.

Deianeira seems strangely pleased by the attention. She is convinced the gods have a purpose for her, after all. Hercules, however, remains more interested in surviving the sea serpent than praising it:

Deianeira: Did you see that? It came straight for me!

Hercules (preoccupied): I noticed.

Deianeira: I told you my place was with the gods.

Hercules: Deianeira, I don't think the gods *hang out* in here!

Deianeira: But they accepted me. That's all that matters.

Hercules: I don't know why you're so excited. We're about to be *digested.*

Hercules and Deianeira navigate past the creature's membranes, every so often bumping into a skeletal leftover from one of its earlier meals. At last Hercules tears his way through to the monster's heart, wraps his arms around a section, and squeezes till it bursts. The creature stops thrashing, and Hercules and Deianeira float up to the surface. As they reach the shore, a magnificent walled city comes into view: They have reached Troy.

A young Trojan sentry, one of the exiles living in a camp outside the city, mistakes the two travelers for spies and brings them before the king, an aged, white-bearded man now too feeble to leave his bed. To everyone's amazement, the king calls Deianeira by name, and bids everyone else leave them. She is his daughter, he says. "You were such a beautiful child that Hera demanded I sacrifice you to her sea monster." But he could not bring himself to do this, and instead sent her away. He alone has known this is the reason for Hera's curse on Troy. He cries at the horror, saying, "I loved you too much. I sacrificed all of Troy for one . . . tiny girl." Deianeira comforts him: "No, you only sacrificed your own heart to keep me alive. I found my way back, as you knew I would." The king dies, content that his cherished daughter is safe.

Deianeira emerges to face her people. Her mission is clear at last: She will reclaim Troy. At her urging, Hercules trains the exiled Trojans in the art of combat. And they gain an unexpected recruit: the once contented slave Waylin, who asks to fight—this time as a free man—for the Trojan cause. It is Waylin who rallies the inexperienced and hesitant Trojans against the fearsome warriors of the blue cult. He cuts one warrior down and it deflates into nothingness, leading him to cry, "If you stand up to them, they don't exist."

Hercules meanwhile tracks the blue priest, who has seized Deianeira and plans to sacrifice her to Hera. The goddess has armed her servant with deadly chains that fly at Hercules, wrapping tightly around his legs, body, and neck. But before the blue priest can kill Deianeira, Hercules breaks his chains and with one blow of his sword beheads Hera's butcher. Even this does not discourage the blue priest, whose headless form rises

and lunges at Deianeira, until Hercules impales him with his sword and uses it to hurl him over a parapet to his death.

Hera is relentless. Deianeira feels herself being lifted off the ground, and Hercules leaps to pulls her back to earth. But then, as Deianeira watches in terror, he is sucked into the heavens by his furious stepmother. Zeus, an onlooker in these grisly events, now appears near Deianeira, who sobs, "She's got him." Zeus assures her, "She won't hurt him," then adds firmly, "She wouldn't dare."

As the victorious Trojans acclaim Deianeira as their queen, back in Greece a figure tumbles out of the skies, landing with a thud that would pulverize any ordinary hero but merely causes Hercules to wince before dusting himself off. He walks only a short way before a villager runs up to him, shouting, "There's a monster, Hercules, you've got to help us!" There is to be no rest from his labors protecting others.

Lost Kingdom is a sweeter film than *Amazon Women*, but in two respects it suffers by comparison. One is that the villains it depicts are not especially imposing. Unlike the fierce, hard-riding, and visually striking Amazons of the first movie, the soldiers of the blue cult appear only briefly, in the final battle, and are quickly exposed by the lowly slave Waylin as unreal: a symbolic test of courage for the raw Trojan recruits rather than a lethal enemy. The blue priest is more menacing, but although endowed with magic powers, he never looks robust enough to provide nearly a match for the son of Zeus. Hera, of course, is a formidable antagonist, but her presence is merely hinted at (often by a feather from a peacock, her symbol), rather than embodied by an actress.

A more glaring void in *Lost Kingdom* is that despite traveling with a woman for most of the film, Hercules lacks a love interest. Renee O'Connor as Deianeira is spirited, funny, and attractive, but her character is depicted as so young that Hercules emphatically rebuffs her one effort to kiss him. The scene upholds his virtue, but suggests that his affection for Deianeira is at most avuncular rather than amorous. Even this bond fades when at film's end Deianeira becomes Queen of Troy while Hercules moves on to new lands and labors.

Despite these problems, *Lost Kingdom* has much to recommend it. Action scenes are varied, lively, and often marked by captivating effects, including Hercules' battle with a giant, his struggle against—and inside—

> **Legendary Facts**
>
> Renee O'Connor, who played Deianeira, wasn't done with Greek myths and heroes after her adventures in *Lost Kingdom*. O'Connor reappears as Gabrielle, sidekick and best friend to Xena.

Hera's sea monster, and his climactic fight with the blue priest. The bright cinematography offers a wealth of locations and sets, ranging from the opulence of Lydia to the mystery of Troy. And Hercules encounters enough colorful characters of diverse shapes, sizes, and qualities to give this "picaresque" tale more than its share of unpredictable turns.

Lost Kingdom also continues the tradition of shrewd casting that so enlivened *Amazon Women*. Once again Kevin Sorbo makes Hercules a hero of many parts: strong, athletic, courageous, but also sensitive, humorous, and, especially in scenes with young Deianeira, gentle. And once again Sorbo's Hercules has a heavyweight sparring partner in Anthony Quinn's wayward but well-meaning father, Zeus. As young Deianeira, Renee O'Connor is thoroughly endearing, however much the terms of endearment are bounded by Hercules' moral scruples. Elizabeth Hawthorne similarly can only hint at Omphale's wilder side, but in her brief screen time she evokes surprising pathos as a stoic widow whose wealth and power cannot erase or fully mask her pain. Portraying a slave proud of his "profession," Robert Trebor manages to convey deep feeling amid the buffoonery. And as the blue priest, Nathaniel Lees intones his evil designs in one of the most resonant baritones since James Earl Jones' Darth Vader.

The sole telefeature written by Chris Williams, *Lost Kingdom* attests to his interest in reworking the ancient myths to explore American values and concerns. Whereas the Greeks wondered how people could best follow their destiny as decreed by the gods, the characters in *Lost Kingdom* must learn to choose their own destinies. For Deianeira, this means rejecting human sacrifice, whether to a water god or to Hera herself, and pursuing instead her own best path: to reclaim Troy for her people. For the slave Waylin, wisdom means spurning servitude, even to so noble a man as Hercules, and instead becoming a hero in his own right.

Legendary Facts

Robert Trebor, who played the slave Waylin, quickly became a regular on *Hercules: The Legendary Journeys* as Salmoneus, a man always in search of the next get-rich-quick scheme.

What sets Hercules apart in *Lost Kingdom* is not simply his physical strength but his strength of purpose: He will set his own course to match the highest ideals, no matter that he must stand alone against humans or the gods themselves. As with that classically American hero, Gary Cooper's indomitable sheriff in *High Noon*, who must face both gunslingers and his own fears and doubts, so, too, Hercules wonders whether he will survive, day to day, as he champions the human race against the cruelty of the gods:

Deianeira: Are you immortal?

Hercules: *You* want to know? [Deianeira nods, enraptured.] So do I. All I can tell you is, when the sun's out, well, I'm going to live forever. And at night, when I can't sleep and the worries start creeping in, well, the next monster's going to get me for sure.

But for Hercules, this burden of uncertainty cannot keep him from protecting others. It is simply the hero's price, which he will pay willingly, every day, for as long as he lives.

Even as Hercules was emerging as a television sensation, trouble was brewing between Rob Tapert and Chris Williams. Questions of credit played a part. Tapert had contributed critically to the initial guiding vision for *Hercules*, along with his partner Sam Raimi, Universal's Dan Filie, and coproducer David Eick, and so felt entitled to at least part credit for having created the television character. But Williams, who had fleshed out this vision, insisted that he had given *Hercules* life (and depth). Dan Filie, whose involvement in these TV movies went back to their earliest stages, sympathized with Williams but observes, "In all fairness, Rob and Sam already had the vision of *Hercules* at this point."

The dispute spilled over into an arbitration hearing before the Writers Guild, which awarded sole "created by" credit to Williams. Tapert was neither surprised nor impressed on hearing that the Writers Guild had sided with the writer.

The partnership between Tapert and Williams finally capsized after striking immovable artistic differences. As Eick recalls the frustrating creative stalemate, "Rob and I would sit with Chris for hours and hours and hours giving script notes, and nothing would change. Rob wanted more plot-driven episodes, a key to feature films. Williams, on the other hand, had ambitions for intense character-driven drama. In *Lost Kingdom* he had a character named Gaylen who was a gay eunuch, and much of the story centered on questions of his identity. It never made its way to the screen." "It was overreaching our goal to write for adults and for kids," Dan Filie recalls, "so we pulled that back a little bit." Williams reacted sharply to this and other deletions from his first couple of scripts, further rending his relationship with Tapert, the show's ultimate creative arbiter.

Filie believes that Williams offered many fine ideas, but that Tapert's editing judgment was sound and even essential: "Right now [*Hercules*] is called kind of a guilty pleasure. You know, people will enjoy it and react, with *surprise* in their voice, 'Hey, *Hercules* is a good show!' There's a quality to this show they don't have even in big action movies, the writing and the dialogue is not stupid, it's sharp, but it's still accessible. You don't need your Cliffs Notes of the Greek myths to get through it. Chris' take on it, I think, was going to be even heavier, [aiming for] more insight. It would have been another level that we all thought would have made *Hercules* . . . a little less accessible to everybody."

Hercules and the Lost Kingdom was itself lost for a time in this conflict of visions. Originally entitled *Hercules: The Journey Begins*, it was to be the first telefeature to shoot and air. But Tapert thought the script sorely needed work, and moved up *Amazon Women* from second to first in the production schedule. By the time filming began on *Lost Kingdom*, Tapert and Williams were associates in name only. "Those things happen," Tapert says. "I hired Harley Cokeliss, a friend of mine for fifteen years, to direct Chris' episode. Harley is the single most tenacious person in the world. If a story line doesn't work for him he just keeps biting and biting and biting away. So through twenty-four-hour-a-day badgering, Harley got that script turned around."

Hercules and the
Circle of Fire

The third telefeature builds on the ancient tale of Prometheus, the wisest member of a race of giants called Titans, who smuggled fire from Mount Olympus so that humans could survive the cold, forge metal tools, and prosper. According to myth Prometheus acted despite a warning from Zeus never to share fire with mortals. For his disobedience he was chained to a rock in the snowcapped Caucasus Mountains, where every day an eagle gnawed at his liver. Every night his liver regenerated so that his torment was endless. For thirty years (some say thirty thousand years, also a small span for an immortal), Prometheus lay in agony, but Zeus could never break his spirit. Then the Titan found unexpected help from another champion of mankind, Hercules. Hercules ended the eagle's savage attacks with a well-aimed poisoned arrow and unchained Prometheus with a few hammerlike blows of his club.

The myths differ as to why Zeus consented to the liberation of Prometheus. Some say that his anger cooled after torturing Prometheus for a few thousand years. Others claim he so admired the courage of his son Hercules that he forgave both the erring Titan and the mortal who dared set him free. A lesser-known story, adapted for *Circle of Fire*, is that Zeus vowed to keep Prometheus bound until an immortal gave up his immortality in exchange for the Titan's freedom. To the surprise of everyone on Mount Olympus, Chiron, the tutor of Hercules and other Greek heroes, happily agreed.

Chiron was among the most admired figures in Greek myth. He was a centaur, a creature with the body of a horse and the head and chest of a human. Most centaurs were savage and dissolute, but Chiron was known for his wisdom, goodness, and knowledge of both martial and healing arts. Hercules was entrusted to his care while a youth, to learn discipline as much as to hone his fighting skills. The two developed a warm bond, but Chiron later fell tragically at the hands of his most renowned pupil.

When a group of drunken centaurs attacked Hercules, he tracked them to their lair and killed them with arrows dipped in venom from the blood of the Hydra. In the darkness he accidentally wounded his mentor, Chiron, who had taken no part in the attack. Although most versions of this tale say that Chiron died after a night of excruciating pain, some sources relate that Chiron was descended from Cronos, the father of Zeus himself, and thus immortal. But although he could not die, neither could he live except as an invalid wracked by suffering. To end his misery, Chiron gladly shed his immortality for the freedom of Prometheus.

Circle of Fire presents Chiron as immortal but, as Hercules observes, living "in constant agony." Chiron further laments his immortality because he knows that one day he must witness the death of his beloved mortal wife and their children. He has never blamed his misfortune on Hercules, who has devoted his life to finding a cure for Chiron's festering wound. The movie opens with Hercules on one such quest, vanquishing a murderous witch who guards a fountain of youth. He brings back a vial of the magic waters, hoping to restore his friend to health.

Legendary Facts

To simplify the costuming, Chiron was rewritten from a four-legged centaur to a two-legged satyr, another mythical creature with pointed ears, a hairy body ending in goat's legs and hooves, and small horns sprouting from its temples.

The potion works, but only briefly: Chiron's wound reappears almost as soon as it vanishes. Hercules vows to keep searching but before he can set out again a larger horror seizes their attention. The fire heating Chiron's home suddenly goes out, as it does in homes all around them. Chiron's children begin to shiver, and Hercules promises to discover the source of this plague and set things right.

A lone flame leads Hercules to a temple devoted to Hera, and there he sees a beautiful woman asking a guard to light her torch so she can share the fire with others. Her name is Deianeira. Hercules is struck by her beauty and amused by her hard bargaining with the temple's gruff but not overly clever sentry:

Guard: I told you I can't help you. This fire is for the great goddess Hera.

Deianeira: Some great goddess, she's not even lifting a finger to help these people. None of your damn gods do!

Guard: You can't come in. (He bolts shut the vent in the temple gate, but quickly unbolts it on hearing the woman's next words.)

Deianeira: All right—what if I pay?

Guard: Exactly what have you got in mind? I'm thinking, uh, one hundred dinars!

Deianeira: *Fifty* dinars.

Guard: Fifty dinars?

Deianeira: All right, fine, then fifty dinars.

Guard: Wait, wait, I said—

Deianeira: You said fifty dinars!

Guard: Uh, I did, but, uh, I wasn't agreeing to, uh, fifty dinars.

Deianeira (feigning exasperation): OK, fine, then *thirty* dinars.

Guard: No, I didn't say thirty, I said fifty.

Deianeira: *You* think of yourself as an intelligent man.

Guard (smiling as the flattery sinks in): I like to think so, yeah.

Deianeira: Well, then, you would think that twenty dinars would be a good deal.

Guard: No, uh, wait, wait.

Deianeira: Fine, then, twenty dinars it is. You drive a hard bargain.

Hercules, however, won't let Deianeira pay Hera's minions. "These fools don't deserve a single dinar," he declares. "I'll get the fire you need." Deianeira reacts sharply to this unwelcome gallantry: "*Excuse* me? I thought I was doing a pretty good job here. What do *you* propose to do?" But the guard, recognizing Hercules, realizes all too well what he has in mind and frantically disappears behind the gate. Hercules is not to be put off, though: Taking Deianeira's torch, he knocks down the gate and steps into the temple.

After sending more than a dozen guards sprawling to all corners of the temple, Hercules lights the torch, but this flame, too, abruptly vanishes. Overhead the temple priestess looks down from her platform and warns, "You fools! That torch will do you no good. Hera is destroying *all* fire. This sickness you call mankind has offended her long enough. Soon your world will be frozen, and not one of your wretched souls will survive!" Deianeira glares at Hercules, who holds her now useless torch, and storms off to seek guidance from Chiron. He tells her only Hercules can lead her to Prometheus, the guardian of fire, and she is overjoyed at the idea: "Hercules! Of course!" But her mood changes when Chiron points behind her to the handsome but meddlesome stranger from the temple:

Deianeira: *You're* Hercules! You *can't* be. (turning back to Chiron with a broad smile:) You must be mistaken!

Hercules: He's not mistaken. I am Hercules.

Deianeira: Then we're in big trouble.

But Deianeira soon realizes he is her sole hope, and informs him, "Fine, then you can take me to Prometheus." "What happened," Hercules teases, "to 'I don't *want* your help, I don't *need* your help'?" Deianeira replies with a sweet smile and a sharp line, "It's turned into, 'I *don't* want your help—but I have no choice.'"

After a long journey that ends with a climb straight up the side of a cliff, the two travelers reach the temple of Prometheus. Two giant gates, each decorated with the sculpted figure of a torch, mark the Titan's great gift to the world. Yet when Hercules forces open the gates, a rush of bitterly cold air escapes. He and Deianeira then see a terrible sight: Prometheus himself, sitting almost immobile, covered by ice and frost. He strains simply to greet his guests, and Hercules urges, "Wait, don't try to speak, I'll free you." But Prometheus replies, "No, it's no use," and instead sets him a greater task, to retrieve the eternal torch that is the source of all fire on earth:

"I took fire from the heavens so that man would have knowledge to help him grow. Don't let my efforts be destroyed! Go to Mount

Ethion. Find the torch. Free it from Hera's evil grasp. . . . If the torch dies, all life dies with it."

As Hercules and Deianeira travel on, their uneasy partnership blossoms into attraction, strengthened by shared adventure and adversity. A child of the woods named Phaedra, wearing ragged brown and green garments and a wreath of twigs and berries, comes across their path and excitedly points out a shortcut. It leads, however, straight toward a monstrous apparition made of branches, soil, and roots, which lumbers toward Hercules and pummels him savagely. After Deianeira concedes that "this is one of those things that responds best to fists," Hercules throws the creature to the ground, shattering it. But it reassembles itself, rises, and attacks once more. At last Deianeira realizes the giant's secret, and what Hercules must do to defeat it.

Locked in mortal combat, Hercules at first brushes off Deianeira's bid to gain his attention, saying, "I'm a little busy right now." But after he is knocked through the air several more times, he listens more attentively as she tells him this is the giant Antaeus, whose mother is the goddess Earth herself. Whenever Antaeus touches the ground, his strength is renewed. Hercules then lifts the giant on his shoulders till his strength is gone, shakes out the lifeless materials, and hurls the remains onto a cross made from the skulls of his many victims.

The way to Mount Ethion is long, and little Phaedra—part waif, part acrobat, part sorceress—finds new ways to make it longer still by confusing and delaying the two travelers. At last Hercules spies Phaedra in a cave within Mount Ethion and declares, "You're working for Hera!" "She is actually working . . . for *me*," says a familiar, cheerful voice, as Zeus appears before his son. Phaedra bows politely to Zeus and skips away. This is too much for Hercules, who has grown accustomed to his father's absences and passivity, but never before experienced his enmity.

Hercules demands an explanation, and Zeus says he's been trying to keep his son out of danger. "Antaeus nearly broke my neck!" Hercules fumes, but Zeus is all smiles: "Ah, but he didn't!" Antaeus simply slowed Hercules down. Zeus warns his son that Hera has placed the torch in a circle of fire so fierce that not even Hercules may survive. This fire, Zeus tells him, "kills immortality."

Hercules will not be deterred. He advances toward the flames, but Zeus hurls a thunderbolt that sends him flying back twenty feet, then calls forth a stone wall to bar his way. "You may be the strongest man in the world," he tells his son, "but remember, I am still . . . the king of the gods." Hercules breaks through the rock, but another thunderbolt crackles just in front of him, searing the ground and once more sending him reeling. "You are pushing me, boy!" Zeus growls. "The next one will not be aimed at your feet!"

"You really could kill me, couldn't you?" asks Hercules, dazed as much by the thought of his father's attacking him as by the thunderbolts themselves. "I'm trying to *save* you!" Zeus shouts. Hercules urges his father to remember the people whose lives depend on his retrieving the torch. "I *care* about people," Zeus answers. "It so happens I care more about you." He turns sadly, and seems older now as he walks away. "Father!" Hercules calls out. "I love you too . . . but I still have to do this."

Hercules leaps into the ring of fire, knowing it will consume his power. He wills himself forward, wrests the torch free, and hurls it with unerring aim and matchless strength across the sky and into the temple of Prometheus, where it once more bestows on humans the gift of fire. Then Hercules collapses, overcome by Hera's circle of fire and his own superhuman exertions. "He's dying!" Deianeira wails to Zeus, and the truant father suddenly becomes a fierce protector of his child. "Hera, Hera," Zeus shouts, "stop this savagery! If you hurt my son, I'll haunt you into eternity!" Then he adds with quiet resolve, "You'll have to take me too!" He steps toward the flames, perhaps to menace Hera, perhaps to save his son—or perhaps to perish with him. But as he advances the fire recedes, then vanishes, and Hercules survives.

Deianeira for the first time sees Zeus—this mischievous, charming, clever old man—as truly king of the gods. But just as Hercules is a deeply human hero, so Zeus, the lord of all creation, is also a loving but harried family man:

Hercules: You saved my life!

Zeus: That's what fathers are for.

Hercules: What if Hera hadn't backed down?

Zeus (reflecting): We'd be in a lot of trouble!

Having saved the world, Hercules can attend to more personal quests. Bearing a flame from Mount Ethion, he lights a circle around Chiron, who stays in it just long enough to be purged of his immortality, reemerging as a mortal—and cured of his wound. Hercules and Deianeira celebrate this happy ending with a kiss.

Circle of Fire is unique among the Hercules telefeatures in portraying the son of Zeus as a daredevil adventurer, an ancient, more powerful fore-

runner of such film heroes as Robin Hood and Indiana Jones. In the opening scene alone, Hercules narrowly survives the iron grip of a witch who seems invulnerable to weapons by tipping over a cauldron containing her beating heart and cutting it with a sword; he then escapes a flood of acid by racing on the tops of benches just before they dissolve and leaping between two spiked walls that are quickly closing—all this while carrying a young woman to safety on his shoulder. Later, at Hera's temple, Hercules outleaps, outduels, and outmaneuvers as well as outmuscles opponents, even parrying sword thrusts behind his back while holding a torch and balancing on two wooden poles that span a pool of water.

The film's kinetic style demanded an extra measure of athleticism from its star, Kevin Sorbo, whose willingness to do many of his own stunts resulted in some real-life close calls. Sorbo remembers the scene where he had to jump through a wall of flames into the "circle of fire" as literally overheated: "The fire marshal tested the flames and said, 'You're going to feel a little warm when you reach a certain point, but you should be okay.'" The stunt coordinator further assured him, "Kevin, you can just leave when it feels uncomfortable." They had a space open for Sorbo to leap through, but he found this gave him a meager margin of safety:

> Well, halfway through the first take somebody yelled stop. I asked what the problem was and they told me that my costume was starting to smolder. . . . They sprayed me down with fire retardant and everything. I got out of there, and my back was [still] smoldering, and within about a minute after that the entire fire alarm system went off in the building, [it rang] 911 . . . the place filled up with water, the fire station showed up, and they just went nuts on us.

The casting of *Circle of Fire* is impressive overall. As Phaedra, Stephanie Barrett is an example of why adults should beware of sharing scenes with child actors. Barrett is by turns sweet, impish, savvy beyond her years, and so amusing as to win sympathy for what is, at heart, an antagonist to Hercules and Deianeira. And the casting of Tawny Kitaen as Deianeira proves a bold stroke that gives *Circle of Fire*, like the two earlier movies, a strong and appealing female lead.

Kitaen had grown steadily as an actress during a ten-year movie career. Her first starring performance, in the erotic French adventure *The Perils of Gwendoline* (1985), revealed a voluptuous body and luxurious auburn hair but limited dramatic skill. Yet as the critic Danny Peary observed, "By the time she made the okay horror film *Witchboard* (1987), playing a violent, possessed woman (speaking in a low, male-devil voice), her acting and energy equaled her sex appeal." As Deianeira, Kitaen adds a flair for comic repartee that affords Hercules a wry as well as lovely foil. Her portrayal of an engagingly independent heroine makes Deianeira's growing love for Hercules in the following two movies even more affecting.

Hercules in the Underworld

The twelve labors of Hercules took him ever farther across the earth. His early struggles against such fierce creatures as the Nemean lion and the Hydra were said to have occurred within fifty miles of his native city, Thebes, in the heart of Greece. The later labors, though, took him to the boundaries of the world known to the Greeks: west to Gibraltar at the edge of the Atlantic Ocean, east to Asia Minor, and south to Africa (where he fought the Libyan giant Antaeus). His last labor sent him farther still, on the longest and most perilous journey any human could take: he traveled to the underworld, the land of the dead that welcomed all mortals in their turn, but never again released them.

In myth, Hercules' twelfth labor involved a command by King Eurystheus of Tiryns to bring back the dread watchdog Cerberus, who guarded the gates of the underworld. Cerberus was no ordinary canine but a huge three-headed terror with a serpent's tail, a beast that would have sent Cujo scampering for shelter. Hercules relied on Athena, goddess of wisdom, and Hermes, patron god of travelers, to guide him to a cave at the southernmost point of the Greek mainland that led down to the chill land of the dead. Then he approached Hades, the god of the underworld, for permission to borrow Cerberus, his prized guardian of the gates. But Hades grimly refused and barred his way.

Hercules clarified his meaning by firing an arrow at Hades and wounding him in the shoulder, making the god roar with pain such as he had never felt. Hades then agreed to let Hercules take Cerberus, but only if he could do so without using weapons. Hercules strode toward the snarling hellhound, choked it into submission before any of its three sets of fangs could tear his flesh, and slung the dazed beast over his shoulder to carry back to Tiryns. When he released the animal at the feet of Eurystheus, the terrified king jumped from his throne, climbed into a large pot, and screamed at him to take the beast back to the underworld. This was Hercules' final labor for Eurystheus, who sensibly decided not to challenge him further.

Hercules in the Underworld relates the tale of the twelfth labor, but adds elements of beauty and passion undreamed of in the original myth. The film opens in a hall filled with lighted candles, where a young woman is ceremonially bathed. When she rises, her clothes, beginning with purest white, then soft browns and reds, are tied around her. Silver bracelets are fitted on her arms, and her long blond hair is combed. Finally, a medallion with a blue stone is placed around her neck, all to the sounds of a slow and haunting Middle Eastern melody. The woman turns toward the viewer for the first time, and her face is beautiful, with delicate yet sensual features; only her wide, expressive eyes seem troubled, a strangely discordant note.

Outdoors the night holds a lethal surprise for two villagers unlucky enough to wander near a hole that suddenly opens in the ground. A greenish light shoots out, hurling dead souls from the underworld toward the sky and turning the two horrified stragglers into charred statues. The desperate villagers make sacrifices and offerings to the gods, but the plague worsens. In desperation they call on Hercules, now a family man

with three children by his wife, Deianeira, to set things right in the underworld. To persuade him to leave his family, travel to their distant village, and risk his life in the land of the dead, they send a messenger named Iole—the woman with the blue medallion, which she presents to Deianeira as a gift.

Deianeira, casting occasional worried glances in the mirror and at the bewitching Iole, still sends her husband off with the young maiden, trusting that his mission of mercy will not also become a labor of love. But her serenity is shaken by an old woman who calls to her in the market, "My deepest sympathy. I'm so sorry for the loss of your husband. My condolences." Deianeira responds that her husband is very much alive, but the woman merely looks gravely at Deianeira's necklace, observing that Nurian maidens give such gifts to those they are about to widow: "When a task need be done, these beautiful virgins can persuade a man to attempt it." Nor can any man resist a Nurian maiden: "From the moment of birth she's trained for this and only this. She knows all there is to know about love, charm, and seduction." When Deianeira denies this could be true, the woman says bitterly, "*I* told myself the same thing once," then drops on the ground an identical blue stone medallion.

Deianeira is overcome by fear of losing Hercules, not to Iole but to the impossible deed she may set for him. She reaches them after a hard journey, and urges Hercules to "please, please come back with me," warning that Iole is a Nurian maiden who will lure him to his death. But Hercules assures Deianeira that he loves only her and will soon return. Holding his wife tenderly, he promises, "There's only one person in the world I'd die for, and that's you."

Her peace of mind restored, Deianeira begins to head home. But her way is blocked by a centaur named Nessus, who bitterly envies Hercules and desires his wife. As Nessus leers over Deianeira, boasting that her husband cannot help her, Hercules hears his wife's screams from across a river, draws back his bowstring to its full length, and fires an arrow that pierces the centaur's body. Sprawled on the ground, the dying centaur remains determined to hurt Hercules. With his last breaths he warns Deianeira to beware young Iole's charm, and offers her a cloak soaked with his blood:

Nessus: My blood is a powerful potion. Give the cloak to Hercules. Once he puts it on he'll never be unfaithful to you.

Deianeira: I told you, I don't doubt him.

Nessus: But you do. You should. Give it to him.

In fact the centaur's blood has powers, but of another kind; Deianeira does not see that where his blood has spilled, flowers wither and die.

Hercules rushes back across the river and, anxious for his wife's safety, decides to end his mission and return home. But Deianeira will not hear of it. Ashamed of her earlier doubts, she insists that he go with Iole to help her village. Perhaps a flicker of worry remains, though, for she presents Hercules with the cloak: "Here, take this, and when it gets cold at night,

I want you to wrap this around you and think only of me." He assures her, "I'll think of nothing else."

Iole sparkles as she walks with Hercules, laughing with girlish innocence at his curiosity about her being a Nurian maiden and why she chose to become one:

Iole: Well, it wasn't really my decision. Before I was born, my mother had a vision, and it told her that one day I'd be called upon to save my village. And in the vision, I was wearing a blue stone medallion. So she and my father sent me off to train as a Nurian maiden. And here I am.

Hercules: What about all those stories I've heard?

Iole (smiling at the silliness of it all): Well, that's nonsense. Fool's talk. You of all people must know how *that* is! I mean, according to the stories of the great and powerful Hercules, you're supposed to be ten feet tall. Some of the crazy things they say you've done! Do you know that you supposedly slew a three-headed giant? And then you killed the Lernean Hydra all by yourself? Or best of all, someone once told me that you killed an enormous sea monster by squeezing its heart until it stopped beating!

Hercules (far from reassured by this comparison): But those stories are true. (Iole smiles.) No, I mean it. I really *did* all those things.

Iole: So maybe Hercules does have a tale or two after all. (She takes his hand and leads him through the forest.) Come on, tell me a few more.

Iole's charm appears to know no bounds. At a tavern along the way she and Hercules come upon a man gone berserk, smashing furniture, thrashing those who try to interfere. At last Hercules grabs a club, but Iole bids him put down his weapon. She walks to the man, palms raised, then extends her arm to pat his head, saying, "There, there, what's the matter?" He begins whimpering and glances down ashamed at a spilled bowl of boiling soup. Iole explains for him, "I think he burned his mouth on his food. He would have said something but he can't speak. Can someone get him some water?" Soon the man is gratefully drinking the cool liquid. Iole looks back at Hercules and says gently, "Not everything needs to be killed. Sometimes kindness can work too."

Hercules and Iole come to her village. The green fire has become an enormous force streaking into the sky. Everywhere around them are signs of plague, scorched earth, and the charred remains of villagers. As Hercules peers quizzically at the hole, his father, Zeus, suddenly appears, explaining that this is the gateway to the underworld. It holds only death, he warns, and if Hercules enters, he can die too. "Go back to your family!" he commands, and for once Hercules cannot simply brush aside his father's caution.

"Iole, I'm afraid I can't help your town," Hercules tells the disconsolate woman. "I stood on the edge of that hole and thought about it long and hard. If I go down there, I may never come back. I have children now and a wife I love. I have to live for them." Iole appeals to his compassion: "Hercules, my people suffer, they need you. I need you." He shakes his head, saying, "Iole, I can't." The Nurian maiden has not exhausted her appeals. "Please, won't you do it for me?" she coaxes as she undoes her hair. She removes her robe and stands naked in front of Hercules, resting her hand on his shoulder and whispering, "Say you'll do it."

Hercules refuses her advances and her plea. Iole, hinting darkly at what the villagers intend for her, vows to go into the hole herself, saying, "I'm dead anyway. I failed in my mission." But nothing can draw Hercules away from his commitment to Deianeira and their children. "I don't want anything more to do with the gods and their games," he says. "I just want to go home."

Stepping into the chill night air, Hercules puts on the cloak Deianeira had given him at the urging of Nessus the centaur. At once it takes on an evil life of its own, tightening around him, choking and burning him. He roars with pain before finally throwing it to the ground, where it explodes and vanishes but for the flash of a peacock feather—Hera's work, again. "The gods will never stop!" he shouts, and this terrible thought makes him leap, with a defiant scream, into the hole that leads to the underworld.

The dying centaur's scheme, having sent Hercules to the land of the dead, now brings a second horror, when a messenger from the village reaches Deianeira. "There was a cloak, a cursed cloak," he relates breathlessly. "Hercules put it on and it tortured him. It drove him mad. His only escape was to jump into the hole." Deianeira is crushed by guilt. She climbs to the top of a mountain and, deluded by Hera into seeing Hercules beckoning, joyfully calls his name, then jumps to her death.

Hercules meanwhile makes his way through the cavernous underworld. Like all new arrivals in the realm of the dead, he encounters Charon the boatman, who for a gold coin (placed in the mouth of the deceased by loved ones) will ferry souls across the river Styx to their final rest. But Hercules has no time for such formalities. Charon grumbles about not getting a coin, then looks again at his robust, tanned guest, and indignantly refuses to give him passage:

Charon: Wait a—what are you doin' here, you can't go across!

Hercules: Why not?

Charon: Why not? Because you're still alive, that's why not! Only the dead are permitted to cross the river Styx, eh?

Hercules: Well, we're going to change that right now, aren't we?

Charon: We can't.

Hercules (seizing Charon): Can't?

Charon (seeing—and feeling—Hercules' urgency): You know, when I say *can't*, I mean, you're a regular kind of guy, we could, uh, maybe talk, yeah, *okay*. Hades is not gonna be happy about this, *let me tell you*. No one alive has ever entered the Underworld before.

As fearsome growls reverberate across the river, Charon mumbles his annoyance at that "damn dog, Cerberus. He's supposed to guard the gates, you know. Keep the dead down here where they belong. But—he's gotten loose somehow. Now he's runnin' around. Causin' all kinds of trouble."

It is in the Elysian Fields, the Greek heaven within the underworld, that Hercules experiences his deepest pain and grief, for he finds that his beloved wife, Deianeira, has joined the souls of the dead. Her new home, to be sure, is a beautiful refuge within this somber kingdom: Deianeira walks peacefully among other white-robed figures amid trees, colorful flowers, and quiet streams. Yet when Hercules approaches, she cannot recognize him, and his urgent descriptions of their past life together bring only regret that she can recall nothing. Then Hercules spies the god Hades, who assures him all is as it must be. But having plunged into the underworld, Hercules is not about to accept things as they are, even at the command of a god.

Though a dread god in the ancient myths, Hades here appears like a

funeral director on a grand scale, attentive and well-meaning but also concerned that nothing disturb the arrangements he has fussed over. He tries to soothe Hercules by explaining that "nothing's wrong" with Deieaneira. "I've merely erased the misery that brought her here, that's all. I've given her peace." He bids Hercules leave, for his time hasn't come yet. "Her time hasn't come either," Hercules insists. "Oh, I'm sorry, my friend, it has," his host explains sympathetically. "I lifted her broken body from the rocks myself." But Hades appears increasingly frightened as he hears Cerberus bellowing in the background, and Hercules realizes that the lord of the Underworld might just be willing to bargain.

"Damn it," Hades says under the strain. "Look, I really would like to stand here forever and debate this, but you've chosen a bad time. I've really got a lot of things to worry about, okay? You should really go back." Hercules instead proposes a deal: "Your Underworld's in chaos. If I'm not wrong, your Cerberus is running loose. . . . I'll catch him and return him to his post if you agree to let Deianeira return with me to the living." Sneering that even his best hunters have failed to tame Cerberus, Hades nonetheless accepts the offer, adding, "But if you fail, she stays here with me forever."

The arms and legs of the Underworld's "best hunters" lie scattered about, suggesting it has been a while since Cerberus last obeyed a command. But Hercules picks up a pole, forces it like a bit into the animal's three powerful maws, and pushes back the giant beast until it topples into a pit. The remaining hunters shout gleefully, eager to see the brutish hound beaten at last. But their blood lust does not sit well with Hercules, who approaches Cerberus without a weapon and says, as if to a frightened collie, "I don't want to hurt you. You just need to go back to where you belong. So what do you say? Will you go?" As the hunters look on in amazement, he reminds them, "Remember that sometimes a little kindness does the trick." Soon he is hammering the end of a chain into the ground, tethering Cerberus to his old post. Petting the now docile animal, he points affectionately at the middle head and orders, "Now, stay!"

As Cerberus is returned to Hades, the lord of the Underworld returns

Deianeira to Hercules. And with Cerberus once more guarding the gates of the Underworld, the hole that had plagued Iole's village with green fire is sealed; her mission has succeeded after all. Back at their home, Hercules and Deianeira watch as Zeus sits delightedly playing with his grandchildren. "Still wondering about your mortality?" Zeus asks his son. Hercules looks at Deianeira, his

sons, Aeson and Clonis, and his little daughter, Ilea, as she happily receives an apple from her immortal grandfather. "To tell you the truth," Hercules answers with a contentment beyond anything he has known before, "I don't think I really care if I live forever. Everything I care about is right here and now."

Hercules in the Underworld, the best of the five telefeatures, also boasts the most finely crafted script. The different myths and labors in each earlier film stand as exciting yet separate tales: Hercules' riveting battles with the Hydra in *Amazon Women*, the giant in *Lost Kingdom*, and Antaeus in *Circle of Fire* are unrelated to his larger adventures with the Amazons, Troy, or Prometheus. But *Underworld*'s young writing team of Andrew Dettmann and Daniel Truly seamlessly wove the stories of Iole, Deianeira, Nessus, Hades, even Cerberus into a single compelling tale. Every scene builds toward sending Hercules to the Underworld, a realm that dooms lesser mortals but yields the son of Zeus his greatest triumph.

Underworld also marks a new level of sophistication in designing the exotic creatures that populate the Hercules telefeatures. Cerberus is a marvel from the K.N.B. EFX group: a full-size model built to the midsection, to allow a puppeteer to work the two side heads from inside, lying upside down. Several puppeteers controlled from outside the more complex center, "hero" head, which could move its jaw, blink, rotate its eyes and head, point its ears, and—most important for a hellhound—snarl. Cerberus also rumbled along in the form of computer-generated graphics by Kevin O'Neill's team of artists, working from a miniature (eighteen-inch) hellhound sculpted by K.N.B.

While Cerberus relied mainly on location-based puppetry, Nessus the centaur involved a more intricate task: the precise merger by computer imaging of man and horse. O'Neill had K.N.B. EFX build an appliance that the actor wore like a skirt that spanned the area between his waistline and a horse's neckline. Computers then synchronized the actor's movements with that of the horse, frame by frame, so that they appeared to be a single creature. Universal had leaned toward cutting the centaur out of the film, doubting that the effects team could solve in time the intricate technical problems. But Rob Tapert pushed for it, and the result was cutting-edge computer-generated imaging, which would become a trademark of the Hercules adventures.

The film affords Kevin Sorbo as Hercules a rare opportunity to delve into the underworld of his emotions, whether in raging at the gods or grieving for Deianeira. Sorbo's generally relaxed approach to the role makes these explosions of raw feeling all the more gripping. And the affection that Sorbo, Anthony Quinn as Zeus, and Tawny Kitaen as Deianeira convincingly express for each other sustains interest in the central theme of the story: Will Hercules risk the bonds of family to save a village of strangers?

As Iole, Marlee Shelton is a wonder. A beautiful woman, she persuades by her very appearance that Iole will be a rival of consequence even to Deianeira. Yet much of Iole's allure lies in the joy and playful humor that Shelton is able to convey, as well as a kindness so deep (helping the man at the tavern) it reveals a beauty of the spirit.

Among the supporting players are two surprising comic turns. Mark Ferguson's anxiety-ridden, hapless Hades scarcely matches the glowering figure of Greek myth, though it serves the story's demand for a god in need. (This same actor, in full beard and rumbling voice, gives Prometheus an abundantly regal aura in *Circle of Fire*.) Michael Hurst, cast as an early victim of the hellfire, also took over as Charon, at the urging of Eric Gruendemann, when the original actor became ill. It was an inspired accident. Hurst improvised a character from two improbable sources: Jimmy Durante, the long-nosed, gravel-voiced singer with a clanging New York accent, and a Los Angeles taxi driver, reflecting Charon's vocation of taking fares for a gold coin.

Underworld stretches to new limits a trademark of the Hercules telefeatures: the willingness to adapt ancient tales to modern times. In the grim original myths Hercules took Iole captive in war and brought her into his home as a mistress. Deianeira's jealousy over Iole left her prey to the schemes of the dying centaur Nessus, not realizing his blood contained poison from Hercules' arrow. The blood-soaked cloak that Deianeira had intended as a love potion sent Hercules into such agony that he had Iolaus burn his still living body on a funeral pyre. Hercules forgave Deianeira, but only on hearing that she had proved her remorse by hanging herself (some say, stabbing herself in their marriage bed). After Hercules died, Zeus carried his son's immortal being to Olympus, though his mortal half, by his mother, Alcmene, remained a shade in the land of the dead.

Here is tragedy in its starkest form: people brought low by flaws in their character. *Underworld* echoes these tragic tales but, in true American fashion, refuses to allow defeat (let alone death) be the final word. The centaur's cloak torments Hercules and sends him into the Underworld, but does not kill him; Deianeira is driven by grief and guilt to take her own life, but is restored and reunited with her husband. Second chances are rare in Greek myth, even for heroes. But *Underworld* reflects a mythic world marked by hope as well as suffering; a world in which every horror offers a chance for redemption, and love is stronger than death itself.

Hercules in the Maze of the Minotaur

our Hercules films were originally agreed upon, but a fifth was later commissioned when another Action Pack movie team failed to deliver its quota. The resulting feature, *Hercules in the Maze of the Minotaur*, relies extensively on flashbacks from earlier movies—a sort of "best labors" highlights reel of Hercules' battles with giants, monsters, and armies. Unlike most such "clip" shows, however, this one features a solid story line, centered on one of the most loathsome creatures from the Greek myths, the half man, half bull known as the Minotaur.

By order of Minos II, tyrant of the isle of Crete, seven Athenian boys and seven maidens were sacrificed yearly to the Minotaur, according to the ancient myths. This fierce and powerful creature fed on human flesh and roamed a labyrinth so complex that no one could find his way out unaided. An Athenian named Theseus managed to enter the labyrinth by offering himself as a victim, then slew the Minotaur with a sword and returned by following a thread he had unspooled to mark his way. *Maze of the Minotaur* adapts this tale by elevating the Minotaur from merely a brute to a far more dangerous schemer seeking vengeance against Zeus for imprisoning him as punishment for his evil deeds. The movie also places Hercules himself rather than Theseus at the center of this tale, as the Minotaur seeks to lure the son of Zeus into the labyrinth and kill him.

Despite limited new footage—the price of supplying an extra movie on urgent notice—*Maze of the Minotaur* offers several fresh looks at its hero. Having settled into family life, Hercules still misses his earlier days battling monsters and giants. The call to save people from the Minotaur comes just in time to rescue Hercules himself, letting him once more test his strength in a worthy cause. The bond between Hercules and Zeus has also grown; Zeus is a friend, an ally, even a supplicant, because the king of the gods urgently wants Hercules to do what he himself cannot: destroy the Minotaur. Only at the film's end, after Hercules slays the Minotaur to save his friend Iolaus, is this creature revealed in his original form—a handsome man who, like Hercules, was the son of Zeus and a mortal woman.

Maze of the Minotaur is notable, too, for the ripening screen chemistry of Kevin Sorbo and Michael Hurst as Iolaus. "I remember making that click with Kevin," Hurst says. "Suddenly we were buddies in an action thing and it really felt good. And I remember my character's being appreciated for the first time for his humor." Both actors improvised much of that humor, at times embellishing their lines, as in a scene where their characters try valiantly but vainly to appear content about leaving behind their heroic days for a new, responsible world of farming:

Hercules: It's all turning out pretty . . . green. How are *your* crops doing?

Iolaus: Oh, not too good. I can't get the hang of this manure thing. You know, it's either too *much* or there's not *enough*—

Hercules: Yeah, yeah, yeah, I can't figure out what to do with manure either. (pensive:) Do you . . . do you *mash* it in?

Iolaus: No, I kind of spread it all around, you know. (excited:) Maybe I *should* mash it in, do you find it works?

Hercules: What I do . . .

Hercules holds out his hands as if about to demonstrate, then suddenly looks up, and both he and Iolaus begin laughing at how unsuited they are to the simple joys of farming.

Iolaus: What the hell are we talking about?!

Hercules: I have no idea. Let's go back to the house, get you something to drink, and we can talk about something we give a damn about.

They soon begin trading stories of old adventures, and dreaming of new ones.

Hurst taxed his vast energy to the limit when the filming went three days over schedule and he found himself alternating between productions of *Hercules* and *Hamlet*, which he directed and starred in. "I was leaving my *Hamlet* rehearsals at six o'clock in the evening, being picked up by the production company and driven straight to somewhere way out of Auckland, and working till two o'clock in the morning, and then going back and starting *Hamlet* again at nine o'clock. And I remember being up at one in the morning, in the middle of nowhere, freezing, being covered in green slime, and thinking, Boy, tomorrow I've got to say, 'Oh, that this too, too solid flesh will melt, thaw and resolve itself into a dew.'"

Hamlet in fact never escaped from *Hercules'* iron grip, as Hurst discovered on opening night of his stage production. As he laughingly recalls, pandemonium erupted when his Hamlet branded the usurper of the throne, Claudius, as "no more like a [king] than I to Hercules": "The whole audience went up, because I'd been in *Hercules*. They're all actors and friends, the opening night audience. I nearly said, 'Shut up! This is Shakespeare!'"

Casting the Minotaur was no easy task. Tracy Hampton, a young woman who cast nonspeaking roles, was assigned to find the right physical type, who would be voiced later by another actor. Hampton recalls, "They came to us and said, 'We want someone who's going to be able to do his own stunts, who's built incredibly well to hold this ox head—it's remote-controlled and incredibly heavy—who'll be able to act, and will not be bigger than Hercules but complement Hercules.'"

Among those who answered Hampton's casting call was a radio announcer and former American football coach named Anthony Ray Parker. Parker had never acted before, but he impressed Hampton as physically right, and with his deep, cavernous voice, there would be no need for the producers to find a second actor to say the Minotaur's lines. "As soon as they heard Anthony Ray Parker speak," Hampton says, "well, he had the most distinctive voice they ever heard, so that was great." (In the end, though, Al Chalk, who narrates the opening credits of the five Hercules films, "looped" the Minotaur's dialogue in postproduction.)

Well before Hercules slew the Minotaur, his exploits were fast be-

coming legend with television executives. Dan Filie found the blend of action, character drama, and humor "something special," and showed a rough cut of the second movie, *Hercules and the Lost Kingdom,* to officials from the syndicated stations. They were impressed enough to launch *Hercules* as a weekly series without even waiting to sample ratings from the broadcast. With the same cast and crew largely in place, thirteen hour-long episodes began filming in the late summer of 1994, and debuted to high ratings in January 1995. After five landmark adventures involving lethal women warriors, centaurs, satyrs, the world of the dead, a ferocious Minotaur, and the fabled kingdom of Troy, the labors of Hercules—and Renaissance Pictures—were just beginning to unfold.

HERCULES

LEGENDS BEHIND THE SCENES

*T*he myths shown on *Hercules* and *Xena* are the product of many unseen legends: Writers, directors, costume and set designers, effects experts, musicians, and other artists all enhance the screen magic woven by the actors. Their stories, though unfolding off camera, are the stuff that TV dreams are made of.

The Writers

*W*riters on *Hercules* face a formidable challenge: to create labors worthy of the world's strongest man. They have responded in part by conjuring such deadly foes as a twenty-foot Cyclops, an army of sword-wielding skeletons, a god made of fire, and "the mother of all monsters," Echidna, whose human face and lizard's body are covered by swirling tentacles. But the writers' vision of Hercules' greatness has proven larger than even these fearsome creatures.

The prologue to each episode of *Hercules* proclaims, "His strength is surpassed only by the power of his heart." And writers and producers strive for ways to show Hercules as more than a demigod of last resort who can be called on to slay the latest ogre. According to John Schulian, the show's head writer for the first two seasons (succeeded by Jerry Patrick Brown in the third season), the key is to offer in every episode "a blend of action, humor, and heart."

Schulian joined *Hercules* after having written for such acclaimed series as *Miami Vice*, *Wiseguy*, and *Midnight Caller*. Earlier he had been a sports columnist renowned for portraying some of the most exalted mythic heroes in American life: prizefighters. Under his keen gaze, boxers came alive as full human beings, carrying scars not only from the ring but also from hard childhoods, demanding fans, and dreams of glory that disappointed or danced just beyond their reach. The skills Schulian honed in finding the sensitive, appealing souls hidden by the boxing world's macho code later helped him portray Hercules as a hero at once courageous and compassionate, physically invincible and emotionally vulnerable.

It was Schulian who, with Rob Tapert's concurrence, had Hera destroy Hercules' family in the opening scene of the first episode. He thereby revealed at the outset of the series that the son of Zeus was subject to pain and loss, like any human. Schulian then built on this tragedy to deepen Hercules' character by having him choose to help others rather than seek revenge.

Schulian also played on the comic possibilities in *Hercules*. In the mythic world he envisioned, even monsters could be farcical, like the clumsy but good-hearted giant Typhon and his mischievous child, Obie. And Schulian found the friendship between Hercules and Iolaus a source of ongoing camaraderie and banter. Paying homage to a famous action "buddy movie," Schulian said of his approach to *Hercules*, "I would do this like *Butch Cassidy and the Sundance Kid*."

Schulian's writing partner, Bob Bielak, came to *Hercules* after writing for *Tour of Duty*, an emotionally gripping action series set during the Vietnam War. In episodes like "The Other Side," Bielak continued to evoke the human side of heroes. "I liked the heart in that," Bielak says of Hercules' poignant visit with his deceased family in the Underworld. "I couldn't have written that episode five years ago, before I had a family. There are things that kids brought out in me that I would have missed before."

A story meeting for a Halloween episode from the second season, "Mummy Dearest," revealed the writers' concern to show Hercules as a deeply human hero, whose father may be ruler of Olympus but whose feelings are very much of this earth. John Schulian hosted the meeting to review a "beat sheet" (or script outline). He was joined by Bielak and the freelance author of "Mummy Dearest," Melissa Rosenberg, who had earlier written scripts for the television shows *The Outer Limits* and *Dr. Quinn, Medicine Woman*. Also on hand was Rob Tapert, low-key in manner but unmistakably at the center of this collaborative process.

"Well, Melissa, you've covered yourself with glory!" Schulian exclaimed warmly. Rosenberg's story brought to Hercules' world such novel touches as an encounter with Egyptian royalty and an homage to fifties horror films. An exotic beauty, Princess Anuket, follows the trail of a stolen mummy

into Greece, and asks Hercules to help her. ("You want me to find . . . your mommy?" "*Not* my mommy. My *mummy!*") Otherwise, she warns, a renegade priest named Sokar will use his black arts to turn the mummy into an unstoppable evil force. Though a newcomer to *Hercules*, Rosenberg had caught the show's tone of lighthearted adventure; now the senior writers, together with Rob Tapert, guided her through the finer points of creating a legendary journey.

In every episode Hercules must do more than fight; he must stand for something. Rosenberg interwove the mummy's tale with scenes of Hercules speaking out against slavery, and at last persuading even the pampered Egyptian princess that her own slaves should be freed. This is the kind of moral lesson *Hercules* looks to convey, especially to young viewers, but the heroine's change of heart seemed too abrupt to both Schulian and Tapert. They suggested that Rosenberg add a "mid-beat," an intermediate scene in which, thanks to Hercules, Anuket begins to question whether slavery is right. The power of Hercules' good character and values must appear as convincing as his physical strength.

Hercules may be pure fantasy, but the show's producers put a premium on helping viewers suspend their disbelief by pruning any loose story ends. When Sokar tried to scare Hercules by creating the illusion of a vengeful Pharaoh's ghost, he brought down not only the wrath of Hercules but a rain of probing questions

Legendary Facts

Notable horror film mummies include Boris Karloff, Lon Chaney, Jr., Christopher Lee, and Peter Cushing.

from the executive producer. "Is there a logic problem with this ghost?" Tapert asked dryly. "How does Sokar even know the image of the man he wants to re-create? I *like* the ghost, it's a Halloween episode, but is there a logical way to do it?"

The mummy, too, had to behave reasonably (for a mummy). Bielak asked Rosenberg to go over the "ground rules" for the mummy's supernatural powers, what it could and could not do. How was it, for example, that the decidedly unheroic merchant Salmoneus could escape—more than once—from the mummy's grasp? Was this creature a real threat or merely comical? The upshot was to trim Salmoneus' getaways, for otherwise, as Tapert and Schulian agreed, "We would have *Abbott and Costello Meet the Mummy.*"

The demands of logic applied to villains as well: they could be as bad as they wanted to be, but their aims should be clear and their schemes clever. Tapert summed up Sokar's ambitions ("OK, he wants to rule the world and marry the girl"), and exhorted Rosenberg to "connect his motives and strengthen them throughout." Tapert and Schulian also questioned a "beat," or scene outline, in which Sokar executed an aide for failing to get him the mummy. "Spare the henchman!" Schulian said with a mischievous glance at Tapert, who jokingly lamented the series' penchant for having a villain slaughter some hapless minion simply to show how nasty he is. "I'm sick of that beat. We've done that beat to death! You know, we reached the zenith in [the episode] 'Let the Games Begin,' " where the villain has *two* of his goons killed. " 'I'm so powerful and so *stupid* I'm reducing my army! Let me kill two of my four men!' "

Although *Hercules* thrives on action, fight scenes must still justify their place in the story or face the editor's pen. Tapert complained of "too many meaningless fights"; he asked about a brawl in the script, "Does it advance the story?" Even then, he noted, they "must lose [cut] a few fights." Rosenberg was politely protective of her opening scene, asking, "Can I keep the fight in the teaser?" This free-for-all pitted Hercules against Princess Anuket's whole entourage, so she could be sure that he was "the right man to find [her] mummy." Tapert nodded, "Yeah, that was a good fight!"

Tapert and the writers spent more time scouting possibilities for comedy than for displays of muscle. "Somewhere there's a beat of humor where Hercules is amazed by the Egyptian practice of mummifying," Tapert observed. "We can play on the culture clash." Also, recalling a popular song by The Bangles, Tapert suggested, "Let's see if we can get the licensing rights to 'Walk Like an Egyptian.' It's a light enough episode. We can do it without the vocals, if Joe [Lo Duca, the composer for *Hercules*] can do his version of it." Schulian added, "And if you can get a line into the script, 'Walk like an Egyptian!' "

The recurring comic figure Salmoneus, who peddles everything from "toga-wear" to "air sandals," is up to his old tricks in "Mummy Dearest." This time, convinced that the public will pay "big dinars" for the privilege of being scared, he plans to open a house of horrors. Tapert conveyed a suggestion from the producer Liz Friedman that Salmoneus ask Hercules' endorsement for his museum. "Yes, it makes him as shameless as possible," Schulian agreed with enthusiasm, adding, "and the actor [Robert Trebor] will play him even more shamelessly. I guarantee you!"

The producers formed a bodyguard around the character of Hercules, pouncing on any dialogue or deed that would poorly serve the show's hero. Schulian pointed to Beat 7 in Act III, where Hercules jumps off a wall down a dark pit: "That doesn't sound smart, like our boy." "I agree," Tapert said, and recast the beat to have Hercules peer over the wall just as Salmoneus accidentally hurtles into him from behind. Above all, the producers were vigilant to dispel any doubts about Hercules' boundless strength.

"Hercules tries to bend the bars, but can't?" Tapert recited with surprise this stage cue from Act IV, and vetoed the image in a word: "No." Schulian explained to Rosenberg, "Hercules doesn't often do feats of strength, at least in our world, but when circumstances require, he can hurl boulders and rip jail cells out of their moorings." A scene in which Salmoneus comes to Hercules' rescue also sent red flares sailing through the meeting room. "Hercules don't need no stinking help!" Schulian declared with a smile. "People don't save Hercules. Hercules saves himself and others." Tapert added wryly, "Dr. Quinn can be saved by other people."

The technical challenges of filming this episode generated a final round of concerns. In one scene, a screaming Princess Anuket leans against a wall, only to have it spin around and send her to the bottom of a pit. "Do we have a wall that can do that?" Schulian asked. Questions also attended a suggestion to have Hercules destroy the mummy by hurling it so that it unravels at high speed. Was this really feasible? On every point Tapert offered an assurance that might well serve as his credo for the scripts on both *Hercules* and *Xena*: "Write it; we can *do* it."

Casting

Casting offices in New Zealand and the U.S. work full-time to fill roles on *Hercules*, from guest villains to huddled villagers. Diana Rowan, who casts most of the featured parts from her home near Auckland, approaches the relentless deadlines with a mixture of good humor and terror:

> Well, every week I have to find forty actors for *Xena* and *Hercules*, forty American-speaking actors. . . . Every episode I think, We're not going to make it, this is not going to happen this time. This is it. Our last episode is being made. And somehow we pull through, and then we face the next script, which usually comes about seven days before we start to shoot. . . . So every seven days I'm casting one *Hercules* and one *Xena*.

Finding the right actor for a role, according to the U.S. casting director Beth Hymson-Ayer, is "totally subjective, a matter of intangibles, and that's why you can't go to any school for it." Her intuition has led to such discoveries as Alexandra Tydings as the goddess Aphrodite, Glenn Shadix as the giant Typhon, Hudson Leick as the crazed warrior Callisto, and Teresa Hill as Nemesis. And sometimes Hymson-Ayer gives her discoveries an extra helping nudge, as with the actress who plays the Golden Hind, Serena, whom Hercules falls in love with and marries:

Legendary Facts

Sam Jenkins has appeared four times on *Hercules: The Legendary Journeys*, as Kirin in "Prince Hercules" and as Serena, the Golden Hind, in the episodes "Encounter," "When a Man Loves a Woman," and "Judgment Day."

> I had cast Sam Jenkins as the hero's high school sweetheart in a pilot episode of a series called *Glory Days*. They were breaking up, and Sam had about seven lines. But I kept track of her because she was not only beautiful but a really nice kid—a young woman now

but a kid then. The first time I tried to cast her on *Hercules* she couldn't audition on the day we had the producers present, so I snuck her in on videotape, in between the people who were auditioning. Although she didn't get the part, I told the producers, Sam is somebody who should be doing the show. . . . And then a part came up that she liked, and once she showed up to audition and everyone saw her, well, what more do you need? She won the role.

The distance from Hollywood to Auckland limits the number of American guest actors to about one an episode. Diana Rowan, New Zealand's foremost casting director, fills the other speaking parts, while a former model named Tracy Hampton sees that the villages Hercules visits are populated by dozens of extras who match that week's ethnic look. Rowan is among a half dozen "lifers," New Zealanders who have been with the production since the first TV movie. She helps set the tone of these adventures by encouraging actors to play modern characters rather than stereotyped ancients:

> The first note I give to all actors is that they should be as natural as if they were on the streets of New York or California today. . . . And with the gods, although they should have a charisma on-screen that raises them a little bit above the average mortal, I still encourage the actors to talk as though they're just going down the path. That makes it more accessible to the audience.

For Rowan the line between gods and mortals is not so sharp as between heroes and villains: "The 'goodies' I make as real as possible and the 'baddies' I encourage to go up a notch or two because I think that makes it more exciting and, after all, we're not talking about reality here in any shape or form."

Because "a script can be cast in so many different ways," Rowan makes a point to learn the director's vision for each character. Still, she will often play with that vision in unexpected ways:

> I don't necessarily go with the first thing that comes into my mind, because I think life's not like that. So if a script says "a huge thug comes over the bridge," I think, Now how else could you cast this? What if you got a little person in the part rather than a

big nasty-looking person? For the same reason, it's quite nice sometimes to have someone who is really evil smile all the time, and appear really charming. In fact, it's really much more threatening. . . . I like to push the boundaries that way, it's one of my quirks!

Set Design

At the entrance to Pacific Renaissance headquarters in Auckland a visitor gingerly opens a large crate shipped from Los Angeles to production designer Rob Gillies. Nestled inside is a dragon's head, six feet long and four feet around, painted brown, red, and orange, for use in an upcoming episode of *Hercules*. Even Gillies' mail, it seems, belongs to an alternate universe.

Palaces, forts, temples, war wagons, dungeons, mazes, "doomsday" weapons spewing fire, and even a modern-day "museum of horrors" have sprung full-blown from Gillies' imagination. A soft-spoken, friendly man ever ready to sketch a new location or prop, Gillies each week provides the son of Zeus with sets and props that convey a sense of grandeur, beauty, and mystery.

"Yeah, I have great fun on the show," Gillies said of his role dreaming up outlandish props for Hercules and other characters. "They're constantly falling through trapdoors and plunging into pits with vipers and things like that." Inspiration for these ingenious devices comes to Gillies from many worlds of fantasy and even, on occasion, reality: "[I draw from] everywhere. Comics, magazines, books, other TV shows, old TV shows, nature—like natural skull shapes, whatever. [I] just mix it all up." While all creatures, great, small, and fictitious, spark Gillies' creative energies, time is his one natural enemy: "The scripts are written a little like *Indiana Jones and the Temple of Doom*—only we have a *week* to get it ready."

As Gillies and a reporter stand on either side of his latest creation—a gigantic sandal-clad foot made of plastic and other nonmythic materials—

the conversation turns to how he came to work on *Hercules*. "What on earth did the producers say they *wanted* from you when they hired you?" he is asked. Gillies looks pensively at his prized foot, worthy of the monsters roaming his TV landscapes, and replies with a twinkle, "They wanted a lot of sole."

Costumes

*L*ike any man, Hercules puts on his pants one leg at a time—but, according to Kevin Sorbo, they weigh almost twelve pounds. The woven leather trousers he sports for each episode suggest a medieval rather than an ancient look. Yet Sorbo recalls donning them with gratitude and relief, for he had feared having to wear a toga. Not everyone was so relieved, however. According to costume designer Ngila Dickson, "It takes two people working full-time for two days simply to weave together the four colors of leather" for a single pair of Hercules' trousers. "A wardrobe expert spends another two days supervising the stitching, and then we spend two to three days more breaking them down to a point where they can be handed over to Kevin." Asked how many pairs of trousers Hercules has on hand, Dickson replies:

> Nowhere near enough! Kevin's got three really good pairs that we keep in maximum condi-

tion, plus we have a pair that we use for anything like going into water, which are a little ripped, and then we've got something like four pairs for stunt doubles.

Why trousers? They do not, after all, immediately call to mind ancient times. Dickson observes, "No, but they're terribly practical!" Then she explains her approach to costuming for the series:

> We do try to maintain a nod toward ancient times, but my philosophy on this has always been very strongly that these are mythical creatures and therefore I should be able to reinvent them. They were invented by the Greeks and the Romans—the gods and all that surround them—and they dressed them in their times the way they saw them. So I just dress them in these times the way I see them.

Dickson had not heard of the "no toga" rule that the producers had decided on beginning with the first TV movies. But it is one that she likes:

> Togas are very difficult to work with. They're incredibly time-consuming in terms of dressing, it's really difficult to get fabrics to achieve the right drape for them, and they take up vast amounts of fabric. So all those things mean that I would use them very rarely, only when we're doing something that requires a certain set style.

Dickson's imaginative outfits have drawn admiring notice from fans and critics alike. Her costumes have ranged across Greece, Rome, Egypt, and other ancient lands, and touched on medieval themes for villagers and for Hercules himself. She even re-created the aristocratic fashions of revolutionary France for the third-season episode "Les Contemptibles." From simple peasant garments to the dazzling white dress of the goddess Aphrodite, Dickson's designs are as unpredictable as they are eye-catching. Her office, piled high with fashion books and magazines, attests to her extraordinary knowledge of dress through the ages. And she relishes the creative freedom the producers have given her, saying, "Each week they will let me go wherever the inspiration leads."

Filming Hercules

*H*ercules is shot on New Zealand's North Island, from windswept Bethells Beach west of Auckland to lush parks within the city and a seventy-acre vineyard to the south. The vineyard, known as Lion Park because of its earlier incarnation as a "safari" theme park, features a castle, a Moroccan marketplace, a Polynesian village, an army camp, and other settings that change color and character each week. Another outdoor set, called Sturges (after a nearby road), has a standard complement of villages plus a boat exterior built for Hercules' adventure with the Argonauts. "We have to create an entirely new world from scratch," the producer Eric Gruendemann says. "And coordinating all the artisans and technicians [for] the kind of show that we've mounted down here has been a mammoth undertaking, to say the least."

Although directors on *Hercules* alternate each week, the series counts on scores of veteran artists for sets, props, costumes, and makeup to ensure a distinctive, high-quality look. It counts, as well, on a topflight camera crew to give *Hercules* a visual style unique among TV action shows.

John Mahaffie, who heads the film team, is among New Zealand's foremost cinematographers, though he recalls having entered the profession "quite by accident." He had been a commercial artist during his late teens when a job opened up in the TV branch of an ad agency, which sparked his love of cameras, editing, and filmmaking. Mahaffie freelanced for two decades as an assistant cameraman, often on foreign productions in locales from Tahiti to North Carolina. His credits include *Mad Max III: Beyond Thunderdome* (1985), an action movie notable for its inventive camera angles and riveting Australian vistas.

Mahaffie's skill with the "Steadicam," a device that enables steady handheld camera shots even on rough terrain, won him a job on the *Hercules* telefeatures. When *Hercules* became a weekly series, Mahaffie was asked to become the director of photography (or DP), an irresistible creative challenge that he soon found "a marathon of a job."

Drawing on his background in feature films, Mahaffie approached

Hercules as if he were shooting a series of hour-long motion pictures. "We gave each episode a dynamic and a scale of logistics beyond normal television," he says. "And that's been true of the whole production, really, whether you look at the wardrobe or the art department or the camera team and equipment. Few episodic television shows have had this scope."

Mahaffie's ambitions for shooting *Hercules* have strained against the show's modest budget, which, at a million dollars per episode, is some 40 percent less than for network action programs and below even that of syndicated series like *Star Trek: Deep Space Nine*. To compensate, Mahaffie says, "I've tried to find constructive ways to break the rules [of filmmaking], to cut the time needed for a feature film but still get feature-film quality." Among many resourceful adjustments, he is a master at shifting a few props to convey the illusion of different camera angles:

> You plan your main shots, your "master" shots, with the camera facing the hero and the sets in one direction. Then when you do your back cuts [shooting characters from the opposite side], you might say to the art department, "Look, it would be quicker if we just removed that little bit of background [scenery], and I'll change the lighting a bit" [to simulate a reverse angle] without actually turning the set around 180 degrees. Now on a feature film you would normally stick to the "geography" of a scene absolutely, but for TV you find ways to cheat on the geography while maintaining your quality shots.

Mahaffie emphasizes the "collaborative vision" that goes into the cinematography, and this is evident on the set of "Mummy Dearest." The first thing a visitor notices on this indoor soundstage is the Egyptian look of the sets and props, complete with exotic vases and decorations on simulated brick walls overlaid with straw. The costumes, too, draw attention, notably a dress worthy of Egyptian royalty for actress Galyn Gorg, who plays Princess Anuket. And the extras have a swarthy look, often heightened and in some instances created by the makeup artists, that seems just right for the land of the Pharaohs.

Legendary Facts

Galyn Gorg, who plays Princess Anuket in "Mummy Dearest," also appeared on *Xena* as another royal figure, Helen of Troy.

The ability to convey the splendor of ancient Egypt on a modest set (really a refitted factory) is extraordinary. Yet just outside camera range, modern reality intrudes. A slender young woman scurries across the set carrying a twelve-foot "stone" pillar and sets it down lightly near other "ancient" artifacts. Another crew member, sporting a brown baseball cap over her braided ponytail, hovers near Kevin Sorbo and buffs his arms with giant sponges to give them what Sorbo laughingly calls the "Hercules sheen."

Much of the day's work involves meticulous preparation by Mahaffie's five-man crew to get the desired camera ranges, angles, and paths for filming. While actors chat, undergo finishing touches on their makeup, or fine-tune rehearsals, Mahaffie directs the laying of tracks for the camera dolly. This mobile platform on wheels supports the camera and its operator and allows a "dolly pusher" to move it along the rails. Under Mahaffie's guidance the camera operator can then pan in for

close-ups, pull back to reveal more of a scene, and track actors as they move across the set. The planning and labor that go into these set-ups, though unheralded and of course unobserved by audiences, actually consume more time than the filming itself.

Mahaffie's interest in feature-film quality is evident in all aspects of his cinematography. The crew uses 35mm film, which provides a breadth, clarity, and accuracy unmatched by *Xena*'s 16mm film, which is cheaper and permits lighter cameras but yields a grainier picture. Also, while Mahaffie at times will employ two cameras to get both a close-up and a mid-range shot of the same subject, he will almost never shoot from different angles at once. That would be self-defeating, he believes, because it tends to compromise the lighting from at least one angle. Mahaffie would rather achieve perfect lighting in one direction and then shift the cameras, a slower approach but one that affords viewers razor-sharp images.

Charlie Haskell, a director who has worked on both *Hercules* and its sister spin-off series, *Xena*, compares the filming of the two shows:

John Mahaffie and his crew are a little bit older and a bit more experienced. And they have a pretty definite style of how to do this.
You find that you don't work as fast as you do on *Xena*, you don't
get as many shots done in a day. But the standard is always very
high. It's quite a high [-quality] precedent—I find that each shot
I do on *Hercules* is always very good. It's pretty to look at. On
Xena, you shoot a lot more, it's a bit more action-packed, fast-
moving cameras . . . it's a little bit wackier . . . and sometimes it
can be a little bit rougher as well, probably as a consequence.

A good director on *Hercules*, Haskell elaborates, must adapt to the
show's emphasis on quality over speed in filming: "You know, you'd be
crazy to go onto *Hercules* and expect to get thirty [camera] setups a day. If
you walk in there for a shot list of thirty setups, well, you might as well
throw it out right away, because you're not going to achieve it. You have
to know what you're going to get, and use [that pace] to your advantage."

The burden of shooting an episode in the allotted time is so relentless
that directors rarely try to change the basic look and tone of the show.
Mahaffie likens the making of *Hercules* to "a machine on the roll, and the
directors sort of jump on board and hopefully they are able to steer it in
the direction they want to go." But their main task, Mahaffie says, is "to
avoid the obstacles rather than say, 'Let's stop and rethink here,' because
there are no brakes on the machine, no stop signs in an eight-day shooting schedule." There is instead a relentless sprint to keep up with the
"shot list." "A good day," says Mahaffie, "is when you finish with just a few
minutes to spare and you're satisfied with the work you've got. And a bad
day is when you're rushing flat out to get to the end and still you are a few
shots short. But that is the challenge and also the frustration of episodic
[TV] versus features."

Mahaffie is a soft-spoken but central presence on the set, who often
draws on his technical knowledge to expedite the director's work. Watching
rehearsals of a fight scene between Hercules and the Mummy, Mahaffie ad-
mires the stunts but frets that the "blocking," or layout of the scene, will require time-consuming installation of special lights for filming the reverse
angles. He suggests instead having Hercules briefly glide out of frame during the fight; the Mummy will look confused about where he has gone, and
then Hercules can spin around and charge again, all with the cameras facing
in the original direction. "That one change in the blocking," Mahaffie tells
the appreciative director, Anson Williams, "should save us an hour."

Happily for both Mahaffie and Williams, Kevin Sorbo plays a quietly heroic role on set as well as on-screen. Perfectly prepared, Sorbo appears equally at ease taking directions and assisting cast and crew members. In a scene early one morning with Robert Trebor as the manic merchant Salmoneus, Sorbo shows why, in the words of assistant director Claire Richardson, he is "as good a star and person as you could hope to work with."

The script calls for Salmoneus to greet Hercules and begin hawking his latest business venture, a house of horrors. Trebor, a cerebral, intense actor, questions Williams for more than ten minutes on the upcoming scene, as crew members look on resignedly. Sorbo merely smiles patiently, glides his hand through the air, and quips, "We're off to a nice, smooth start." Shortly before the cameras roll, Sorbo asks Williams, "Do you want me to stare at [Salmoneus] the whole time till he gets here and spots me?" Williams approves and calls, "Action!" Trebor becomes increasingly distraught on missing several lines but Sorbo calms him, feeds him the lines, and remains good-humored through six takes.

Unlike many a star, Sorbo proves receptive to ad-libs by other actors. In a burst of comic inspiration, Trebor exclaims, "Ooh, that must have hurt!" as he steps over the "Egyptian slaves" bowing on the palace floor. Afterward Sorbo tells Williams, "I think it's a funny line! Why don't we leave it in?" Sorbo later explains, "Bob Trebor is a very funny man, and if he can come up with something cute and quaint, that's great, because [making] *Hercules* has got to be a team effort."

At the helm of this team effort, director Anson Williams finds ways to make his mark while relying on the star and crew to keep the production machine rolling. In directing the climactic scene when Princess Anuket cries over the death of a slave and realizes that slavery is wrong, Williams yells at Galyn Gorg to bring more emotion. Gorg just wants Williams to say "cut" so she can get ready again. Instead he keeps the cameras rolling and keeps yelling at Gorg, "Do it again! Do it again!" Gorg later recalls, "I had never experienced anything like this, and I was getting *so mad*! And you know what? I didn't know what he was doing, but then my performance just kind of came together, and I was blown away by it! Afterward I told him, 'You know, you really made me mad,' and he said, 'Good!'"

Legendary Facts

Anson Williams, the director of "Mummy Dearest," may be better known as Potsie on *Happy Days*, in which he co-starred with the future director of *Apollo 13*, Ron Howard.

For everyone involved, the routine on set is physically and emotionally taxing: twelve hours of painstaking work each day to complete, if all goes well, six to seven minutes of finished dialogue. Yet the cast and crew manage a lighthearted tone, at least in between their labors. Sorbo is "a total professional who *never* misses a line," said Galyn Gorg, but he is also "fun-loving." On several occasions he teases Gorg off camera until, at last, she chases him across the set as the crew bursts into laughter. And Robert Trebor, who as Salmoneus provides much of the broad humor on-screen on "Mummy Dearest," offers memorable comic relief off-screen as well.

Trebor rehearses a scene in which the Mummy, played by the towering actor Mark Newnham, creeps up from behind and grabs Salmoneus, who calls to Hercules in a panicky, high-pitched voice, "Help me!" Trebor changes tone with each reading and frowns between shots as he searches for just the right approach. But right after Mahaffie gets their last take on film, Trebor begins humming a rendition of "Tea for Two" while leading Newnham, swathed in bandages, in a dance across the set. His impromptu musical number brings a round of appreciative chuckles from the cast and crew. Then Williams readies for the next scene and the "dance floor" instantly reverts to a hushed set. Sorbo, Trebor, and Newnham move seamlessly back into character, crew members spring to their tasks, the cameras roll once more, and Hercules resumes the serious business of saving Salmoneus from the Mummy.

Stuntwork

With three major fights plus a number of smaller skirmishes to stage each week on *Hercules*, stunt coordinator Peter Bell has been one of the show's indispensable off-camera heroes. Bell is a veteran stuntman who once climbed a rope hanging from a plane 4,000 feet high and drove a car from one roof onto another for a Hong Kong action flick, *Mad Mission 4*. He describes his mission on *Hercules* as "keeping the fights fresh and making viewers *feel* the action."

Bell's stunt team numbers around forty men and women, about a dozen of whom see action every day. Most of his "stuntees," he says, "come with one special skill or other, whether it be martial arts, boxing background, gymnastics, mountain climbing, or perhaps they were good wheel men," or drivers. Allan Poppleton, for example, was recruited from a martial arts school at age twenty-two for the TV movie *Hercules and the Amazon Women*. (He doubled for Amazons in fight scenes, his face concealed by a large animal mask.) Bell retooled his skills "so they would look good for the camera and what we want to do on the series." And once on Bell's team, Poppleton went to gymnastics class and learned stunt riding and falls as well.

Despite the hazards, most of Bell's stuntees have been with him for many years, and Bell regards even those with five years of hard knocks as "recent arrivals." This, he explains, is because "you can never, as we say, buy experience," which is crucial to making the shift from the gym to a film set. "We can show them what to do," Bell says, "but as far as the fight scenes go in both *Hercules* and *Xena*, a big part of doing the stunts is getting the timing right: When you come in, how you sell the hits to the camera, the flying through the air, and the impact on the ground are all important things of a fight scene. And that takes *experience*. And so once you know, really know, how to fall properly, you can keep going in this business for quite some time."

Bell designs the fights on *Hercules* as imaginatively and precisely as a choreographer would a dance, using a "four-line" system of his own devising. After sketching two stick figures face to face, each in a fighting stance, Bell draws a line between their shoulders, a second between their stomachs, a third between their knees, and a fourth, which he calls the "visual line," about three feet above their heads. Then he orchestrates fight moves that involve the viewer in all four zones:

I take the "punter's" [viewer's] eye line and I raise and lower the fight moves up and down those lines. So, let's say, I may start a fight with moves at shoulder level. Then I will shoot down and I will do a backspin kick or something [else] to bring the punter's eye line down around the knees-to-feet area. I'll then bring it back up to the stomach level. I'll then shoot it way up above to the visual line. I'll put in a somersault or I'll have Herc pick somebody up above his head, spin him around, and drop back down. But I keep playing the lines up and down, so there's never just one level. That makes the fight look more interesting and more spectacular.

Having planned and performed stunts for over two decades, Bell has found that fight scenes are the greatest challenge to sell to an audience:

You can crash a car, you can do a high fall, you can set yourself on fire, and they all look visual. And it doesn't matter what you basically do, that stunt is always going to look good. When it comes to a fight, however, you have to *make* that look good. So I've always been a stickler with all my stunt people that whenever they do a fall, whenever they hit the ground, it must be with a good, solid hit.

Landing on the ground is the icing on the cake for a fight. It makes the punter *feel the pain*. You have all the visual side of the fight, with the person who is throwing the blow, whether it be on *Hercules* or *Xena*, doing a spectacular move, you have the hit, you then have the stuntee flying through the air or flipping through the air. This is all part of the visual. Then you have the landing, and we try and make that look as spectacular as we possibly can!

When a guy takes a hit, he doesn't just fall over. Instead, his feet will fly right up in the air and he'll come crashing down on his back. Or he'll flip right over and land on his stomach, or he'll flip out toward the side. So the landings are what I call the "feeling" part of a fight. When the stuntee hits the ground, the people watching him feel it and cringe. They say, "Oh!" and it makes them feel as if they're in the fight!

Another reason Bell values a good fall is that when a stuntee is knocked down in a fight, he seldom gets up again. "Sometimes we have 'two-dimensional' fights where the two parties trade blows and move backward and forward. But ninety percent of the fights are 'one-dimensional.' That is, the stuntees will come running in, take their hit, and go flying and crashing down."

According to Bell, stuntees must be able to do three basic falls for fight scenes: an Irish whip, a back fall, and a half gainer. The Irish whip requires the stuntee to change direction in mid-fall. "Let's say you get a punch across the face," Bell says. "So you turn your head to the side that the punch is going, so your body will flip that way. Then you'll do a flip—a forward somersault—in midair and come crashing down right on your back."

The back fall involves less of a flip than the Irish whip, but Bell calls the landing "spectacular":

When the stuntees get hit, they throw their feet right up in the air so they come crashing down on the ground. And the first part that hits the ground is the top of their back and shoulders. So it's really a dramatic fall and makes it look as if it's really hurting.

The third fall, the half gainer, features both a great visual and a hard landing, according to Bell:

This fall would be used, say, if Hercules "coat-hangers" an attacker. What happens is the stuntee comes running in, he will take a hit in the chest, do a complete flip right up and over, 360 degrees, and come back down and land facing the same way. . . . Yeah, he'll do a complete somersault backward and come crashing down on his stomach. . . . Probably about eighty percent of the stuntees can do that gag.

Charlie Haskell, who shot dozens of action scenes as the show's second-unit director during its first season, praises Bell's savvy in filming as well as fashioning stunts:

Peter is always so aware of the cameras. He doesn't just set up stunts without regard for how they can be filmed. I found in working with him, he would offer you suggestions about camera angles. And so often he was dead right!

Kevin Sorbo perfectly complements Bell's inventive staging of fight scenes with his star presence, athleticism, and readiness to mix it up with the stuntees. In preparing for the physical demands of his role, Sorbo absorbed the "white lotus" system of martial arts expert and fight choreographer Douglas Wong, whose screen credits include *Dragon: The Bruce Lee Story*.

Wong is known for adapting an actor's natural abilities, and he found in Sorbo an ideal pupil. In six weeks of concentrated effort, Sorbo developed skills normally acquired only after four years of training. Wong taught Sorbo to perform falls and rolls, hand-to-hand techniques, and moves with the sword and staff. Wong also built on Sorbo's years as a football defensive end for scenes where Hercules cuts past or simply bowls over groups of warriors.

Bell describes the fights he creates for Hercules as tailored to both Sorbo's all-around physical gifts and his character's great strength: "Kevin is a big man but also extremely active and he has good body coordination. And I'd say the style that I've done with Kevin is that because he's the strongest man, when he hits people, throws people, they really fly." Bell also shows off Sorbo's surprising agility for a big man, "as when Hercules grabs a foe's elbows and rolls over his back. So it's a combination of Hercules being the strongest man in the world and a sophisticated John Wayne, with a slight acrobatic tinge." Bell works hard to keep all those elements in play for the camera:

> With Hercules' fights I still use those four lines, but when he hits somebody, I'll make sure that I've got some guys who, when they take a hit, exit the frame completely airborne. And we'll show them flying through the air, going long distances, and crashing down either through roofs or onto tables or whatever. Herc also grabs hold of guys' wrists and we do the "bam-bam," where he flips them backward and forward over his head, down onto the ground, and then swings them around over his head. That is all mechanical effects, and that is his style.

Lacking Hercules' power, Iolaus emphasizes speed and an anything-goes attitude. "I have styled his fighting along the lines of Jackie Chan," Bell says, referring to Hong Kong's most popular martial arts film star. "He is fast and he uses anything he can get his hands on. I've tried to keep away from having Iolaus be acrobatic because that starts to get into the [realm] of *Xena*. But he does some acrobatics. A number of times Iolaus is caught between two guys and they'll grab him, and all of a sudden he'll flip over backward while they are holding him." It helps, says Bell, that Michael [Hurst] is "an extremely active actor and very good" at picking up skills. "And because he's a small man, his moves are all very quick."

Legendary Facts

Jackie Chan draws on his training in Chinese opera as well as the martial arts to perform all his own stunts. Michael Hurst prefers boxing to singing arias.

Hurst thrives on the action scenes and, like Sorbo, keeps in top condition. "Kevin and I are both physical," he says, "we both train hard. I like [developing] endurance. I train, I do boxing at the

moment. And that's all about endurance, putting yourself in a situation where you need to go further." Hurst recalls a third-season episode, "Not Fade Away," where his character is beaten and has to do "that classic staggering across the desert" to get to Hercules:

> It was very easy for me to go out there and stumble and get up with a mouthful of sand, and stagger on. They'd say, "Do a little stumble down the sand dune." And I'd think, Great! I'll risk breaking my arm because I know I'll tuck and roll, and what the hell! [That attitude] is not about muscles or strength. It has to do with being able to stand up to [anything]. Now, I don't know where that comes from in me. Perhaps from my working-class upbringing in the north of England.

Most stunts on *Hercules* depend on sheer physical ability, but Sorbo cheerfully points out that when Hercules knocks a foe a dozen feet or more through the air, larger forces are at work. Bell custom-designs rigs and harnesses that enable stuntees not merely to roll with the punches Hercules throws, but to fly with them.

The air ram is Bell's most frequently used mechanical device. As soon as a stunt man stands on it, the platform will shoot up in the air and send him flying anywhere from ten to twelve feet high and twenty-odd feet out, depending on the pressure he puts on it. He can trigger the device by running onto it or by standing on it going either backward or forward. Because landings are rougher on the stuntee than for a normal "flip fall," Bell places crash mats to cushion the impact. According to Bell, the second-unit camera crew will employ the air ram to enhance fight scenes that the main unit has already filmed with the principal actors.

> Now in the fights on main unit, if I have a number of the stuntees selling the hit and flying out of shot airborne, I will now pick them up with the second unit as the air ram carries them away, which will look as if Herc has hit them and they are flying through the air.

Another of Bell's inventions is a Russian swing, which lets the stuntee generate his own momentum for a long airborne trip. Bell compared it to a bench suspended like a swing in a playground, which a stuntee can rock forward and backward but "with a slight modification in the design." The stuntee actually stands on the front of the bench, another stuntee stands behind him, and both push it higher and faster till they get it up to "quite a tremendous height." At that point one of the stuntees sails off the Russian swing, "traveling quite a long way and crashing down into an air bag."

Unlike the air ram and the Russian swing, which are designed to give the stuntee altitude, the skip pan simulates the ground-level effects of a punch by the world's strongest man:

> The stuntees come running in and Hercules palms them in the chest, and the next minute you see them skidding back across the ground. You don't actually see their feet, but they stay rigid and [pulled by the skip pan] they shoot back along the ground as if they're standing.

Bell continuously strives to improve on his mechanical designs. Since the second season he has increasingly used the air ratchet to show off Hercules' power:

> The ratchet is a machine that I attach a cable and a harness to, and I have a "pick point" out where I want it to go. And depending on how far I want to take them, I'll vary the amount of pressure I put on them. The advantage of the ratchet is that you can see Hercules hit the guy, and I can then fire the stuntee with the ratchet and take him twenty-odd feet up in the air and land him down forty to fifty feet away. Or I can take him up in the air and can send him down through a roof. And I can use the ratchet in other ways, like the time I put in a gag where Hercules grabs somebody by the wrist, lifts him off the ground, and throws him backward and forward over his head and back to the ground again. A "bam-bam" gag. Well, that is all done by the rachet.

Among the most enthusiastic fans of Bell's latest invention is Sorbo himself. He exclaims that thanks to the air ratchet, "When I hit a guy while I'm still in frame, you see the guy flying about fifty feet through the air. And it looks fantastic. It requires some CG [computer-generated] editing to take the wiring out. But it looks unbelievable on film. It's going to be fun. People are going to say, 'Wow, how do they do that?'"

Although Bell's stunt team, according to Poppleton, performs in a "carefully controlled environment," dying on *Hercules* is not without risk.

On the set of a third-season episode, "Prince Hercules," four horses bolted as they were pulling a "war wagon" with a stunt man inside. The man barely managed to leap to safety before the wagon careened off course, crashed, and was destroyed. Bell nonetheless recalls only a handful of injuries to his crew in literally hundreds of fights on *Hercules* and *Xena:*

> A stuntee broke his little finger while rolling down a hill. Another was doing a stunt fall from a castle when part of the set gave way, and he over-rotated when he hit the air bag and hit his head on the camera right in front of it. And we had a stunt girl get burned, not badly but she did get burned, when we were ratcheting her off a tower in an explosion where the timing was off from the special effects. When we ratcheted her off, they set the explosion off a little bit too soon and she got caught in it.

All three stuntees, Bell remarks, quickly returned to action. "Of course, the guys are always carrying bruises and bumps, but that really just comes with the territory because of the falls they're doing. But as far as having an injury where you can't work for a few days, no, those are the only ones we've had in four years."

The action scenes also demand considerable physical courage from the lead actors. Michael Hurst broke his right wrist filming a crossover episode of *Xena*, and for several weeks on *Hercules* he appeared with his arm in a sling while continuing to fight and fence with his other arm. Kevin Sorbo has endured an assortment of injuries from falls and fights. In "The Warrior Princess" Hercules bests Iolaus in a duel, but in real life Sorbo required nine stitches after Hurst clipped the back of his head with an aluminum sword. The unscripted carnage led the prop department to reconsider its use of metal weapons. "We switched to plastic after that," Sorbo says, but adds that despite such mishaps he relishes doing his own stunts:

> I'm still pretty gung ho about this. Sure, accidents can happen and I've had my share of them. I have to admit it is foolish in a way. There are so many action stars in the movies who do very few of their own stunts, to protect their careers. And it makes total sense. But for me, maybe it's a mixture of ego, pride that I can still do it, and also that I really enjoy it, I get a kick from it! And I

think that people who watch the shows can tell that Michael and I are actually in there doing our own fights.

The conclusion of filming in New Zealand is by no means the end of work on an episode. Many specialized tasks go on for weeks after the last reels of film arrive in Los Angeles, including editing, adding the music, visual effects, and sound effects, revoicing much of the dialogue, and mixing the different sound tracks. Since the first *Hercules* movie, Bernadette "Bernie" Joyce has coordinated all the aspects of postproduction that determine the look—and sound—of the series.

Editing

The two senior editors on *Hercules*, Steve Polivka and David Blewitt, receive as much as 50,000 feet of 35mm film for a single episode, some eight to twelve hours of material, which they must drastically trim and order. They work on a computerized system called Lightworks, a notable improvement over editing on 35mm film, which once was standard practice for TV shows and movies. The chief advantage of computers, Joyce says, is that editors can cut and assemble scenes much more quickly and precisely with digital technology than by the old method of manual cutting and splicing.

An editor takes the raw "dailies" of an episode (the film just shot in New Zealand), feeds them into a computer, and cuts them into coherent scenes. He will then assemble these scenes into a full "editor's cut" of the show, after which the director will specify any changes. This "director's cut" then goes to the producers, who send the editor notes on what they want to see changed, shortened, or at times added for continuity (perhaps a shot of an arm reaching for a sword or a horse galloping into the picture). When the producers approve a version, the show is considered "locked," and the editor makes a master copy on broadcast-quality tape. With the addition of special effects shots, the editor's work on the episode is complete.

Although editors are often thought of simply as technicians, their work involves ongoing creative decisions. They must choose the best of several takes for every shot; whether to use close-ups or wide-angle coverage; when to use quick cuts to give a scene more energy and when to linger on an actor for more emotional power. And because the filmed material far exceeds what could ever fit into a forty-four-minute episode, editors, together with the director and the producers, must decide which scenes or lines to keep and which to cut. At the heart of their craft is always the desire to tell the best possible story.

Special Effects

The monsters and other supernatural terrors that stalk Hercules have all escaped from the computers of Kevin O'Neill and his team of "FX" (special effects) artists. As children O'Neill and his coworkers were entranced by adventure movies featuring effects by Ray Harryhausen, a pioneer in the use of stop-motion puppetry. Harryhausen dazzled moviegoers with such creatures as the Cyclops and dragon in *The Seventh Voyage of Sinbad* (1958); Poseidon, the seven-headed Hydra, and sword-wielding skeletons in *Jason and the Argonauts* (1963); and Medusa's serpent-laden head in *Clash of the Titans* (1981). "We all grew up watching films like this," O'Neill says of Harryhausen's work. "I think he inspired a whole generation of effects technicians that work in the business now."

Legendary Facts

While Ray Harryhausen has influenced generations of special effects artists, his own career choice was decided when an aunt took him to see *King Kong*.

In 1993 O'Neill, then a veteran of several FX studios, was finishing work on Universal's movie *Dragon*, about the martial arts legend Bruce Lee. The film's story line of a mythic hero battling both mortal and supernatural warriors provided ideal training for O'Neill's next assignment. That summer Rob Tapert ran into O'Neill on the Universal lot and invited him to supervise the visual effects for the *Hercules* movies then in preproduction. O'Neill's flair in creating a bestiary of centaurs, multiheaded Hydras, and other mythical wonders for the TV movies led to ongoing work on the series *Hercules: The Legendary Journeys*.

In order to handle the relentless pace of episodic television and still produce quality FX on a modest budget, O'Neill decided to forgo a central studio building and instead hire a "garage band" of artists who would work out of their homes while sharing images over the internet. O'Neill's "virtual studio," linking coworkers electronically, was perhaps his greatest FX illusion, permitting his team to do the work of a large studio at a fraction of the overhead.

O'Neill benefited from superb timing, for *Hercules* came along just when a "desktop revolution" was making powerful FX software programs widely affordable for the first time. Individuals could now create whole 3-D worlds on their home computers, and O'Neill was intent on taking full advantage:

> The only way we could produce these effects in the time and budget allotted was to do it on desktop [computers]. The series *Babylon 5* had actually been doing it for a year, creating entire en-

vironments in outer space in a computer. Now at *Hercules*, we take original photography and add things to it, which is often harder to deal with. Because if you have an entire 3-D environment, as on *Babylon 5*, you have complete control over the art direction, and if something is failing technically you can adjust the look of something a lot quicker. But once you photograph something, as on our shows, everyone expects it to look a certain way: Even if viewers have to imagine what a creature looks like, they knows it's still the same grassy landscape, so that limits the adjustments you can make.

O'Neill recruited artists who had worked for top FX studios on A-list feature films. Kevin Kutchaver, whose credits include *Return of the Jedi* and *The Addams Family*, "was especially crucial for us," O'Neill says, "because of his special skill in combining live-action photography with computerized 3-D creatures." O'Neill also hired Doug Beswick, a 3-D animator who had worked on *Gumby*, *Star Wars*, and *Aliens*. For the second season of *Hercules*, O'Neill, Kutchaver, and Beswick formed the company Flat Earth and brought in as 3-D superviser Everett Burrell, whose Optic Nerve studio had won an Emmy for makeup effects on *Babylon 5*.

The roster of talent in Flat Earth has shifted each year, but O'Neill continues to follow a basic rule in hiring that values art over electronics. "I found," he says, "it was better to hire people with creative backgrounds than to hire people with computer backgrounds to do creative tasks."

Some of Flat Earth's standard procedures would still be familiar to earlier generations of FX artists, such as blue-screen photography and compositing. Filming against a nearly iridescent blue screen remains the method of choice for extracting an actor's image so that it can later be placed into a scene. Compositing, which involves superimposing images shot in different places and at different times into a single shot, is a process nearly as old as filmmaking itself. But O'Neill's team relies chiefly on digital electronics to create and manipulate images, an approach on the cutting edge of FX technology.

While no two monsters on *Hercules* spring to life in exactly the same way, certain approaches are common to many of Flat Earth's operations. Kevin O'Neill first confers with the director and the producers—Rob Tapert and often Liz Friedman—on what a creature should look like, how it will figure in the action, and what effects should be practical within the budget and time available:

The director will sit down with the storyboard artist and me, mapping out what FX we'd like to see. Those storyboards are distributed to the producers, the director, myself, and the production crew on location. I will then work through a production schedule for each of the items we will need: complex 3-D shots [generated by computer]; mechanical shots, which are shots done on location without any postproduction effects; and matte paintings, which are 2-D backgrounds. All of these will eventually be composited together.

Once Tapert approves the basic concepts, the technical work of making a creature begins. A three-foot sculpture of the creature plus a detailed sculpture of the creature's head are built as models for the computer to replicate. Andy Clement, a 3-D animator, doubles as the artist who makes and paints most of the sculptures for Flat Earth. Beswick checks to see that the creature is being sculpted in a "flat" position, arms at its sides, feet slightly apart, to make it easier for the computer to process accurately. Otherwise, a dynamic pose might stretch the creature's limbs and create distortions when it is made into a computer model.

Bryan Blevins then takes the sculpture, called a maquette, draws a detailed grid on it, and, as O'Neill explains, touches each point "with a sort of pen attached to a 'digitizing arm' that translates all of this three-dimensional data into an object in the computer that looks just like it does when you hold it. Each point on the grid becomes a point in 3-D space in the computer, until you've got a 3-D object that replicates the sculpture you've been digitizing."

The digitized object goes to 3-D superviser Burrell, who, O'Neill says, "has a makeup background and a sculptor's eye for how to paint and light our characters." Burrell inserts a "skeleton" in the computerized creature using a software program called Bones, which gives the creature multiple joints and determines how it will move. In earlier decades Ray Harryhausen would insert a physical armature into his puppets; now the skeleton, like the rest of the creature, exists wholly in the realm of digital electronics.

Beswick now animates the creature according to the scripted action, after which it goes, along with film of the live action and any other background images, to Kutchaver. His task is to combine all the images into a single scene, so that the computerized creature blends into the action so fully as to appear not merely alive but on set with the "other" actors. According to O'Neill, the entire process from the first designs to the final compositing takes six to eight weeks.

The centaur in the TV movie *Hercules and the Underworld* was, in O'Neill's words, "the effect that started it all, in terms of whether or not we could do weird stuff like the compositing, or combining, of humans and animals." Kevin Kutchaver guided the compositing process safely past all technical snares. Fan reaction was overwhelming and spurred encore appearances by two, three, many centaurs. And while most creatures on *Hercules: The Legendary Journeys* appear in only one or two scenes, the centaurs have trotted through several episodes and been viewed from a multitude of angles, interacting with other actors in both long and close-up shots.

Legendary Facts

Centaurs have appeared in *Hercules in the Underworld*, in "As Darkness Falls," "Outcast," and "Centaur Mentor Journey."

Making a centaur for *Hercules* requires merging shots of a real person and a real horse in order to create the illusion of a single fabulous creature. The process begins with the background, or action, plates. A trainer walks around the set with a horse on a lead. All the actors work around the horse with the understanding that an actor will later be added to these sequences.

The centaur-actors wear appliances that replicate the neck of a horse. They are used for close-up shots that don't require the horse half of the centaur. However, for the wide-angle vistas that show the entire centaur in motion, the shots are designed as digital composites—that is, a blending of different shots using digital technology.

Once the scenic backgrounds are photographed and reviewed, a blue screen is shot with the actors. From that point on it's just a selection process. All the possible takes are reviewed, from the perspective of trying to come up with not only the best take but also the best lineup of action between the horse and the actor. In all, the FX team works with three pieces of film: A scene of the horse on a lead with the trainer, generally shot by the production in New Zealand. Then, a blank plate, which is only the background without the horse—or humans—on which all the pieces of the scene will be superimposed, or composited. Finally, the actor in his centaur-appliance, shot in front of a blue screen so he can be extracted and placed in the new background.

Once these pieces have been selected, the FX artists prepare the background. Typically, there are things in the background that must be eliminated from the final image: viewers clearly should not glimpse the trainer or the lead lines for the horse, or the horse's head. First, a kind of wire removal procedure gets rid of the lead; then the trainer and the horse's head are "removed." Each element that is eliminated is replaced with a piece of "clean background." The result is an image of a horse walking around the background with no head—a good start.

The actor who will play the centaur (or at least, his upper half) stands or walks in front of a blue screen so that his image can be extracted from the background. The camera movement is corrected a frame at a time to match the moves and prompt the actor to follow the horse's action. Then the FX artists create more background work to blend the horse-appliance into the real horse.

Marks drawn on the horse in chalk permit the FX artists to later track its movements a frame at a time, constantly lining up the horse's anatomy with the actor's, and keeping them lined up so they're in constant sync. This is called a match move—the two must go together flawlessly. Then hours of fine-tuning ensure that the actor and the animal appear as one.

Since the birth of the first centaur in Flat Earth's computers, O'Neill has fine-tuned the process. "We've changed the appliance worn by the actor so that it blends in more naturally. We've also changed the way the actors move, because a lot of times they weren't quite mimicking what a horse did as much as they were just hopping up and down." The most advanced digital technology is at work in compositing the centaur, but the actor must help by "learning to move like a real horse."

Pyro, a creature made of fire, was another landmark for Flat Earth and, in O'Neill's words, "one of the coolest things we've done." In a second-season episode, "The Fire Down Below," Pyro tries to destroy Hercules by searing him with flames that shoot from his body. "This was a really tricky one," O'Neill says of Pyro:

> We actually shot every sequence twice. We had a guy dressed in a green suit just so we could have the animators actually see a human being moving in the action that the director wanted. We photographed that once, choreographing the action with Kevin

Sorbo. We then took that man out of the scene, and we photographed it again without anybody playing the Pyro guy. Instead we had Kevin Sorbo acting out his part. That material was then sent back to the cutting room and a sequence was cut with the guy in the green suit.

The animators took this film and added a 3-D object of a human being to the guy in the green suit. We then took the plate without the guy in the green suit and composited a man—a humanoid figure based on the animation that the animators supplied us. We actually wrapped burning fire and burning white elements of fire wiping across the 3-D object. And that made an odd, self-illuminating, glowing object.

In order to make the creature look like walking fire, not like a man *on* fire, but like a man made *of* fire, our 2-D department actually made animated fire trails that radiated off his arms and legs. And then we composited real fire over that image, making sure it matched the creature's movements.

Like most FX artists, O'Neill considers the crowning achievement of his hero, Ray Harryhausen, to be a battle between the Greek Argonauts and seven deadly skeletons in the film *Jason and the Argonauts*. Paying homage to this classic scene became O'Neill's challenge for a second-season episode, "Once a Hero," which Rob Tapert directed. "I'm a huge Ray Harryhausen fan," said Tapert. "The guys [at Flat Earth] gave me as a Christmas present an autographed picture of Ray holding one of the little skeletons he animated."

O'Neill and Tapert went back to the source, watching *Jason and the Argonauts* to appreciate Harryhausen's style and plan how it could be embellished. Harryhausen had carved seven miniature skeletons by hand from real bone and plaster. Within each one he placed an electric armature that could be activated by hand or by motor, and adjusted the positions of each skeleton, frame by frame, to synchronize them with the actors playing the Argonauts, who had already been filmed wielding swords and shields. Finally, Harryhausen magnified the images of the skeletons and superimposed them opposite the Argonauts. Animating the sequence took Harryhausen four and a half months for a few minutes of footage, but the result was one of the screen's most memorable battles.

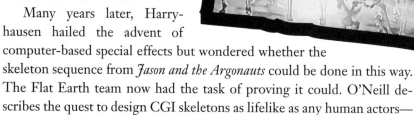

Many years later, Harryhausen hailed the advent of computer-based special effects but wondered whether the skeleton sequence from *Jason and the Argonauts* could be done in this way. The Flat Earth team now had the task of proving it could. O'Neill describes the quest to design CGI skeletons as lifelike as any human actors— and as dazzling as Harryhausen's magnificent seven:

> The way we plotted all this out was to do exactly what Ray [Harryhausen] did. We actually had stuntmen representing each skeleton, wearing T-shirts numbered one to eight, and then the scene was photographed once with the guys in the T-shirts, and once again *without* the guys in the T-shirts but with all the human characters. And the whole scene was cut together using the guys in the T-shirts. We then matched the skeletons to the movements of each actor. Our artists animated to the background plates without the guys in the T-shirts, rendered out the skeleton animation, and composited those images with the shots of Herc and Iolaus and Jason and the Argonauts.

Although dragons were rare in Greek myths, one flew into

Legendary Facts

The Greeks didn't have many dragons in their myths. However, the most famous was Cecrops, who was half man and half dragon. He was also the first king of Athens.

the world of *Hercules* during a third-season episdoe called "Lady and the Dragon." O'Neill describes how his team brought the dragon Braxis to life:

> We designed on paper and then sculpted a variety of different looks, and had the producers sign off on one particular look. Then we sculpted a full-size dragon head and had an articulate paw made for actual live-action coverage on the set, which would give us more footage of the dragon even if it was just little pieces. We then made a sculpture of the entire dragon as we had conceived it on paper, and digitized that into a 3-D model.
>
> We then animated the dragon and we also had a performance reading by the person who did the voice for the dragon. We videotaped that and studied it, had the animators study it, and then broke it down into what are called animation X sheets, which are cue sheets that the animators use to create the different mouth movements. We created about thirty-two heads, different phonetic heads in the computer for all the vowels and consonants that the creature was using to speak. And those heads were blended, or morphed, together to create the actual lip sync of dialogue.
>
> We rendered out all the animation so that the dragon performed in sync with the voice as it was recorded. We then started the process of compositing the dragon into the scenes, which included a series of composites [film that combines different shots into a single scene]. This involved blue-screen work so that we could place the actors into the scene, and rotoscoping, a process where we actually remove certain people and objects from a shot, place the dragon behind them, and then composite them back in again. Once there was an actual rotoscope machine, but nowadays we do it all in a computer. You take a pen and draw on the pad that's connected to your computer, which then draws a line around the image on the screen you want to remove from or put back into your scene.

O'Neill traveled to New Zealand to choreograph the action with Kevin Sorbo, Michael Hurst, and the dragon before the actual filming. Occasionally the two actors played scenes with the sculpted dragon head or the paw, but often they were paired with a pole that had a mark for the dragon's eye line. But while O'Neill's dragon remained largely invisible to the actors, in the final composited scenes it talks, breathes fire, holds Iolaus in one of its paws, and soars memorably into the clouds.

Part of the challenge the dragon posed for the FX artists, O'Neill says, was "to figure out how to create that image on the Herc budget, which was a big hurdle to get over." But Braxis soared past that barrier, appearing in four minutes of footage for less than $200,000, whereas the creature in the movie *Dragonheart* appeared on-screen for some fifteen minutes at a cost of around $20 million.

Some of the most crucial effects on *Hercules* are the ones viewers never see. Flat Earth handles the unheralded "cleanup" detail when the production uses wires or cables for stunts in which Hercules knocks someone into another town or lifts someone by the arm and bounces him up and down. Wire removal is a painstaking process that occurs entirely in the computer. "We have to come up with things to put in place of the wires," O'Neill explains. "You have to grab pixels [the smallest points on the computer screen] from around each wire and pinch them in and paint them over."

For O'Neill and his fellow FX artists who give *Hercules* much of its mythic aura, the series has provided an exhilarating opportunity to take the work of their idol, Ray Harryhausen, to new levels. "I think that's probably the most exciting aspect of it," O'Neill said. "It's something that I wished all my life to emulate, and . . . now, finally I produce this, in conjunction with a team of really talented, motivated people." Nor is O'Neill's team resting on its laurels. "There are always new challenges, new things we want to try," he says, confident that the next generation of FX discoveries lies just ahead.

Music

*J*oseph Lo Duca, the composer for both *Hercules* and *Xena*, was a versatile composer and performer from the Detroit area when he met Sam Raimi and Rob Tapert, then completing their first horror film and "looking for someone who could make frightening music." Lo Duca's score for *The Evil Dead* was scary enough to forge an ongoing creative bond with the two producers. A dozen years later they asked him to score their TV movies about Hercules.

Originally Tapert had envisioned an exotic musical score for *Hercules*, possibly with Arabic roots. "Rob was very taken by a lot of ethnic and Third World music he had heard," Lo Duca recalls. "Also Peter Gabriel [the British pop musician who drew on Yemenite melodies and instruments in scoring *The Last Temptation of Christ*]." But, Lo Duca explained, he and Tapert changed direction as it became clear that Kevin Sorbo's Hercules was no exotic figure but a down-home American, transplanted to an unspecified age of adventure:

> "We had a hero who had no real Greek roots in any way, shape, or form, except for the mythology. The costumes looked medieval to me. The landscapes were beautiful, but so lush they had no bearing on ancient Greece." Neither did the theme Lo Duca composed just an hour before boarding a plane to meet with Sam Raimi. "It came very quickly," an upbeat, stirring melody suited equally to an epic in ancient Greece or the American West, "for an affable, likeable hero."

The broad comic tone that features prominently on *Hercules: The Legendary Journeys* also encourages Lo Duca to compose playful variations of familiar musical themes:

> There is a lot of cutting up in the script and on the set. There's a lot of physical comedy. Musically we haven't shied away from

that. We have actually gone over the top and commented on it. We have the clumsy giant Typhon kissing Echidna, "the mother of all monsters," so I write *The Honeymooners* [theme] over a big, sappy, romantic screen kiss. [The goddess of love] Aphrodite is windsurfing, so I write surfin' "oud" [Arabic lute] music along with some broad nods to the beach comedies of the sixties. The music is as good-natured as the show. We get in on the fun and I hope it's fun for the listeners.

The score for *Hercules* delighted fans but still left Lo Duca hungry to experiment. "I was in love with the original idea of doing something exotic," he relates, "and so I tried to work other kinds of music in: We refer to this as 'surrounding Herc with hummus.'" Lo Duca incorporated Greek, Middle Eastern, and other melodies less familiar to Western audiences, mainly for "the villains of the week, the love interests of the week, the new gods of the week. Those characters get expressed musically in some strange ways."

Lo Duca recalls that for the first telefeature, *Hercules and the Amazon Women*, he roamed far from the Hollywood norm in searching for music to represent the Amazons:

My first solution was to write something more East European in meter, and I hired a group of female gospel singers to sing this chant, knowing that their version would be throatier and zestier and more warlike, but still feminine. And that happened to be a wordless chant. In Brazil they tend to sing "lay ah la, lay ah lay ah," and they work with those syllables. And being a big fan of Brazilian music, I found this was something that, without inventing a language, I could teach to a group of singers—and it worked. It was just based on those samba and other melodies that they sing, using those syllables, and I thought, "I can use that. I can make this work." Lo Duca grafted this Brazilian chanting style "onto an Eastern European rhythmic and harmonic base . . . not unlike what [the theme for] *Xena* has become."

An early episode of *Hercules: The Legendary Journeys* allowed Lo Duca to press his musical forays into Brazil even further. In "The Festival of Dionysus," drunken maidens are programmed to assassinate a king with their daggers. This surreal, orgiastic scene invited musical innovation, and

Lo Duca received Rob Tapert's encouragement to dare something completely different:

> Rob said, "You know that samba in [the Brazilian movie] *Black Orpheus*? . . . It's one they play every year during Carnival?" Well, I pulled in some musician friends, we took a samba rhythm base, and I wrote an Arabic melody over the top, and that melody was played and sung with the "ah lay ah la" chant, but in Arabic. We used a mixed group of singers at that time . . . and then the melody was played on Middle Eastern instruments as well. . . . We also played Arabic rhythms and I had a couple of musicians playing conch, you know, the seashell, and my direction to them was, "You're the JB [James Brown] horns." We do this kind of thing all the time.

Lo Duca's work routine in composing for *Hercules* and *Xena* begins when he receives rough cuts of episodes at his home near Detroit, and exchanges notes with the producers about where music is needed and what kind. He described these shows as requiring "a lot of music, perhaps thirty-five minutes of a forty-four-minute episode. They're not sitcoms, or dramas like *Law and Order*, they're action-adventure fare. If a few minutes go by and there is no music, people get nervous. The producers are conscious of [how viewers go] channel-surfing, they want [music] to keep the show moving." Lo Duca laughs. "Maybe there's too much music sometimes!"

Composing on a tight schedule has conditioned Lo Duca to trust his instincts:

> There is just enough time to get your first inspiration and run with the ball. I have had to score long action sequences with computer-generated monsters that I have never seen. There was an episode [of *Xena*] . . . where Gabrielle was playing a flute. I had to put notes into her fingers and into her breath where none existed. There have been scenes where we have had to make dancers dance to music that we didn't have access to.

Adjusting to widely varying resources makes for an added creative challenge. "The music is sometimes written for orchestras, sometimes for synthesizers, and sometimes for ethnic musicians," Lo Duca explains. The largest budgets are keyed less to the needs of particular episodes than to times of intense ratings competition: the "sweeps periods" in November, February, and May. According to Lo Duca, "Those are the shows that have the most punch, like 'The Warrior Princess' debut [on *Hercules*] during May [1995] sweeps."

For all the pressures and constraints involved in composing for television, Lo Duca freely acknowledges that compared with most other musicians, he has entered the Elysian Fields in terms of support for his creative impulses. "I am given the resources of an entire symphony orchestra," he says. "That's uncommon for a composer in any field."

Lo Duca also employs cutting-edge technology at each stage of his work on *Hercules* and *Xena*. He composes and synchronizes to picture using his personal computer, sends files electronically to his copyists, and prints out music using notation software. Computers dispatch the performances cross-country to studios in Los Angeles over digital phone lines and cue melodies to points in each episode with split-second precision. "While the setting of the shows is BC," Lo Duca observes, "the music is made in ways that look to the millennium."

Sound Design

If the footsteps, horses' hooves, rustling leaves, clashing swords, and crashing boulders on *Hercules* sound "natural," this is a sign of painstaking effort, well after filming ends, to mimic or outdo these sounds. Only the actors' voices are preserved from the original production in New Zealand, and even these must often be redone. Passing planes, cars, and trucks, strong winds, and the incessant chirping of cicadas that breed in February and March require actors to "loop," or revoice, much of their dialogue. In a process known as "automated dialogue replacement" (ADR), actors may spend hours in a recording studio in Auckland or Los Angeles, synchronizing their speech to the images of their characters.

According to Sam Clark, a postproduction supervisor, Kevin Sorbo is "phenomenal" in looping dialogue, "getting much of it on the first take." Lead actors, Clark says, generally excel at this task, partly from the intensive hours they put in each week. "Some actors, though, don't have much practice, and it shows. The process takes much longer, and we don't get the same quality."

One of the very best at looping, according to the crew at Digital Sound and Picture, is Hudson Leick, who played the evil Callisto in a third-season episode called "Surprise." Having spent an entire Friday afternoon in the recording studio to revoice her character's lines, Leick returned on Monday for a second marathon session. About half of a nine-page list of eighty-eight cues remained to be done, beginning with a stretch of dialogue that had given Leick and the sound crew fits the previous week. Sam Clark, a postproduction supervisor, exhorted her, saying, "Hudson, this passage is the bane of your existence. If you nail this, it's downhill from there!"

Clark called for Cue 54, which was instantly retrieved through digital programming. A scene of Callisto walking with Hercules flashed on a large overhead monitor. Leick watched from her soundproof recording studio, then began to revoice her character's dialogue. In a manner at once taunting, humorous, even melodic, she intoned, "I think the first thing I'm gonna do . . . is find the good Xena . . . rip out her tongue just to hear her whistle an apology!" It is an inventive reading, but not perfectly in sync with the picture. "Hudson, I think you're just a little behind it," Clark told her, then added encouragingly, "Great first try!"

Leick's second reading brought more compliments but someone broke the news, "She started a little early on 'rip out.' The second part, though, was excellent, maybe we can use that." A third take was nearly flawless but "just a little late at the top, then gets a little bit ahead at the word 'rip.' " Clark implored Leick, "Let's try one more."

A dozen takes and ten minutes later, the crew members were exultant. Clark declared like a sportscaster after a touchdown pass, "Hudson, the crowd's going nuts in here. . . . That's gonna fly." Leick cheered. After-ward Clark explained, "This cue is probably going to be an amalgamation of takes from Friday and today. It's basically what Hudson had done in production [in New Zealand], except the sound is cleaner, better."

Leick knows her character so well that when she objected to saying every few seconds, "Hercules, hurry!" Clark invited her to improvise her own dialogue. He asked Leick, "What else would Callisto say?" "She would call him 'Stupid'!" Hudson replied at once. Soon she was playing angry, desperate variations on her insult. "Hurry! Stupid man! Hurry up, run!" Clark smiled as he relates, "I love doing this with Hudson because she really gets into character!"

Leick spent much of her studio session looping non-verbal sounds, as in a scene where Callisto is grabbed by a vine. Varying her tone and intensity, Hudson gasped and screamed, choked, and called for Hercules, wailed and struggled frantically. After a few "readings," Leick paused to ask, "Well, if I'm choking, how is it possible for me to say, 'Hercules, hurry!' and to give more yells and struggles? If I'm choking isn't it going to be hard to get words out at all?" Clark conceded, "No, you're exactly right," but added:

> We've got to have something that motivates Hercules to run to save you. That [screaming] we were playing out before, that's the "Act Out," it's sort of a tease, to get people to come back after they've gone to the fridge. So now Herc knows where you are, with your one motivating sound. It's the crucial "fridge factor"!

Tim Boggs of Digital Sound and Picture, who supervised the ADR sessions, suggested to Leick, "Why don't you hit little parts of [Hercules' name] while you're struggling?" Leick nodded agreement at the idea of a halfway scream. "I can do that," she said, "but it's gonna be light." Perhaps this would be enough, she added, "because Hercules is a semi-god so he could hear me anyway!" Leick delivered her lines with just the right mix of desperation and anger, and Clark exclaimed on behalf of the whole crew: "That was great!"

In addition to dialogue replacement, many other sounds are added during postproduction. Joseph Lo Duca digitally transmits his musical score from his home in Detroit, and a music editor may supplement this from a library of Lo Duca's past compositions. A team of four or five "Foley artists" re-creates sounds of body movements. To simulate the flapping of wings, a Foley artist blows rhythmically into a microphone. For a scene in which Iolaus is lifted onto a bed after being wounded and begins shaking, two Foley artists beat and press on wooden crates.

Boggs and other technicians contribute an array of sound effects. Often they draw on sounds stored in a digital library, though they also are constantly searching for new sounds. And, according to Boggs, the art of creating sound effects often involves using familiar noises in unconventional ways:

> So many sound effects are natural sounds that have been slowed down or speeded up, or reversed. For example, the unearthly roar of the giant "deathstalkers" in *Star Wars* is actually a pig's squeal, reversed and slowed down, with some electronic enhancement. We used to do that sort of thing on *Hercules* and *Xena* for the monsters. Often you may not even be aware of it. But we put [in just enough] to give a darker feel to the creatures or people that are more animalistic. . . . And we like to play for humor. . . . In "The Apple," where arrows are rounding corners, we added tire squeals! We love putting in modern sounds to be funny, we love to laugh at ourselves.

Boggs believes that the right sounds can enhance any scene, and that these sounds are out there, awaiting discovery through inspiration or sheer hard work.

The final stage of mixing is to combine the many sound tracks onto a single master tape containing stereo tracks. Josh Schneider, who helped mix "Surprise," explains, "We normally use sixteen tracks for Foley and backgrounds, eight for dialogue, eight for music, and up to fifty or more for hard sound effects. It runs around a hundred tracks per show—give or take a dozen." Bernie Joyce adds, "Obviously, the more action in an episode, the more tracks you're going to have." "The monster episodes, the sword-fight scenes," Schneider observes, "will have a hundred or so elements going at once."

Bernie Joyce says that all the technical features of postproduction have one basic goal: "to create [for the viewers] the illusion of reality." For a show dealing in myth and legend, that illusion must be especially compelling. And, Joyce adds, by making each story as exciting as possible, "We hope to sweeten that reality."

LEGENDARY
STARS

KEVIN SORBO

Hercules

7hey didn't tell me how to play Hercules," Kevin Sorbo says of his screen role as the world's strongest hero. "I think I brought a lot of myself and a lot of my own ideas to the character. He uses his brain before resorting to brawn. He's willing to talk people out of things and he's willing to listen to people. And I was that same way." Sorbo relates an example from his twenties:

When I worked as a bouncer in a bar, I used to talk to guys [who were out of line]. You know, I probably would have been in ten fights a night instead of one a month, which is what I was in, and those just couldn't be avoided. But every night I could talk most of these guys out of fighting. . . .

Yes, it helps [to be a big man], but only up to a point. But it also helps if you just point out the reality of the situation to these

guys and say, "Look, you don't want to hit me. Then you'll go to jail for the weekend." I'd say, "Come on, she doesn't want to dance with you. What's the big deal? There's so many bars you can go to." And they'd start listening to you because you'd talk to them as a friend instead of being a tough guy with them.

Kevin Sorbo has indeed stamped the character of Hercules with his own good nature, gentle humor, and sense of fun. And at six-foot-three, 215 pounds, with long brown hair and bright blue eyes, he has boosted *Hercules* to Olympian ratings with looks as well as charm. Sorbo has gained cult status among male and female viewers of all ages by convincingly portraying the rarest of heroes: someone people would love to know as well as admire.

The ruggedly handsome actor was born on September 24, 1958, in Mound, Minnesota, a suburb of Minneapolis. Before his parents retired, his father taught at the local junior high school and his mother was a nurse. "I can honestly say I had the perfect Norman Rockwell upbringing," Sorbo says. "I'm the fourth of five kids, I had a great childhood in a fantastic neighborhood, and most of my best and closest friends now are the ones I've had since high school."

The desire to be an actor struck early but bloomed late. Sorbo was eleven when his parents took him to see a high school production of the musical *Oklahoma*, and he decided that acting was the profession for him. But in a neighborhood where boys were considerably more respected for toughness, especially in sports, than for acting ability, Sorbo kept largely silent about his professional goals while proving an eager and talented athlete.

"You name it, I played it," Sorbo recalls. Football, baseball, golf, tennis, but above all, basketball. "I lived for that game," he says. "I was hardcore in Minnesota. In high school I used to chip the ice off the driveway in the middle of February so I could shoot hoops outside in twenty below weather. . . . Yeah, I was a maniac!"

After studying marketing and advertising at the University of Minnesota, he left in 1981 to begin a career in acting. At age twenty-four, while working with a stage troupe, taking acting classes, and shooting commercials, Sorbo fell in love with a model in downtown Dallas. "She dragged me over to Europe for what was going to be three months and ended up being over three years," including eight months in Italy, a year and a half in Germany, and six months in Paris. "Oh, I had a great time, I am so grateful for her coming into my life, just to open that world to me. And for me, traveling now is just such a way of life."

During a three-and-a-half-year stay in Europe, Sorbo studied, read books of all kinds, attended plays, but let his acting ambitions take a distant second to love. "I took it as a time to be with this woman and also have a great time seeing Europe. And I would go back and do it in a heartbeat. But it just reached a point where I felt, 'I'm ready to get back into acting.'"

Sorbo's first dramatic part after settling in Los Angeles in 1986 was on the prime-time soap opera *Dallas*. "I had two lines," he says, "but I got my [Screen Actors Guild] card through all the commercials I did." He later joined the daytime soap opera *Santa Barbara*, playing a Swede named Lars Stedwell, a modest stretch for a man whose roots are "One hundred percent Norwegian." Sorbo also had a recurring part on the HBO football comedy *First and Ten*. Although his career advanced slowly, Sorbo never considered quitting:

> People kept telling me to go back and get my degree so I'd have something to fall back on. But "fall back on" was such a dirty phrase to me. It just fueled the fire. Because I'm the type of person who, if ninety-nine people said, "You're great," and just one said, "You can't hack it," I'd show that one person that he's wrong about me. I know I have a lot to prove, not only to myself but to others. . . . I want to leave a mark.

Sorbo supported himself during the late eighties and early nineties by appearing in over 150 TV commercials, for everything from Diet Coke to Prell Shampoo. Outside the U.S. his face was famous for a Jim Beam commercial he had shot in New Zealand, playing a character out of a Clint Eastwood Western who glares at a bartender as he pours his drink on the floor, saying, "This ain't Jim Beam."

Although these commercials fell well short of Sorbo's acting ambitions, he looks back on them fondly:

> Thank God for commercials! They allowed me to stay in classes and do showcases and really go after my dream. And I didn't have to bartend, I didn't have to wait tables—I think I'm one of the two actors in L.A. that didn't have to do that. So I was very fortunate.

Other actors used to make fun of me, [saying], "Oh, you're not a real actor, you do commercials." Well, commercials are tough. I once spent ten days shooting a thirty-second spot, they were so precise. And I learned a lot about being on the set, and about discipline, and got very comfortable in front of the camera. So when these guys would tell me I wasn't a real actor, I'd say, "Well, Paul Newman, Dustin Hoffman, and Richard Dreyfuss have done commercials. So talk to them about not being a real actor!" And when I'd go on a date, the same guys who were making fun of me were there as my waiter. "And *that's* why I do commercials, pal!" So I can save that sixty hours a week and do other things.

Among the other things Sorbo did for seven years was study acting with a succession of teachers. He found the experiences valuable, yet not until he dropped out of acting class in 1992 did his career begin to take off. "I was becoming a professional student," he says. "And the minute I dropped out, I got rid of those voices telling me that I'm doing this wrong or that wrong. I started trusting myself and listening to my own instincts."

During the early nineties he appeared in episodes of *Murder, She Wrote* and *The Commish*, and in a movie with Scott Glenn, which was shot in Utah and Ohio and went straight to video. "It was a rip-off of *Silence of the Lambs* and not very good, but it was a great way to begin." Sorbo then won a lead role in a TV pilot for NBC called *Critical Condition*, a medical drama that he calls "very well written and two years ahead of *ER* and *Chicago Hope*." The network promised a thirteen-show pickup, but programming executives worried whether a dark hospital drama could survive in the ratings, and the series expired on the scheduling table. Sorbo moved on to another TV pilot, *Aspen*, "which was a kind of like *Cheers* meets *Dynasty* on the ski slopes!" That, too, crashed before becoming a series.

By 1993 Sorbo was coming tantalizingly close to winning lead roles on network shows that became hits. He was one of two finalists for the role of Superman in ABC's *Lois and Clark*. Sorbo even received word that he'd gotten the part: "I was higher than a kite because not too many shows come with a twenty-two-episode guarantee." But twenty-four hours later the producers reversed themselves and gave the role to Dean Cain. Sorbo was disappointed but not discouraged. "I knew in my heart that Dean Cain was right for the role of Superman, he really fit the part better than I do," he says.

Sorbo also narrowly missed starring roles on two groundbreaking shows, *The X-Files* on the Fox network and *NYPD Blue* on ABC. Then the *Hercules* script came along, though Sorbo had his doubts:

> I told my agent, "All right, I'm athletic, I'm kind of a big guy, but they're going to want an incredibly large guy for this. I'm not right for this part." He said, "Just go read for it." And I said, "Well, send me a couple more scripts. So I read the first one and said, "Let's go for it!"

Sorbo recalls the producers telling him they wanted a thinking man's hero, not a musclebound giant: "They had in mind a decathlete as Hercules, not just a shot-putter; a Joe Montana quarterback type, not an offensive or defensive lineman." Despite Sorbo's impressive first audition, the casting sessions dragged on:

> I lost track—I may have read for them seven or nine times in three months. Every time I went in, there was a room full of people. I remember reading for one casting director and going straight from her to read for a group of "suits." Rob [Tapert] was one of them. And they put me on hold, oh, forever. And on my birthday, believe it or not, I was shooting an episode of *The Commish*, and then boom! That's when I got the call. They said, "You got the part." On my birthday. Pretty weird!

Sorbo prepared for the physical demands of his role with an accelerated program of martial arts training. He still lifts weights and works out for ninety minutes after his twelve-hour day on set, then runs in the evening to build endurance. On occasion he finds time for a swim or a game of basketball. And he takes pride in literally plunging into his show's action scenes.

> The second unit comes in and cleans up the really tough stunts, like falling down five flights of steps, why risk it? But Michael [Hurst] and I are doing our own fights. You know, I'm like an old athlete who still thinks he can go out there and play with the twenty-year-olds. But in a lot of cases, I can. . . . Am I a world-class athlete? No. And if I took on a guy who knew how to do karate, I'd get my butt kicked. I'm certainly honest enough to

know that I couldn't do it. [But] I think I could learn to do it. I still think it's never too late.

The burgeoning success of *Hercules* in the U.S. and many other countries astonishes Sorbo, who jokes about it and doesn't quite believe it. He recalls giving an interview to the Japanese media after *Hercules* became one of the few American shows bought by Japanese television:

> They asked, "How do you think you'll do?" And I said, "Godzilla is toast!" And they loved it, they absolutely loved it! . . . I think the show has definitely turned into a cult hit [in the U.S. and other countries], and I think it's going to have a long life. But it's all very surreal. I see my photo on billboards and toy boxes. I look at it and just—it doesn't seem real to me, you know?

A measure of Sorbo's soaring popularity is his starring role in a $35 million fantasy-adventure film, *Kull the Conqueror*. Filmed in the former Czechoslovakia while Sorbo took a three-month leave from *Hercules* in 1996, *Kull* was produced by Raffaella de Laurentiis, whose father made the *Conan* movies that launched Arnold Schwarzenegger's film career. The role of Kull, Conan's warrior father, was originally offered to Schwarzenegger, then passed to Sorbo, who says that his big-screen character is a darker figure than Hercules that will reveal new facets of his acting.

Sorbo remains devoted to playing Hercules. He remarks on his delight at filming action scenes, like a duel with sword-wielding skeletons, that recall his childhood days watching films with dazzling special effects. Sorbo also remarks that everyone on the show "has found the humor in it, and even the fights are done with a little wink." Amid this fun and adventure, Sorbo says, the series must continue to show Hercules as a vulnerable human being in order to stay fresh:

> I think Hercules still has lessons to learn. It may be through the eyes of a child, the voice of a child, that he learns something else that he needs to. Something that could change his personality or the way he looks at life.

Sorbo would also love to see Hercules vent his frustrations at the gods, perhaps in a climactic episode:

> There's an episode I want to write, where we finally see Hera. And my character goes to Mount Olympus, where the gods are larger than life, and he has to defend himself [in a trial]. Maybe the gods have decided to make me all mortal or all god. So it's one way or the other. And I go up there and present my case, saying, "Look at the things I've done." And afterward their first thought is, "No, we're going to strip you, make you mortal." And at the very end, they say, "Okay, you're right. We're going to make you a full god"—much to Hera's dismay. And I stand up and, you know what? I say, "Forget it! I don't want anything you have to give me. I just wanted to prove a point." And I walk out!

MICHAEL HURST

Iolaus

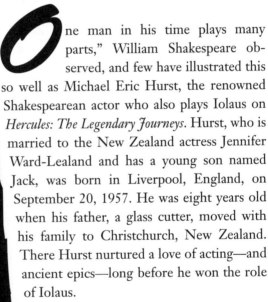

"O ne man in his time plays many parts," William Shakespeare observed, and few have illustrated this so well as Michael Eric Hurst, the renowned Shakespearean actor who also plays Iolaus on *Hercules: The Legendary Journeys*. Hurst, who is married to the New Zealand actress Jennifer Ward-Lealand and has a young son named Jack, was born in Liverpool, England, on September 20, 1957. He was eight years old when his father, a glass cutter, moved with his family to Christchurch, New Zealand. There Hurst nurtured a love of acting—and ancient epics—long before he won the role of Iolaus.

"My favorite picture of all time," he says, "is *Ben Hur*," a four-hour adventure set in ancient Rome that held his interest through fourteen viewings at age ten. Hurst later acted in school plays while practicing stunt fights with a friend in the foyer of movie theaters during intermission. In one routine, he would topple down a flight of carpeted steps and collapse at the bottom before a shocked crowd. Hurst recalls, "All my stunt skills were developed by the time I left school."

After a year at the University of Canterbury, Hurst was accepted at age nineteen into the training program at Christchurch's Court Theatre. Two years later, in 1979, he moved to Auckland for a seven-year stint with Theatre Corporate, playing dozens of parts, from Scrooge in *A Christmas Carol* to Shakespeare's *Macbeth*, and becoming the company's chairperson in 1985. He also starred as Mozart in *Amadeus* and King Herod in *Jesus Christ Superstar* at the Mercury Theatre in Auckland.

Hurst's physical grace and daring became a trademark of his acting. In 1985 he starred in a play set in a wrestling ring, and he performed grueling stunts that he learned from his agent, a former professional wrestler. Two years later Hurst portrayed the dashing D'Artagnan in the Melbourne Theatre Company production of *The Three Musketeers*, and choreographed the play's fighting and fencing scenes. During a production of Thomas Mann's *The Holy Sinner* in 1994, Hurst would climb to the high roof and swing from the rafters. But he broke his wrist rehearsing a fight scene when he was slammed into a concrete wall. No matter: Hurst refused to have the arm placed in a cast, and performed his action scenes by relying on his good left hand.

Hurst also became renowned for his daring as a director. He remarked that every generation reinvents Shakespeare, and he has amply proved the point: His *Macbeth* took place in a bomb site during World War I, while in *Romeo and Juliet*, Verona's Mafia leaders carried mobile phones and briefcases while Lady Capulet relaxed in a spa pool built into the stage.

As an actor, Hurst totally immerses himself in a character. He shaved his hair and eyebrows for one role, wore makeup and a black tutu for another. To prepare for the part of Touchstone in a 1981 production of Shakespeare's *As You Like It*, he painted his face and went clowning in the street. There is only one thing he will not do in preparing for a part. "If you're going to play Hamlet," he remarks, "the last thing you want to do is see someone else play Hamlet! You should make the role totally your own."

By the early nineties Hurst was one of New Zealand's foremost authorities in interpreting Shakespeare, a leading acting teacher, and cofounder of the Watershed Theatre in Auckland, known for its inventive productions. He appeared in films and TV series as well as in plays, and thrived on finding unconventional projects. In 1993 Hurst wrote, directed, and starred in *Jack and the Beanstalk*, a children's pantomime now being performed throughout New Zealand. That same year, Hurst became the first actor cast when Renaissance Pictures set up in New Zealand to retell the adventures of Hercules.

Diana Rowan, the New Zealand casting director for *Hercules*, relates, "We already knew Iolaus had to be shorter than Hercules. And when I read the first script with Iolaus the first person that came to my mind was Michael." Rowan believed that Hurst could make this character much more than a routine sidekick:

> There were only two ways to go with the character of Iolaus: you could either make him seriously weak, but then you would wonder why Hercules was carrying this baggage around, or you could find somebody who could contribute enormous energy, and Michael doesn't even have to act it. He just radiates energy and enthusiasm and ability.

Hurst was immersed in theater projects and hesitated to audition, but Rowan's enthusiasm did not flag. She pressed his agent and finally persuaded Hurst to read for Eric Gruendemann, who was supervising the production in New Zealand. Hurst dutifully showed up with one of his steel double-handed broadswords and performed a scene that he also directed. He recalls:

> There were lines about monsters that you had to take seriously or it would never work. Well, I took it so seriously it became kind of humorous, and before I knew it, I got a call asking if I could meet with the director and producer. I remember walking into a room full of six *very* tall Americans [Hurst is five-foot-seven]. We had a meeting, and finally they asked me to do the American accent, which I did, and there was a great sigh of relief all around, and I got the part.

Hurst's performance as Iolaus soon won the adoration of fans, who loved his energy and intensity, his reckless abandon in fight scenes, and, not least, his rugged good looks. Iolaus has also provided a comic foil for Hercules, which he calls a welcome challenge:

> I love comedy. Yes, I play a lot of tragedy in theater [but] I've had to fight the fact that I was typecast for my first ten years when I

did comedy, comedy, comedy, comedy. I played all of Shake-speare's fools, among many other comic characters. You name it, that was me, so I wanted to explore the other side.

Hurst and Sorbo also convey a crackling screen chemistry that reflects a genuine friendship, according to Hurst:

Getting to know Kevin [Sorbo] has been a big plus. Al-though our back-grounds differ, both of us have struggled in our own ways. Also, we're both physical. We're almost identical in that, because we both train hard, and we both like to get in there and do our own fighting [scenes]. And we both have a childlike side. You probably wouldn't see it on first look, but neither of us is afraid to let the [inner] child come out.

Hurst looks forward to seeing Iolaus continue to grow in the coming seasons:

One way would be to have him face the truth of what it is to be a womanizer. Iolaus is always looking at and chasing women, and it's done in a very lighthearted and funny way. But I'd love for him to have an encounter where it costs, to see the consequences of his actions.

Something we never mention is Iolaus' wife and children, which I had in [*Hercules and the*] *Amazon Women,* but in [*Hercules in the*] *Maze of the Minotaur* I say my wife, Ania, died and [I'm raising] two boys. . . . I'm not saying bring them back, but I'm saying that consequence or involvement [is important].

We've never really played the truth of regret. I had an idea that either Hercules or Iolaus begins the show, and it's as if it's twenty years later, and one of us is dead, and it was so pointless. And the idea is, what price heroism? ... And the whole thing would have to be a fantasy or dream sequence that can let the character show regret and real rage and anger. ... Can the show take it? I don't know. But we are trying to push the boundaries. Our [executive] producer Rob Tapert said today we are going to see some really dark episodes peppered among the more humorous ones.

Hurst also wants to see both Hercules and Iolaus face even greater challenges. He concedes that they have fought terrifying creatures, but adds:

You know you're going to win if you fight a monster—it's Hercules, for heaven's sake! But what if a force came out from the East—a dancing Shiva or a Kali from India or maybe a Chinese demon—a force that didn't respect the Greek pantheon of gods, so therefore those gods had no power? Then we would have to face it in a different way and rely on other skills!

Hurst's interest in Iolaus' growth is not simply a matter of his devotion to wringing every facet of a role. To a surprising extent he also identifies with Iolaus:

Iolaus is a comfortable character to put on, because he's just me. Some of the things Iolaus does are Michael quirks. Iolaus gets bored easily, and so do I when people are not getting to the point. I'm just like Iolaus, I guess, or he's just like me! And sometimes I do attack things. Not literally, but I think, "Oh, let's just get in there and do it!" Every year, not in the theater or films, I like to do something risky. This year we did the abseiling [rappelling] into the caves. You know Kevin [Sorbo] and Eric Gruendemann and I abseiled 350 feet down a rope into a cave in Wytoha and [climbed] our way out. We had guides, but that was pretty risky and adventurous. I've done bungee jumping. Every year I'd like to do something that is on the edge. I guess, vaguely life-threatening.

Hurst also savors the epic themes and the sheer scope of *Hercules*, a feeling he first experienced on the set of *Hercules and the Amazon Women*:

> It suddenly hit me, "Hey, I'm in a real action movie, an American one!" I remember very clearly my exhilaration at that. And the first scene we shot, where Kevin and I first arrive at the village, and I say, "Why do I get the feeling we're not getting the whole story?" and Kevin says [Hurst slips into a John Wayne tone], "Because we're not." I thought, "Wow, we're heroes!" I also remember a fantastic sight of thirty horses with armed Amazon women galloping down one of the sand dunes, and I could only think, "Wow! This is so *big*!"

ROBERT TREBOR

Salmoneus

Robert Trebor plays Salmoneus, a man who
awakens each day with a
new get-rich-quick scheme and who
peddles everything from air sandals
and sundial watches to "celebrity bi-
ographies." Salmoneus lives to
"make a fast dinar" as he chases the
Ionian Dream of the good life, filled
with wine, women, and wealth. Trebor said that viewers can laugh at
his character but also identify with
him: "They admire Kevin [Sorbo as
Hercules], they admire Michael [Hurst as Iolaus], they *are* me."

Born in Philadelphia into a close-knit Jewish family, Trebor early decided to become an actor despite receiving some heartfelt parental advice:
"Please, do it on the side, you're going to starve to death!" After attend-
ing Northwestern University, he moved to New York City in 1976 and
honed his gift for character improvisation in companies like Second City
and the Ensemble Studio, while also appearing in plays, TV commercials,
and films. In 1985 Trebor drew critical praise for his intense stage (and
later screen) performance as the serial killer Son of Sam in *Out of the
Darkness*. He increasingly appeared in Hollywood productions, notably
the crime thriller *52 Pick-Up* (1986), based on the Elmore Leonard novel.

In 1994 Trebor won the role of the slave Waylin in *Hercules and the
Lost Kingdom*. He describes the difficult casting process:

Originally they wanted somebody like the butler in *Arthur*—an elderly guy like John Gielgud—or a street comic like Eddie Murphy. . . . They really didn't know what they wanted! I got to audition because the casting director had worked in the Ensemble Studio and knew I could improvise comedy. And it turned out that Rob Tapert, who is a good friend of Elmore Leonard, liked my work a lot from *52 Pick-Up*. I didn't read from the script in the audition, I improvised a character.

According to Trebor, when *Hercules* became a series, the head writer and coexecutive producer, John Schulian, created Salmoneus with him in mind:

John saw my work as Waylin and told me point-blank, "I wrote this based not on Waylin but on your comic energy." John put many elements into that first episode with Salmoneus ["Eye of the Beholder"], particularly the drive to sell to whoever comes along. He also built in that slight lecherousness [when the daughters of King Thespius chased Hercules, then set their sights on Salmoneus]—I'll be happy to romance fifty women if it's for the cause!

Trebor's manic expressiveness and comic brilliance have helped make his character a recurring foil for Hercules, appearing in about one-third of the episodes. According to Rob Tapert, Trebor improvises many of his own lines:

Bob's totally off the wall. . . . He probably says only twenty percent of what's written for him, the rest he makes up. . . . In "The Gauntlet" [a first-season episode], he totally made up a song for Xena. He called and said, "This episode is so dark, can I do this funny song?" And I said, "Bob, go for it."

John Schulian, the series' head writer through the first two seasons, was less amused by Trebor's ongoing alterations of his staff's work. Trebor, for his part, acknowledges Schulian as "a fine writer," but insisted that actors must sometimes change lines to give a fully believable portrayal. He cites an instance in the episode "Unchained Heart," when Salmoneus becomes too frightened to move after a cave-in. Trebor departed from the script by conveying his character's panic through understated gestures rather than his usual boisterous conduct:

> The whole purpose of acting is to make it come alive, not just do my comic shtick. John [Schulian] had wanted me to say during the cave-in, "We're all doomed, we're all going to die!" First of all, I don't know if people really say that. . . . I thought, "Salmoneus is usually so talkative, what if instead we see me mute and just rocking a little bit?" So in the read-through, I said, "Can we just cut all this stuff?" And the director liked it. . . . I love the chance to do that, to just be a real person in a situation.

Trebor's directorial debut came in *Hercules'* third season, in the episode "A Rock and a Hard Place." This was ironic because Trebor is known for his comedic abilities, but directed one of the most intense episodes in the series.

Trebor's character has become so popular that Toy Biz has even manufactured a Salmoneus action figure for children. For Trebor, who honed his craft through some lean years in New York and Los Angeles, his emergence as a fan favorite has been especially gratifying. His parents, long worried for his future, have also taken joyful notice, he says: "They'll tell everyone to watch Salmoneus, no matter what the subject of conversation. 'Speaking of Bosnia, have you seen *Hercules*?' So yes," he adds warmly, "they're very proud of what I've done."

BRUCE CAMPBELL

Autolycus
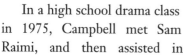

Bruce Campbell, who plays Autolycus, the self-styled "King of Thieves," was born on June 22, 1958, in Royal Oak, Michigan. He grew up in Birmingham, a suburb of Detroit, and recalls taking an early interest in acting:

> At age eight, I watched my father perform in a production of *The Pajama Game*. Realizing that adults could also participate in this form of make-believe left a lasting impression on young me.

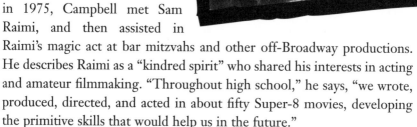

In a high school drama class in 1975, Campbell met Sam Raimi, and then assisted in Raimi's magic act at bar mitzvahs and other off-Broadway productions. He describes Raimi as a "kindred spirit" who shared his interests in acting and amateur filmmaking. "Throughout high school," he says, "we wrote, produced, directed, and acted in about fifty Super-8 movies, developing the primitive skills that would help us in the future."

Disappointed by his film classes in college, which he says "failed to compare with my recent hands-on experience," Campbell dropped out and tried to break into TV and movies. During this period he met Rob Tapert, who was rooming with Sam Raimi's brother Ivan at Michigan State University. Tapert and Sam Raimi soon joined Campbell as ex-college students, and in 1979 raised money for their own low-budget film, *The Evil Dead*. Like his two partners, Campbell shouldered many aspects of the production:

> We all really had to wear a lot of hats on that film because our crew kept getting smaller and smaller. We wanted to finish the film and were willing to do anything in order to do it. I did my own Foley footsteps for the film. I was the music editor, and Sam and I recorded a lot of the sound effects for the film.

The Evil Dead was released in 1983, with Campbell as star and coexecutive producer. Over the next decade he appeared in two sequels plus a string of genre films like *Maniac Cop* and *Sundown: A Vampire in Retreat*, and the offbeat comedy *The Hudsucker Proxy*. Campbell added to his cult following by starring in *The Adventures of Brisco County, Jr.* (1993–1994), a sly Western series on Fox television, and doing guest turns as the evil billionaire Bill Church on ABC's *Lois and Clark: The New Adventures of Superman*.

Campbell first worked on *Hercules: The Legendary Journeys* as a director ("The Vanishing Dead"), then appeared at the start of the second season as the thief and all-around mischief-maker Autolycus. Asked if the role was created with him in mind, Campbell first replies deadpan, "The truth is: all roles are created for me; I just don't have the time to do them all." Then, more seriously: "The role wasn't created for me. But Rob Tapert thought I would be right for it. Originally, I saw 'Auto' as an Errol Flynn type. The hammier the better."

Married, with one son and one daughter, Campbell continues to work in varied film and TV projects as an actor and a director. He has directed several more episodes of *Hercules*, and his character Autolycus has also created havoc and won fans on *Xena: Warrior Princess*.

LIDDY HOLLOWAY

Alcmene

*L*iddy Holloway, a gracious woman who has gained distinction as an actress and a writer, plays Hercules' mother, Alcmene. A native of New Zealand, Holloway spent much of her childhood in England with her mother. At eleven she won acceptance to the Royal Festival Ballet, and stayed in "a very beautiful old building" at a country boarding school in Hartfordshire. There she studied all aspects of dance and drama, then returned to New Zealand to complete her education.

Holloway joined a theater company in 1971 and worked with it on and off for many years while raising three children. In Australia during the late seventies and early eighties, Holloway acted and started writing for television. Her first show as a writer was called *Cop Shop*, and Holloway recalls thinking, "My God, what do I know about cops and robbers? You could write what I know on a book of matches." But she learned quickly by reading and "hanging out with police," even riding with them in their squad cars. Holloway has written over eighty hours of television shows, including *Deepwater Haven*, a children's program coproduced by Germany, France, Australia, and New Zealand.

In 1994 Holloway appeared in *Hamlet* opposite Michael Hurst at the Watershed Theatre in Auckland. With Hurst directing and starring as Hamlet, Holloway played emotionally charged scenes as his mother, Gertrude. "Sometimes we stood just millimeters from each other, and the intensity was so great that one night he had tears flooding down his face. And you could feel the audience just holding its breath." Holloway recalls Hurst as "such an unconventional Hamlet. You never knew where he was going to appear from. Which was great for the actors, because you're on stage thinking, Where is he going to come from tonight? And you have to keep alert."

Holloway won the role of Hercules' mother, Alcmene, in 1995, during the series' second season. The character had earlier been played by Jennifer Ludlam in the TV movies and by Elizabeth Hawthorne during the series' first season. Holloway says of her approach, "I tried to be as in sync as I could with what the earlier actresses had done without mimicking, which would have been impossible anyway because I don't even look like either of them." Instead she modeled Alcmene on "the American mom," as played by wholesome actresses like June Allyson.

The demands of the role have included physical stunts, which Holloway approaches with enthusiasm. On occasion Alcmene has even fended off thugs, which Holloway greatly enjoyed:

> It's probably because I'm a middle-aged lady, and here is a challenge to show that ladies of a certain vintage can still handle the physical aspects of a role. . . . Yes, fighting, and tossing one guy down a cliff over my shoulder. Of course, the stuntman did all the work, bless his heart. I just hung on!

Holloway has also done her share of reacting to imaginary monsters. In a second-season episode, "The Mother of All Monsters," the creature Echidna wrapped her tentacles around Alcmene. Holloway recalls this was a challenge because, of course, there was no creature:

> I'd never done that sort of thing before. There was a tentacle wrapped around me, and I had to think, Okay, what do I do if a tentacle comes out and wraps around [me], what is my physical response? And then I had to do the whole action in reverse, so that when the film is played in reverse it would look as if the tentacle were sliding around me rather than falling off.

The heart of Holloway's role, of course, involves playing opposite Kevin Sorbo as Hercules. She describes how she brings to these scenes her own experience as a mother of two grown-up sons: "Hercules is Alcmene's son, and she loves him. So I'm always thinking, How would I feel if this was one of my sons? How would I respond? I try to overlay that on Kevin so that I'm emotionally responding as I would to one of my own boys if he were in trouble." On hearing someone say that Hercules is lucky to have her as a mother, she responds brightly and without hesitation, "He's very lucky."

TAWNY KITAEN

Deianeira

*J*ulie "Tawny" Kitaen, who sparkles as Hercules' wife, Deianeira, is equally lively and humorous offscreen. Born on August 6, 1961, in San Diego, Kitaen recalls getting an early start in the entertainment industry "by jumping in front of every tourist's camera. It just seemed so natural. And once talkies came around, I was ready!"

Kitaen's first role was as Tom Hanks' fiancée in the comedy *Bachelor Party* (1984). There followed roles in *The Perils of Gwendoline*, based on a risqué French comic strip and shot in France, the Philippines, and Africa; the CBS soap opera *Capitol*; the horror flick *Witchboard* (1987); and other films and TV series. During the early nineties she was the voice of Anabelle on Fox's Saturday morning cartoon show about a wisecracking housecat, *Eek! the Cat*.

Kitaen won the role of Deianeira by accident. Reading for the female lead in *Darkman II*, she impressed the producers Sam Raimi and Rob Tapert, who thought she would be right for the part of Hercules' love interest in three TV movies then in preproduction. For Kitaen, who had played gorgeous and sultry women yet was also a doting mother of a baby girl, the role of Deianeira seemed perfectly timed: "Yes, she represents who I am right now, without a doubt. Because she wears some pretty skimpy outfits, but she's a mom, she's not trying to pretend she's not."

In three TV movies, beginning with *Hercules and the Circle of Fire*, Kitaen brought a beguiling sense of fun to the part of Deianeira. She recalls that in approaching the part, she kept in mind what Jack Lemmon said—that good acting is about playing a character, not about gimmicks. "How do you play a drunk? By not playing drunk," he said. Kitaen applied that to her role as the wife of a demigod in a Greek mythic setting:

> Lemmon's words always stuck in my mind. So what I tried to do for Deianeira in this role was not to play the era, not to play some [imagined ancient time]. Just play like it is 1994 and it will play as though it's whenever Hercules and I lived. Of course, there are limits. Your character can't all of a sudden start dancing the macarena. But you can still bring yourself and your times to the part. For example, Deianeira rolls her eyes at some things Hercules tells her. Because she's a real person to me, and whether or not a woman in those ancient times would react that way to something her husband said, it's what I felt a real person would do now.

Kitaen enjoyed acting with Kevin Sorbo, whom she describes as having "that perfect balance of being absolutely dedicated to what he does yet not taking himself too seriously." She also praises Sorbo's openness to improvising, as in their first movie together, *Hercules and the Circle of Fire*:

> Our characters come to a fork in the road and the script has us choose one path, then the other. I suggested playing it so that we first hesitate, then look at each other like we're really clever and we know what we're doing, and of course we really don't. So we played off each other for that . . . There's also a scene where Kevin is holding a rope [on a cliff] and I'm on his back, I'm climbing up his head. I wind up stepping on his face and you can see him reacting to this. I did all that on purpose and that wasn't in the script! You know what I call it? I call it jazz.

Asked what Sorbo was calling it while she stepped on him, Kitaen admitted he might have chosen different words.

In *Circle of Fire*, Deianeira reacts to various mythical beings, an acting challenge Kitaen found amusing:

> There is a scene where we are talking to the "ice god" [the frozen Prometheus]. Well, you just resort back to when you were a kid and you were just making things up and talking to imaginary tea-party people. There's no science to it. There's just the ability that some people have to stand there in front of fifty crew members acting like a complete fool, and not caring about those who don't.

Kitaen was invited back as Deianeira when *Hercules* became a series, but she declined to commit to the demands of an hour-long series. Her character was then written out of the show, killed by the vengeful Hera. The producers have brought Kitaen back for select guest appearances, as when Hercules visits Deianeira in the underworld in the episode "The Other Side." Her career remains filled with possibilities, but for Kitaen, recently married and absorbed in raising her young daughter, "Being a mom is at the top of my list."

LUCY LAWLESS

Xena

Lucy Lawless became an adventurer long before she starred as one. The fifth of seven children and the oldest girl, Lucy was very much a tomboy who, like her four older brothers (and most other New Zealanders) thrived on rugby and other sports. But acting soon proved a more enticing pastime.

As a ten-year-old student in a Catholic convent she got her "first real part," playing a saleswoman in a musical about the Prodigal Son. As befitted someone who loved singing even more than acting, she later lost all memory of the role, but "I remember some of the songs. I was a much better singer in those days than I am now."

Lawless' singing was good enough to lead her away from early thoughts of becoming either a marine biologist or a pathologist, and she spent three years training for the opera. In 1986 she enrolled in Auckland University to study languages and opera, but left school after a year. "I knew what I wanted to do, it wasn't to get a useless degree. . . ." She remembers, "I just wanted to travel. . . . And it's the best thing I could have done."

At eighteen she picked grapes on the Rhine in Germany, then moved to Switzerland and, with her boyfriend from New Zealand, Garth, traveled through Greece. When the money ran out, the couple left for Australia, where Lawless worked as a gold miner in the outback.

Lawless kept at this grueling work for eleven months, later calling it "a way to make good money, for people who weren't otherwise qualified—a way to get back to Europe." Then, thinking of the grueling, dirty labor, the harsh terrain, and the isolation, she adds with a laugh, "I don't know, just a bit of madness." Her plans took another unpredicted turn when, in 1987, she discovered she was pregnant. She and Garth married and returned to New Zealand. The following year her daughter, Daisy, was born, and Lucy began working again. She wrote plays, which Garth produced, and made videos for audition tapes.

At first Lawless starred mainly in TV commercials, until joining a comedy troupe on a New Zealand TV show called *Funny Business*. The audition went smoothly: She and another woman showed up just after two key actresses had walked off the set; both were hired at once. Lawless worked at the show for two and a half seasons. She followed this with guest roles in episodic TV, including an outing on the science fiction cult hit *The Ray Bradbury Theatre*. Then, despite limited acting opportunities and uncertain prospects, Lawless moved to Vancouver, Canada, in 1991 to spend eight months at the William Davis Centre for Actor's Study.

Returning to New Zealand early in 1992, Lawless became a cohost, or "presenter," for *Air New Zealand Holiday*, a travel magazine show broadcast in New Zealand and throughout Asia, which took her around the world. She entered a second season as presenter just as Renaissance Pictures set up in Auckland and began casting *Hercules and the Amazon Women*. New Zealand's foremost casting director, Diana Rowan, joined the company and immediately offered two strong suggestions: Michael Hurst would be ideal as Iolaus, and Lucy Lawless would make the perfect Amazon queen.

"I remember her audition for that part vividly," Eric Gruendemann related. "This was back when we had the time to see some people live—not just on tape, like now—and she just sort of lit up the room. . . . She had a power and a presence, even though only twenty-five years old, and a maturity."

Despite this impressive showing, Lawless could not overcome a reluctance to cast a foreign actress with limited credits. Rob Tapert recalls, "We went, 'You know, we really don't want to go with a Kiwi [a native of New Zealand] in the title role.' We didn't have any experience or anything."

Lawless won a smaller role in the film as Lysia, second-in-command to the Amazon queen.

When *Hercules* became a series, the producers asked Lawless back to play Lyla, a centaur's human lover, in the episode "As Darkness Falls." A sharply different character from Lysia, Lyla is free-spirited, playful, seductive, and manipulative rather than fierce. She is ruthless enough to drug Hercules into a state of blindness, but later repents her action and helps him.

When the Renaissance team began debating who should play Xena, the Warrior Princess, David Eick pressed to cast Lawless in the role. But although Rob Tapert and others were also struck by her presence, questions remained. Should a Kiwi rather than an American actress play Xena? And was Lawless a seasoned-enough performer? "We all noticed her," Dan Filie recalls. "We absolutely said she is really something. Who is that, wow! But we weren't smart enough to figure out that Lucy was our star character. . . ." One executive summed up the doubts about casting her as Xena saying, "Ah, she's a lieutenant, she's not a star."

There was also the matter of name recognition. Universal wanted someone well known, the better to lure viewers to *Hercules*. And, as Eric Gruendemann recalled, "Sam and Rob were then pitching to the studio an idea for a possible spin-off: a ruthless female warrior [who] becomes good. [So] the studio was looking for someone who had a TVQ [popularity quotient] in America."

By January 2, with the start date for shooting the first *Xena* episode drawing ever closer, Tapert was determined to find Lucy Lawless. Lawless, however, was deep in the New Zealand bush. "Well, I decided that nothing *ever* went on in New Year's," she says. "Everyone went away, nothing happened, certainly no work comes up. So we had gone off together on this jaunty holiday to give our daughter the camping experience, traveling the length and breadth of New Zealand in a tiny French beetle type of car that you could wind down the roof on, and stopping at various relatives on the way. The producers tracked us through the relatives. 'No, she went to so-and-so, she's not here, but. . . .' "

The casting director in New Zealand joined the frantic hunt and, as Lawless recalls, "phoned up my parents desperately trying to get hold of me because my agent didn't know where I was, I'd just left." So had her parents. "But my brother happened to be stopping by that day to pick up some mail, he was only there for five minutes, and caught the phone call, and somehow found the number of my husband's folks, who found the number of where we *might* be next—and we just *happened* to stop by that day, we had changed our plans and gone to that particular location, and there I was contacted."

Musing on the fragile set of coincidences that led—just barely—to her winning the role of Xena, Lawless says, "It almost makes me sick to think of it now." But perhaps other forces had also been at work. Lawless recalls that just before learning about her new role she came across "one of those New Year's features the country paper puts out—five days of horoscopes for everybody, and mine was this outrageous claim of 'overseas travel predicted, fame and fortune are on their way.' And we were *laughing* our heads off about it, and the next day that phone call came. . . . Yeah, I have it, I photocopied and enlarged it, because it was such a hoot."

RENEE O'CONNOR
Gabrielle

Whereas *Hercules* often teams its hero with a fellow warrior-adventurer in Iolaus, Xena's sidekick, Gabrielle, is younger and has a wide-eyed naiveté, idealism, and sweetness that play against the harsh past and hardened nature of the warrior princess.

Renee O'Connor at once became a standout among the actresses who auditioned for the part of Gabrielle. Two years earlier O'Connor had impressed Rob Tapert with her performance as the naive but spirited young woman Deianeira in *Hercules and the Lost Kingdom,* the second of the five telefeatures.

A native of Houston, Texas, O'Connor began studying acting at the age of twelve at the city's Alley Theatre. "Luckily for me," she says, "they had a children's program, and so we would use these wonderful costumes and amazing clay sets. And it's funny, because everything was make-believe, and here I am again, you know, at twenty-five years old and still doing it. I think that's where it all stems from—you know that sense of play."

O'Connor's first, unconventional acting gig came at sixteen, prancing through a Six Flags amusement park as a succession of costumed cartoon characters. It was, she recalls, "the funniest thing you'd ever imagine! But it was wonderful because you are larger than life and can play comedy and it was very physical. So we would do shows where we would actually dance and have music and the voices would be over the top."

After a stint at the High School of the Performing and Visual Arts in Houston, O'Connor, then seventeen, moved to Los Angeles to hone her sense of play as a professional actress. In 1989 Disney cast her in the first of two serials on the *Mickey Mouse Club*, "Teen Angel," reviving an old series favorite, "Spin and Marty." That same year, stretching from G-rated fare to HBO horror, O'Connor appeared in an episode of *Tales from the Crypt*, directed by Arnold Schwarzenegger. In the nineties she played Cheryl Ladd's daughter in the miniseries *Changes*. "It was a Danielle Steel novel," she volunteers with an embarrassed smile. She then starred as one of a group of students washed away by a river in the NBC movie *The Flood*. "It was based on a true story in Texas but filmed in Australia, which was so funny, especially since I'm from Texas. But it was pretty exciting."

Other feature films and TV roles followed. She appeared in another Disney production, *The Adventures of Huck Finn*, with Elijah Wood and Jason Robards. "It was a small part but it was wonderful, filled with humor, a nice period piece set in Natchez [Mississippi]." A guest appearance on *The Rockford Files* "was one of the highlights for me because I was—and am—such a fan of James Garner." Sandwiched among these and other performances, O'Connor appeared in two mythic action films for Renaissance Pictures: *Hercules and the Lost Kingdom* (1994) and the direct-to-video release *Darkman II: The Return of Durant* (1995).

Beth Hymson-Ayer, the U.S. casting director for both *Hercules* and *Xena*, felt that O'Connor brought qualities that were perfect for Gabrielle: "a wild sense of humor, an intelligence, and with all that still a youthful quality. Remember, in mythological times, Gabrielle could not be twenty-five, twenty-six years old and still living at home and dreaming of going off on adventure. The life span at that time was not that great, so that youthful look was important, and even though Renee may not be eighteen, she definitely still has a wide-eyed, innocent freshness to her." Hymson-Ayer also viewed O'Connor's aura of intelligence as crucial to the character: "Gabrielle is definitely not an equal to Xena in a lot of respects, but at the same time she is as clever, in her own way."

O'Connor describes her approach to Gabrielle's character:

> They [Rob Tapert and R. J. Stewart] were looking for somebody spunky, spirited, who could hold her own with Xena eventually, and so that was the guideline I began with. And then I took the idea of her being a storyteller and really clicked with that. Everything that she hadn't seen before but had only heard through stories and from her readings, she now could see herself living through Xena. And I made her very romantic, sentimental, and sympathetic, full of the wonder and mystery of life. So she would be the opposite of Xena but want to be like her. And where Xena could be dysfunctional and Gabrielle would be the opposite, together they make one person!

Casting the role was difficult, but Dan Filie remembers, "We decided, 'Let's get the best actress as Gabrielle,' just as we had with Kevin [Sorbo] as Hercules. And in reading the scenes, Renee was just the better actress. There's just a feeling, a good quality to her that comes across on screen. And it's funny, because we cast Renee for one reason, and now I think she's an incredibly attractive, very sexy character as well."

For good measure, Renee also counted a staunch supporter among Universal's extended family in Dan Filie's six-year-old son, Steven. "My son had seen *Lost Kingdom* about, oh, four hundred times. And he's a big fan of Herc, and he *loves* Renee O'Connor. So I'd say, "Stevie! You know Xena's sidekick? You think it should be Renee O'Connor? And he'd say, 'Dad! It *has* to be Renee O'Connor, it has to be young Deianeira!' " Three grueling weeks and several hundred auditions later, Stevie's judgment prevailed.

KEVIN SMITH

Ares

While other actors have played the brother of a hero, only Kevin Smith has played a hero's two half brothers. As Iphicles, he appears as Hercules' mortal twin, and as Ares, a son of Zeus, he is the god of war. It is a tribute to Smith's talent that fans have asked each other on the Internet, "Can the Kevin Smith who plays Iphicles be the same Kevin Smith who plays Ares?"

During his early twenties Smith was a guitarist and singer in a punk rock band that cut three albums and enjoyed a cult following on New Zealand's South Island. He also played rugby, until in 1987 he suffered his third concussion and feared he was becoming "punchy." While he was sidelined, his wife alerted him to an ad for an actor to star in a touring production of *Are You Lonesome Tonight?: The Elvis Presley Story*. Armed with years of experience "doing Elvis impersonations at parties," Smith won the role. "I got a real charge out of it," he says, and although the musical closed in six weeks, he decided on an acting career.

After spending several years with a theater company in Christchurch and playing villains on TV, he won the role of Iphicles in a second-season episode of *Hercules*, "What's in a Name?" Smith's character masquerades as his famous half

brother, Hercules, in order to impress a woman he is courting. Smith wryly explains Iphicles' attitude:

> He figures, Hey, I've paid my dues. I'm going to be Hercules for a while now. Hey, no more waiting for a table in a restaurant! And I get valet parking! Yeah! So that's all he wanted.

Smith says that because New Zealand productions don't often do this kind of fantasy costume drama, he especially enjoys his role:

> It was my first encounter with the *Hercules* set, and I thought, Man, this is cool! I get to wear a rock 'n' roll wig and a groovy leather lounge suit costume. I get to have sword fights and rescue a princess. It doesn't get better than that, you know? When you're a kid and you imagine what an actor does every day, this is it.

Playing the villainous Ares presents a different set of challenges, but Smith finds that Ares' villainy and his godhood both offered exciting dramatic possibilities:

> You can go to town. You can really explore the dark corridors. And, of course, as a god, there are no rules. There's no need to say, "Hey, gods don't do that." You're making up the rules as well. I think Ares does not see himself as a villain, but as absolutely necessary in the larger scheme of things. He thinks, The world can't function without me being here. He's comfortable with who he is. And he's worldly, as gods go. In the first episode with Ares ["The Reckoning," on *Xena*], we see Ares' bachelor pad. Man, it has a Jacuzzi! A Jacuzzi! Here's a guy who likes wine, who likes to eat, who lives the good life.

While Iphicles is insecure, Ares projects supreme self-confidence. It's a part of TV convention, Smith explains:

> Bad guys are generally played with more smiles than good guys. It's something that's reasonably stylized, like wearing a black hat in a Western that signals, "I'm the bad guy." With Ares, at least, it's black leather—it gives you a clue. Ares is like other successful villains in that he's sure of his place in the universe. And his smile

shows his anticipation of ultimate victory: "Okay, it's not happening now, but it's going to come. Every defeat is just a bloody nose. You're going to come back strong."

The villain's going to lose ultimately, of course. But in some ways villains have the emotional memory of a goldfish that swims in a bowl with a rock, thinking, Hey, nice rock. Hey, nice rock. Hey, nice rock. And I think with a villain, too, there's an enormous ego. So they're thinking, *This* time! Otherwise, you know, there would be scenes of Ares just holed up in his pad [crying]!

Smith briefly lived in North Hollywood and has worked in Australia, but he remains attached to his native New Zealand, saying, "This is my home, my spiritual base. I've got a couple of young sons, and in terms of quality of life, New Zealand may not be the perfect place, but after having a look around the world, we feel there's a lot of places worse to bring up kids than New Zealand."

JEFFREY THOMAS

Jason

*J*effrey Thomas plays Jason, the Greek hero who led the Argonauts on their voyage to find the Golden Fleece. The Welsh-born Thomas speaks with a crisp diction reminiscent of Wales' most famous actor, Richard Burton. As a student at Oxford, Thomas fell in love with a woman from New Zealand and eventually married her. He was teaching English at the University when he was offered a role in a play. He accepted because he thought it would be a useful experience, as someone who hoped one day to be a playwright. "So I started acting on a whim," he says, "and found I loved it."

Thomas pursued a wide-ranging career in the arts. His drama *Playing the Game* was staged in New Zealand and then was produced in Wales, London, and London's West End. He also performed in a play called *Someone Who'll Watch Over Me*, in which an Irishman (played by Thomas), an Englishman, and an American are held hostage in Beirut. The characters are chained to a wall throughout. At one point, he says, the American is led out, never to be seen again, and the audience assumes he's been shot; at the end, the Irishman is released; the Englishman remains. Thomas also wrote, raised funds for, produced, and directed a thirteen-minute film that was shown at film festivals and given a theatrical release in Germany.

Thomas has peppered his acting résumé with TV villains, including appearances on both *Hercules* (in "Gladiator") and *Xena* (in "Chariots of War"). But it was as Jason that he became a recurring character—and a member of Hercules' family. In "Once a Hero," Thomas appreciated the writer's development of his character, with Jason beginning as a drunkard and regaining his dignity in the process of regaining the Golden Fleece. He recalls enjoying his emotional scenes in which Jason confesses his fears to Hercules. "Afterward, members of the crew gave me nods and winks, as if to say, 'Good job!'"

Thomas finds the sword-fighting on *Hercules* a refreshing departure from most of the work he's done: "I like the physical side of acting, but most modern dramas are set in an office." Still, Thomas felt some trepidation in the episode "The Wedding of Alcmene," when he was supposed to swing on a rope some ten to fifteen feet off the ground. Although he wore a harness for safety, he still found it "scary" because, he says, "I couldn't help thinking of Christopher Reeve." Thomas handled the stunt without difficulty, though he had more trouble with a scene in which Jason and Hercules hack their way through the innards of a sea monster. "We were both smeared with sticky stuff, which was quite uncomfortable," he says.

Asked about his proudest accomplishment, Thomas bypassed his acting and writing achievements, and says, "I built a doll's house for my daughter for her twelfth birthday. The drawers open, with bank notes and scissors inside. She's eighteen now."

ERIK THOMSON

*A*lthough the Greek myths portrayed Hades as a gloomy presence, the writers on *Hercules* had in mind a more complex and spirited character. Diana Rowan, the New Zealand casting director on *Hercules*, told the producers about Erik Thomson: "It's a case of whether you can grab him between his stints in the theater. But we ought to hook this guy ahead of time because you'll really like him." Thomson won the role and became a staple player in the pantheon of Greek gods featured on the series.

Thomson's journey to the Underworld began in the Scottish Highlands, where he was born in 1967. He emigrated to New Zealand at age seven and later gained admission to the country's sole national drama school, in Wellington. Since graduating in 1990, he has worked widely on stage and in TV coproductions. That helped him perfect an American accent for Hercules.

I've had a fairly good association with and understanding of America and American people through all the plays I've been doing and also through my travels. I've spent about five months in the States, visiting friends from Massachusetts to Colorado and California, and all the way down to Alabama to see my sister.

He appeared in an early episode of *Hercules*, "The Vanishing Dead," as Dolan, a king turned against his sister by the god of war, Ares. During the next season the role of Hades came up, and he was written as a spirited, wry, but overworked god, never having "enough staff" to classify all the dead, especially during rush periods like wars.

At times Hades has appeared unable to cope despite his great powers, often calling on humans like Hercules and Xena to set things right in the Underworld. Thomson thought this an intriguing part of playing this powerful but vulnerable god:

> Hades has been given this huge responsibility. And it gets him down sometimes. And sometimes he loses his edge, he loses his power. I really enjoy playing that character because he has human qualities too. He has his faults. Now I really don't know why the writers had him fight Hercules rather than zap him with lightning, but I like to think it's because he felt like a bit of a fight. He wanted to prove his love for Persephone without using his godly powers. Things like that make the character a little bit more accessible.

Thomson's experience in stage and TV fighting has been especially prized on a show like *Hercules*, where gods as well as mortals regularly see action. In "The Other Side," Hades battles Hercules nearly to a standstill in a confrontation that rocks the Underworld. Like Kevin Sorbo, Thomson did most of his own stunts:

> Peter Bell trained me for an hour on the basic steps; it was like learning a dance. And the basic techniques I'd already picked up on other productions, like how to "sell" a punch for the camera. They had a stunt double standing by, all dressed up like Hades, just in case there was anything I couldn't do. But fortunately I was able to do everything except for the flying through the air. And the funny thing about that massive fight is that in the next episode, "Highway to Hades," I simply zap Hercules with a bolt of lightning. I was thinking, Well, why didn't I do that in the first place?

As Hades, Thomson grumbles frequently about being confined to the Underworld, but off camera he marvels at what the production crew has fashioned:

> New Zealanders are famous for their ability to improvise. We have a saying that New Zealanders can do anything with some number eight fencing wire. I think *Hercules* and *Xena* show that, because the designers and the crews have managed to achieve a great deal.
>
> The Underworld is basically chicken mesh wiring. All the stalagmites and stalactites in the caves use that as a basic structure. Then the crews cover it in a fireproof paper and paint it to have that rocklike appearance. And then the set is all lit and covered with smoke—we use lots of smoke machines.

Although Thomson has delighted in his role on *Hercules*, he recalls his astonishment on discovering the show's far-flung celebrity—and his own:

> Bobby Hosea, who plays [Xena's lover] Marcus, told me he was in downtown L.A. to make a payment on his car, and the woman there said, "What are you doing on *Xena*?" And he told her, "I'm going down to the Underworld." She got excited at this and said, "Oh, if you see Hades, tell him I think he's gorgeous. Could you get a photograph with him?" And then I received a couple of fan letters from America. It's nice, but very strange!

ALEXANDRA TYDINGS

Aphrodite

"Totally!" "Tubular!" "Bummer!" Aphrodite, the Greek goddess of love, has never been so hip, so mod, so surfer-Valley girl-Californian as on *Hercules: The Legendary Journeys*. And Alexandra Tydings, the blond, blue-eyed, funny and free-spirited actress who plays her, has proven a casting match made on Mount Olympus.

Tydings was born into a distinguished political family. Her grandfather, Millard Tydings, and her father, Joseph Tydings, both served as U.S. senators from Maryland. She grew up in Washington, D.C., where early on she mastered a dance form that has since swept the nation:

> My mother tells me that I saw Irish dancing at an outdoor theater in Virginia when I was about four. It's all the rage now, but almost no one had ever heard of it back then. I fell in love with it and kept nagging my mother until she found me an Irish dancing teacher. And I got really heavily into it. You know, ballet is all about *The Nutcracker*, but Irish dancing is about competitions.

Tydings represented the United States at the Irish Dancing World Championships in England

and Ireland, and also became involved with ballet "because they said ballet will make you more graceful." This led to an audition at age eleven with the Royal Ballet of London, with which she performed at the Kennedy Center in Washington, D.C. Tydings dreamed of a career in ballet, "but then I shot up like a weed, so that [idea] crumbled."

Tydings also performed in plays until her early teens. Then in high school, she says, "I sort of went through a rebellious stage which hasn't quite ended yet. I was just too punk rock to be in plays. I had purple hair and green hair. And that's hard to cast, you know."

At Brown University Tydings took courses in art and film that she found exciting but of limited practical value:

> We saw a lot of films that no one has ever heard of, and we learned a whole vocabulary to talk about things that no one speaks. Feminist theory, Marxist theory, all that kind of stuff. When I came to Hollywood after graduation, I had to [discard] all of that and learn how to talk to human beings.

Tydings relates that when she told her fellow majors in "Art Semiotics" that she was heading for Hollywood after graduation, "they thought I was completely insane":

> You see, my whole major is incredibly critical of popular movies and TV, and we acted so smart and knew all this jargon, and could just shred anything that anyone did. So when I started telling people that I was going to participate in the "machine" that was producing everything that we were taking apart and laughing at, they couldn't believe it. They said, "Are you nuts? Why would you subject yourself to that kind of torture? And you know, we're going to have to shred you, too."

Determined to break into acting, Tydings moved to Los Angeles in 1993. She quickly landed a role in Showtime's sophisticated cable series *Red Shoe Diaries*. Among the movie and TV roles that followed, she played Woody Harrelson's rich, spoiled wife in *The Sunchaser*, which dazzled at the Cannes Film Festival in 1996 but fizzled in America.

Early in 1996 a script for *Hercules* that Kevin Sorbo was directing, "The Apple," featured the goddess Aphrodite. Beth Hymson-Ayer, the U.S. casting director, believed that Tydings was a natural for the part:

When we got the script with Aphrodite, it was such an offbeat character and story—so modern and still quite mythological—we needed someone to have fun with the role, and Alex has that personality. I had cast her in another Universal series [*Vanishing Son*], and she is just this open, fresh, whimsical, totally uninhibited person. And fortunately for us she was also a beauty, so it was one of those casting choices that really fit.

Tydings had never before seen *Hercules*, and she recalls having to get her bearings on how to play Aphrodite:

When I read the script for "The Apple," I told my agent, "I don't really understand this. It's an action-drama-comedy?" And she told me, "Just have fun with it!" . . . Kevin Sorbo, who directed the episode, was really sweet and encouraged all of us. . . . For one scene Kevin said I could bring more energy to the next take, and I couldn't figure out what he meant. He explained, "Oh, you didn't do that laugh. I like that laugh. Do your laugh again."

On her next take, Tydings gave a laugh that was joyful, flirtatious, and utterly charming—the perfect symbol of her character in this and later episodes.

"The Apple" proved one of the series' most popular episodes, and Aphrodite became a recurring character who showed increasing depth to match her physical appeal. Tydings was delighted to return to the role, and to New Zealand:

When we filmed "The Apple" it was winter here and it was summer there. So I really felt as though I had stepped off this hellish thirteen-hour plane ride into paradise. It was gorgeous. And we shot the first four days at these giant west-coast beaches with black sand, and at the end of the day I would take off my costume and give them back my wig, put my bathing suit on, and run and jump in the water before they drove me back to my hotel. You can't ask for better than that!

Tydings, who has begun to write screenplays and would like one day to direct and produce, relaxes by dancing and going to the movies. And she takes a special delight, she says, in "hanging out with my dogs":

I grew up with giant dogs, yeah, and one of my dogs now, Stella, is a full-blooded blond English mastiff. And Maggie is a dog we rescued from the side of the road. She was super-skinny and limping. We thought she was a full-grown Rottie but it turns out that she was a half-grown Neapolitan mastiff mix, and she's still shooting up. They are giant, gorgeous creatures, and I love them both.

Tydings adds with a smile worthy of Aphrodite, "They are just awesome."

HERCULES

THE VIEW

FROM

OLYMPUS

This is the story of a time long ago
A time of myth and legend, when the Earth was still young.
The ancient gods were petty and cruel
And they plagued mankind for their sport.
Plagued them with suffering and
Besieged them with terrors.
For centuries the people had nowhere to turn,
No one to look to for help.
Until *he* arrived.
He was a man like no other.
Born of a beautiful mortal woman
But fathered by Zeus, king of the gods,
Hercules possessed a strength the world had never seen,
A strength surpassed only by the power of his heart. . . .
No matter the obstacle,
As long as there were people crying for help,
There was one man who would never rest—
Hercules!

—from the Prologue to the *Hercules* films

The ancient Greek gods and goddesses were immortal and possessed great powers, but were otherwise much like humans. They felt the same desires, including jealousy and anger as well as love and passion, and they sometimes acted spitefully toward mortals and each other. The gods divided among them the seas, the sky, and the earth, and each watched over activities of special interest, from poetry and healing to theft and war. Twelve major gods ruled from Mount Olympus, a snow-covered peak in northern Greece.

7he world of the gods was violent, and those who ruled were the most powerful and cunning fighters. The gigantic race of immortals known as Titans seized power from their tyrannical father Uranus, the sky. The youngest Titan, Cronos, wounded Uranus with a sickle and banished him from Earth. But he proved as cruel as his father, even swallowing his children at birth to make sure they did not rebel against him.

Cronos' horrified wife, Rhea, hid her youngest child, Zeus, and instead fed Cronos a stone with swaddling clothes, which he swallowed whole. On reaching adulthood, Zeus tricked Cronos into drinking a potion that made him cough up his other children, who then joined Zeus in a battle against their father and the other Titans. After ten years, the Titans were defeated and thrown into Tartarus, the deepest pit in the Underworld.

Wise as well as strong, **Z E U S** was chosen by his brothers and sisters as king of the gods. He hurled his thunderbolt to punish the wicked, but shared his power with the other gods. Zeus made his sister Hera his queen. Their wedding celebration lasted three hundred years, but their marriage was stormy, for Zeus had other wives and lovers—goddesses, nymphs, and mortals—and many children by them. Hera was jealous of them all. She especially hated Hercules, for he was not only the mightiest of all mortals but Zeus' favorite.

The five *Hercules* movies portray Zeus as a lovable old rogue who delights in humans, especially if they are beautiful women. Though a kind and just god, he has long neglected his son Hercules, who says of his father in *Circle of Fire*, "He's got the heavens and earth on his shoulders, and he never had time to think or care about me." But Zeus' affection for his son is clear as he visits from Olympus to lend a helping thunderbolt and offer fatherly advice. At the close of *Hercules in the Underworld*, we glimpse the poignant twilight of a god as he sits beside Hercules and Deianeira and lovingly plays with their children—his grandchildren.

Everywhere [Hercules] went he was tormented by his stepmother, Hera, the all-powerful queen of the gods.
Hera's eternal obsession was to destroy Hercules,
For he was the constant living reminder of Zeus' infidelity.

—from the Prologue to the *Hercules* films

HERA, who is blamed for just about everything bad that happens on *Hercules*, was beautiful but vain, taking as her sacred animal the peacock. Zeus seduced Hera by trickery, turning himself into a cuckoo and flying into her arms. Hera was the goddess of marriage and childbirth. She also protected women—except for those Zeus found attractive.

Hera is never seen on *Hercules* except for her glowing eyes, but her attempts to destroy Hercules are at the center of his legendary journeys. Even Zeus speaks of Hera in whispered, worried tones, appearing less the king of the gods than a henpecked husband. Although he occasionally stands up to Hera, more often he simply urges Hercules to stay out of her way. His advice usually goes unheeded and does not do much for father-son relations. At the start of the series, Hera kills Hercules' wife and children with a fireball. In later episodes, she tries to kill Hercules himself with the aid of robotic female Enforcers ("The Enforcer," "Not Fade Away"), monstrous Mesomorphs ("Let the Games Begin"), Death Squad assassins ("A Star to Guide Them"), the lizardlike mandrake ("What's in a Name?"), and many other deadly creatures. But, as in the myths, Hercules overcomes every foe.

APHRODITE, the goddess of love and beauty, rose out of the sea on a cushion of foam when blood from the wounded Uranus touched the ocean. (Homer claims that her father was Zeus, who had an affair with yet another goddess, Dione.) Aphrodite was carried in a giant scallop shell to the shores of Cyprus, where roses bloomed on her arrival, doves and sparrows flocked around her, and the four seasons greeted her and dressed her in clothes and jewels. A famous painting by Botticelli from the fifteenth century, *The Birth of Venus* (as the Romans called her), shows the beautiful blond goddess poised delicately on a giant shell, as the West Wind guides her toward the shore.

Unlike the other gods, who had many tasks, Aphrodite had no duties other than to be beautiful, which she did better than anyone. Her very aura inspired love. And while other Olympians carried special weapons, Aphrodite instead wore a magic girdle that made her irresistible to gods and mortals alike.

On *Hercules: The Legendary Journeys* Aphrodite uses her scallop shell to surf the waves, strums sixties beach-party music on a guitarlike Arabic instrument called an oud, and speaks the latest, hippest lingo ("I'm maxed out on the love gig! I'm shifting my career gear! Time to find a new energy field!"). Yet this Aphrodite is, at heart, the same goddess worshiped by the ancient Greeks. Beautiful and sensual, she is also willful and irresponsible. She affectionately refers to "Herc" as her half brother.

Aphrodite's winged son **EROS**, or **CUPID** (as the Romans called the Greek god of love), did her bidding but he was even more fickle than his mother. Eros flew about, shooting golden arrows that made people fall in love, often with unsuitable partners. The Greeks understood that love knows no limit, for which they thanked Aphrodite, and no logic, for which they blamed Eros.

HEPHAESTUS, the god of fire and metalworking, was a son of Hera, who according to some tales conceived him without help from Zeus or any other male. Born weak and lame, he so repelled his mother that she tossed him out of Olympus. Hephaestus fell for a day and was rescued by the sea goddess Thetis. He grew up to become a craftsman of matchless artistry. When Hera saw a magnificent brooch he had made, she called him back to Olympus. There Hephaestus became smith to the gods, for whom he built golden palaces, chariots, weapons, and tools. He married Aphrodite, though this did not stop her from taking other lovers among both gods and mortals.

In "Love Takes a Holiday," Hephaestus limps about his underground forge, his face badly scarred from the fall from Olympus. A sensitive but tormented god, he hammers objects with infinite skill: a panther that springs to life, a shield that makes its bearer invisible, and—his proudest creation—a golden likeness of Aphrodite, for whom he has pined for three hundred years. "Even an ugly god can dream," Hephaestus tells her. He is rewarded when Aphrodite, touched by his art and his devotion to her, assures him, "Beauty's not just what you look like. It's also what you are inside," then gasps in amazement at her own profundity.

ARES, the only son of Zeus and Hera, was the god of war. A brute and braggart disliked by all the gods except Aphrodite, Ares delighted in bloodshed. Yet his own exploits often ended in failure. Twice Ares attacked his half brother Hercules, who knocked him down four times in a battle at Pylus, and later wounded him in the thigh.

Ares' earliest appearances on *Hercules* were in keeping with the Ares the Greeks knew and despised. A repellent creature, he battles Hercules in "Ares" and is beheaded. But decapitation proves no more than a temporary setback. Ares returns in the third season as a handsome, devilishly clever schemer. In "Encounter" he chides an aide, "Stop thinking short term!" And when Hercules indignantly exclaims, in "When a Man Loves a Woman," "Are there no limits, even to your treachery?" Ares replies with a smile, "Why have limits?!"

The dark-browed **HADES**, a brother of Zeus, ruled the Underworld, the kingdom of the dead. His three-headed dog, Cerberus, made sure no souls escaped. Everything about Hades was somber, from his ebony throne to his chariot drawn by coal-black steeds. Hades owned all precious metals and jewels (for these were underground), and so the Romans called him Pluto, meaning "wealth."

The most famous myth about Hades is retold in an episode of *Hercules* called "The Other Side," in which Hades kidnaps the lovely Persephone, whose mother, **DEMETER**—his own sister—was the goddess of fertility. As Demeter mourned for Persephone she neglected the fields and let crops wither, bringing starvation. Hercules, in the series, or Zeus, in the original myth, compromised between the two feuding Olympians, arranging for Persephone to spend part of every year on earth with Demeter and part with Hades in the Underworld. Whenever Persephone returned to her mother, spring would come and crops would grow again, but her descent back into the Underworld brought the first chill of winter.

Hades as depicted on *Hercules* bears little resemblance to the shadowy figure of myth. The movie *Hercules in the Underworld* presents an almost comically weak god, who is terrified of his dark realm—and especially his escaped hound, Cerberus. Hades fares better in the series, looking every inch a king as he thunders up from the underworld to carry off Persephone. Unlike the ancient tales, though, *Hercules* presents him as a dashing figure; no wonder, then, that Persephone secretly loves him.

Running the Underworld is no easy task even for a god as commanding as Hades. In "Highway to Hades" he complains to Hercules, "Last year Ares had six wars going, and I had a staff of four. This year, *thirteen* wars and Zeus has cut my staff to two. Go figure!" And he grumbles, "I got inventory [of dead souls] coming up." All things being equal, the lord of the Underworld would rather be relaxing in Athens.

The other Olympians have yet to be glimpsed on *Hercules* (except for a single, fleeting appearance by Athena and Artemis in "The Apple"). But they, too, were among the major gods and goddesses.

ATHENA, the daughter of Zeus and his first wife, the Titaness Metis, was the most important goddess after Hera. She was still in the womb when Zeus swallowed Metis as a precaution against having a son who might later depose him. Soon afterward Zeus suffered an unbearable headache and ordered Hephaestus to split open his head with an ax. Out sprang Athena, full grown. She immediately became her father's favorite adviser.

Athena became the patron goddess of the city of Athens, to which she gave her name. The animals sacred to her were the serpent, the cock, and the owl. Though invincible in war and often portrayed in full armor, she preferred reason to bloodshed. Athena also invented the flute, the trumpet, farm tools, and the olive tree. Although kinder than many other gods, she too could be merciless: When a mortal woman, Arachne, boasted of being a greater weaver than Athena, Athena challenged her to a weaving contest and then turned her into a spider, in which form she continued to weave her webs.

ARTEMIS, the daughter of Zeus and the Titaness Leto, was the goddess of the hunt and wildlife. She aided in the birth of her twin, Apollo, when she was just minutes old. A deadly archer, quick to strike down humans who gave offense, she liked to travel with Apollo. Some myths equate her with the goddess Selene, who brought the moon across the sky in a chariot drawn by silver stags.

Handsome **APOLLO** was the god of the sun, archery, music, poetry, and healing. A patron of wisdom, he encouraged people to know themselves and to live in moderation. Apollo foretold the future and counseled mortals by speaking through the oracle at Delphi in the mountains of central Greece, overlooking distant valleys and the sea. Once he clashed with Hercules, who had become impatient with Apollo's oracle and seized her sacred tripod, but Zeus separated his two sons with a thunderbolt. Still, Apollo and Artemis admired Hercules, even permitting him to take one of Artemis' prized Golden Hinds for his third labor.

POSEIDON, a quick-tempered brother of Zeus, was lord of the oceans. He spent most of his time in an underwater golden palace with his queen, the sea goddess Amphitrite. Poseidon's scepter was a trident, and he rode in a chariot drawn by dolphins or seahorses. When he shook his trident, storms and floods followed, and when he struck the earth, mountains trembled. But he could also be kind, as when he turned Thessaly from an enormous lake into dry land.

Although Poseidon has yet to show himself on *Hercules* after three seasons, the god of the sea has appeared on *Xena*. A powerful, deep-voiced apparition formed of water, he has plotted against Xena and will likely be no friendlier toward Hercules.

HERMES, messenger of the gods, was the son of Zeus and the Titaness Maia. He was a favorite of the Olympians despite his thieving ways. Hermes made the first lyre out of a tortoise shell and the gut from one of Apollo's cows, which he had stolen. Apollo was furious, but Hermes escaped punishment by offering Apollo the lyre as payment for the cow. A charming youth who wore a winged helmet and winged sandals, he became Zeus' trusted messenger and helper. Hermes also guided the souls of the dead to the Underworld and brought good luck to travelers.

HESTIA, the eldest sibling of Demeter, Hera, Hades, Poseidon, and Zeus, was the goddess of the hearth. She protected every household on Earth and was honored by both gods and mortals. The gentlest member of her family, Hestia gave up her place as one of the twelve Olympian gods to Dionysus so she could spend her time by the hearth.

DIONYSUS was the son of Zeus and a mortal woman, Semele, who was struck dead by lightning before he was born in an accident caused by the jealous Hera. Zeus rescued him and sewed him up in his own thigh, where he stayed until he was born. Hidden from Hera, Dionysus grew up among nymphs and wild animals, but eventually Hera found him and drove him mad. Wrapped in a panther skin and crowned with vine leaves, Dionysus traveled the world, teaching the art of wine making. His wild religious rituals drew women who danced in a frenzy, for Hera had driven them mad too. Later Dionysus recovered and, despite Hera's protests, was welcomed into Olympus as the god of wine and vegetation.

The immortals, as the Olympian gods were known, often interfered in the lives of humans. They sometimes took humans as lovers but when displeased were quick to kill them or turn them into trees or animals. They might blight the earth and cause a famine, as Demeter did to get her daughter Persephone back. Or, like Ares, they might provoke wars simply to revel in the destruction. Yet the age of gods was also an age of heroes who displayed extraordinary strength and courage. And Hercules, son of Zeus and champion of justice against gods, monsters, and mortals alike, was the greatest of them all.

The First
Season

1. The Wrong Path

Writer	John Schulian
Director	Doug Lefler
Original Air Date	Jan. 16, 1995

Guest cast

Iolaus	Michael Hurst
Aegina	Clare Carey
Lycus	Mick Rose
She-Demon	Nicky Mealings
Alcmene	Elizabeth Hawthorne
Thoas	Martyn Sanderson
High Priest	Eric Gruendemann
Deianeira	Tawny Kitaen
Pilgrim #1	Patrick Wilson
Pilgrim #2	John Watson
Temple Guard	Gordon Hatfield
Tavern Thug	John Dybvig

Story: Hercules is overwhelmed by grief and rage after his stepmother, the goddess Hera, hurls two fireballs that engulf his wife, Deianeira, and his three young children. Unable to understand why his father, Zeus, the king of the gods, has allowed this, Hercules renounces his love for him, burns his own home, and vows revenge on Hera by destroying each of her seven temples. After forcing his way into the first, he rescues a beautiful slave girl, Aegina, from a sacrificial slaying, and pulls down the temple walls. Aegina makes Hercules see that his path of vengeance will not honor his family, and he recovers his senses in time to save Aegina's village from a She-Demon whose tail turns people to stone. Hercules outmaneuvers the creature so that her lethal tail whips back on her body and petri-

fies her. With the demon's
spell broken, her stone pris-
oners slowly come back to life;
in a sense, so too does Hercules, who sets off with a renewed sense of purpose, to help
others in need.

Mythic connections:

In myth, Hercules slays his wife
and children in a fit of madness
caused by Hera. "The Wrong
Path" makes clear that Hercules is
the target but never the tool of his vengeful stepmother.

Highlights:
In ten seconds of off-screen horror, the writer John
Schulian destroys Hercules' family before the opening credits. The aim,
said Schulian (not one for half measures) is to free Hercules to roam
Greece, unencumbered by family obligations. Also, the opening scene features the definitive barroom brawl, which shows off Kevin Sorbo's agility
as well as brawn, and Michael Hurst's daredevil energy.

Kevin's take:
Of all the shows we've done, I still think it has the
two best fight sequences in the series. The opening scene, when Michael
and I walk in on the thugs [saying], "We were in the neighborhood, we
just had to say hello!" and then the fight scene when I rescue Clare Carey
[Aegina] in the temple. I end up carrying her and fling her around my
neck a couple of times [knocking down several henchmen] and pole-vault
with her [holding on to me]. Great fight! The director, Doug Lefler, is
very good at action. And I think because it was our first time back [after
the TV movies], we had a week's worth of rehearsals before we shot those
fights. Now we don't have that luxury.

Michael's take:
The opening fight is just wonderful and very
funny. I don't think it's the best episode by any means, [because for] the first
few, you're just finding your way. But I remember a scene after Hercules
loses his family, in which Kevin and I were both going for the tears. That
doesn't happen very often, that you see, in a hero show like this, two men
actually cry together. And then we joked about it: "Did you get a tear?"!

Hercules shows off some
memorable skills in this
scene from *Hercules in the*

Sometimes even Aphrodite, the goddess of love, needs advice from her big brother Hercules.

In "Encounter," Hercules must save the Golden Hind, a creature that is half woman and half deer, from an evil warlord.

When Aphrodite asks Hercules to talk to Cupid, she never suspects that the two will become rivals in love.

Echidna, the mother of all monsters, blamed Hercules for the deaths of her children, including the Hydra and the Nemean lion.

With Hercules' encouragement, Xena sets off to change her life and right the wrongs of her past.

Necessity makes strange allies when Hercules has to team up with the evil Callisto to save his family and friends.

In "The Enforcer," Hercules works his charm on an old love, Nemesis, but . . .

. . . he finds that charm useless against Hera's evil Enforcer.

Hercules with the catch
of the day.

A trip to the Underworld
reunites Hercules with his
wife, Deianeira.

A shipwreck leaves Hercules fighting for his life against a vicious mercenary.

When Hercules is accused of murdering his wife, Serena, Iolaus and Xena help prove his innocence in "Judgment Day."

Hercules is about to prove the old saying that two heads are better than one.

Hercules swings into action, taking on two palace guards at a time.

Hercules demonstrates that sticks and stones may break your bones, but fists can really hurt you.

Iolaus tries to explain exactly how he got covered in mud.

Hercules enjoys a quiet moment between adventures.

Hercules and Iolaus never know where the next cry for help will lead them.

In a change of pace, prerevolutionary France is the setting for a lesson about the adventures of Hercules.

Hercules battles the Hydra, a fearsome creature that grows two heads when one is cut off.

The bigger they are, the harder they fall.

Hercules and Autolycus discover a king's ransom in gold.

Salmoneus picks a bad moment to try to interest Hercules in another of his get-rich-quick schemes.

Hera tries to disrupt Alcmene's wedding by sending a sea serpent to swallow the groom and the bride's son.

A sea voyage gives
Hercules a brief
rest from his
labors.

A time-travel accident reunites Hercules with his love, Serena.

Hercules struggles with a centaur.

Hercules tries to housebreak Cerberus, the three-headed dog of the Underworld.

A fearsome serpent blows Hercules away.

2. Eye of the Beholder

Writer	John Schulian
Director	John Kretchmer
Original Air Date	Jan. 23, 1995

Guest cast

Salmoneus	Robert Trebor
Scilla	Kim Michalis
Cyclops	Richard Moll
Atreus	Ken Blackburn
Myles	Jim McLarty
Evander	Donald Baigent
Castor	Michael Mizrahi
The Ferret	Derek Ward
Glaucus	David Press
Executioner	Ray Woolf
Head Sister	Nancy Schroder
Inn Keeper	Ian Watkin
Lout	Arch Goodfellow

Story: A twenty-foot Cyclops diverts a village's water supply to irrigate Hera's sacred vineyards and literally crushes anyone in his way. Hercules battles the creature, skillfully avoiding its blows by realizing that the one-eyed bully lacks any peripheral vision and is defenseless against attacks from the side. He defeats the Cyclops but instead of killing him, asks why he is so angry. The Cyclops reveals that because of his grotesque looks, he has suffered years of persecution by the villagers. Hercules wins the Cyclops' trust, which leads Hera to summon her most feared executioners to destroy her stepson once and for all. Together Hercules and the Cyclops defeat Hera's assassins in a spectacular battle, after which Hercules persuades the villagers and the Cyclops to live in peace.

Mythic connections:
The Cyclopes (Greek for "round-eye") were giants with only one eye. Hercules never fought these creatures; in fact, Cyclopes built the walls of Tiryns, the city where he was raised. The Cyclopes were loyal servants of Zeus who forged his thunderbolts as well as the trident of the sea god Poseidon and the helmet of invisibility of Hades, lord of the underworld. The most famous Cyclops, Polyphemus, was a cannibal, whom the Greek hero Odysseus blinded.

Highlights:
This episode introduces a strong comic element that will become a trademark of the series.

Casting coups:
Robert Trebor makes his first appearance as the fast-talking peddler Salmoneus; Richard Moll, the fierce-looking but comical bailiff on the TV sitcom *Night Court*, is the misunderstood Cyclops; Kim Michalis, as the lone villager who sees past the Cyclops' frightening form, previously appeared in three *Hercules* movies.

Kevin's take:
That was our first funny episode. I really enjoyed working with Richard Moll—I used to watch him on *Night Court*. And that was our first episode using forced perspective [using camera angles to convey the illusion of great size], for the Cyclops.

3. The Road to Calydon

Writers	Andrew Dettmann and Daniel Truly
Director	Doug Lefler
Original Air Date	Jan. 30, 1995

Guest cast

Tiresias	Norman Forsey
Jana	Portia Dawson
Broteas	John Sumner
Ephadon	Peter Rowley
Leda	Sela Brown
Teles	Stephen Papps
Odeon	Andrew Kovacevich
Hesame	Maggie Tarver
Ixion	Christopher Saunoa
Bounty Hunter	Julian Arahanga
Leucosia	Emma Turner
Old Man	Bruce Allpress

Story: Hera sends a raging storm when a chalice is stolen from her temple. A group of refugees take shelter in the ghost town Partus and their leader Broteas wants them to remain there. But Hercules learns from the seer Tiresias that Partus has been cursed by Hera, and he persuades them to move on to the protected city of Calydon. Among the new pilgrims is Jana, a lovely but outcast villager who takes care of a feisty orphan named Ixion. Hercules protects them from the other travelers while also fending off a group of Hera's assassins. When the pilgrims reach the

Stymphalian swamp that lies before Calydon, a huge pterodactyl-like bird swoops down. Broteas scrambles for cover and drops the stolen chalice. Meanwhile, Hercules saves Jana and Ixion from the winged beast, finally burying it in a pit of quicksand. He then hurls the chalice toward the horizon and watches the hapless thief Broteas futilely chase after it. On delivering the settlers safely to Calydon, Hercules bids Jana and Ixion a fresh start and a happy life.

Mythic connections:
Tiresius was struck blind by Hera but given the gift of unerring prophecy by Zeus. Even after he died and went to the Underworld, his shade retained the power to foretell the future.

The Stymphalian predator figured in the sixth labor of Hercules, when he rid Greece of birds that infested the wooded shores of Lake Stymphalus and killed people with their steel-tipped feathers. Hercules scared the birds into flight by swinging a bronze rattle forged by the god Hephaestus and procured for him by Athena, the goddess of wisdom. As the birds darted skyward his deadly arrows brought them down.

Highlights:
The bird of prey is marvelously lifelike, right down to its final, struggling descent into the Stymphalian swamp.

Kevin's take:
Fighting that bird was pretty amazing: It was a great creature, but for most of the filming I was really fighting nothing! I mean, even in [the first TV movie] when I fought the Hydra, they had the heads and they had the tail for me to look at. Here they had the head of the bird but they rarely used it. So I was grabbing onto nothing, I was throwing boulders at nothing, I had to [pretend to] whack it on the head and stop my hand in midair, like I hit it off his head, you know. Oh, it was great! The only bad thing about the filming was that the location was *unbelievably* muddy. If you watch it, you'll see me running and feeling like Fred Flintstone starting his car!

4. The Festival of Dionysus

Writers	Andrew Dettmann and Daniel Truly
Director	Peter Ellis
Original Air Date	Feb. 6, 1995

Guest cast

Tiresias	Norman Forsey
Nestor	Jonathan Blick
Pentheus	Warren Carl
Marysa	Katrina Hobbs
Gudrun	Todd Rippon
King Iphicles	Noel Trevarthen
Queen Camilla	Ilona Rodgers
Ancient Priest	Martyn Sanderson
Clarin	Darren Warren
Cletis	Danniel Warren
Old Drunk	Bernard Moody
Thug #1	John Mellor
Thug #2	Michael Dwyer
Pyturis	Arch Goodfellow

Story: A premonition of evil leads Queen Camilla of Meliad to summon Hercules. As the city's annual festival of Dionysus, the god of wine, gets under way, the seer Tiresias tells Hercules that the celebration will be joyous so long as Dionysus deems the king worthy to rule another year. But if not, the ten beautiful virgins chosen for the festival will become drunk on the first wine of the new harvest and slaughter the king in his bed. Meanwhile the king's power-hungry eldest son, Pentheus, plots to overthrow his own father, beseeching Ares, the god of war, to change the wine and cause the virgins to slay the king. To keep Hercules from thwarting his scheme, Pentheus springs a trapdoor that drops the hero into a dungeon, where he is attacked by a ten-foot lizard. But Hercules strangles it and uses it to lasso a rock and climb to freedom just in time to stop Pentheus and save the King.

Mythic connections: Dionysus, the god of wine, was a popular deity of the later Greek world. He inspired cults, mainly of women who danced wildly on the hillsides, clad in fawn skins, and who carried torches and staves wrapped in grapevines and crowned with pinecones. The deadly eel-like creature recalls the two giant snakes Hera sent to kill Hercules in his infancy; instead the toddler choked them to death and displayed them proudly to his parents.

Highlights: The frenzied dance of the virgins seems to end in bloodletting, until Pentheus discovers to his dismay that Hercules has spirited away the king and hidden wine beneath the royal pillow.

Casting coups: Warren Carl, the dialogue coach for New Zealand actors, is the evil Pentheus.

Kevin's take: In the [humorous] opening scene, Hercules is lying in bed, recovering from a hangover. I didn't want [my character] to get drunk, I didn't think that would send a good message, and I fought on that point, and I lost. The producers said, "Oh, come on, it will be fun." So I played the scene, and sure enough, when the guys at Universal saw the episode they went nuts! They said, "You've got to protect your hero, you can't be having him get drunk!"

5. Ares

Writer	Steve Roberts
Director	Harley Cokeliss
Original Air Date	Feb. 13, 1995

Guest cast

Atalanta	Cory Everson
Janista	Marise Wipani
Aurelius	Callum Stembridge
Titus	Peter Malloch
Ximenos	Taungaroa Emile
Fallen Soldier	Peter Muller
Ares	Mark Newnham
Voice of Ares	Al Chalk
Kid #1	Kelson Henderson
Kid #2	Nick Clark
Woman #1	Rebecca Hobbs
Woman #2	Rebekah Mercer

Story: Hercules, aided by the alluring and powerful blacksmith Atalanta, confronts his wicked half brother Ares, the god of war, who uses a band of boy soldiers to quench his thirst for bloodshed. Hercules makes the children realize that they do not really want to commit murder, and must throw off Ares' wicked spell. Then he tracks Ares to his lair and sees him rise from behind a pool of blood, his bulbous skull-head atop a body of mangled corpses of fallen warriors. They battle, and Hercules beheads his foe.

Mythic connections: Ares, one of the twelve great Olympian gods (known also by the Roman name Mars), was the only son of Zeus and his wife, Hera. His greatest pleasures were battle and bloodshed. Ares attacked his half brother Hercules to avenge the death of his son Cycnus. A murderous highway robber, Cycnus had tried to waylay Hercules as he searched for the golden apples of the Hesperides (his eleventh labor). Instead Hercules slew Cycnus and then wounded the charging Ares. Atalanta was the sole mortal woman of Greek myth who bested

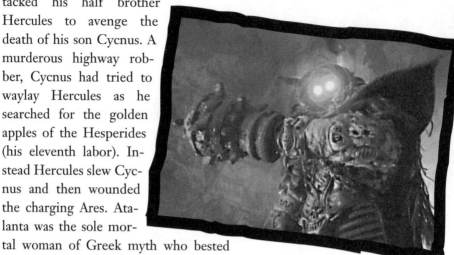

any male she competed with, as a huntress, a wrestler, and a runner.

Highlights: The scene in which Atalanta slyly "defeats" Hercules at arm wrestling by diverting his attention to other facets of her anatomy is not to be missed.

Casting coups: Cory Everson, who played Atalanta, is a world-class body builder.

Kevin's take: This is one of my least favorite episodes; the writing didn't work as well as some others. But I love that [arm wrestling] scene with Cory. And she is a funny, wonderful woman—a sweetheart.

6. As Darkness Falls

Writer	Robert Bielak
Director	George Mendeluk
Original Air Date	Feb. 20, 1995

Guest cast

Salmoneus	Robert Trebor
Nemis	Cliff Curtis
Penelope	Jacqueline Collen
Lyla	Lucy Lawless
Deric	Peter Muller
Craesus	Mark Ferguson
Marcus	Matthew Humphrey
Tyron	Buzz Moller
Cheris	Fiona Mogridge
Mother	Maya Dalziel
Brother #1	Jonathon Bell-Booth
Brother #2	Mervyn Whitley, Jr.

Story: As the town of Nespa prepares to celebrate the wedding of Penelope and Marcus, Nemis the centaur prays to Hera for a way to win the fair Penelope for himself. Then a burst of flame reveals a fearsome iron-spiked cudgel: Hera's gift to wield against Hercules, the man responsible for the death of Nemis' twin brother, Nessus. At the wedding festival, Nemis and two other centaurs gallop in

uninvited, and Lyla, the human girlfriend of one centaur, laces Hercules' drink with a drug that induces blindness. Although Hercules narrowly avoids Nemis' deadly attack, he cannot prevent the centaurs from abducting Penelope. Guided by the merchant Salmoneus, Hercules sets out for Nemis' lair. En route he encounters Lyla, who repents her action and tells Hercules that his blindness is only temporary. But she cannot persuade Hercules to wait before trying to save Penelope. At the cave of Nemis, Hercules splashes a cauldron of steaming liquid onto the campfire: Now both must struggle in darkness. Hercules mortally wounds Nemis but their battle triggers a rockslide. In a dying act of love, Nemis holds up part of the cave while Hercules leads Penelope to safety.

Mythic connections: Centaurs were invited to a wedding in northern Thessaly but became so intoxicated by the wine they attacked the women, and one tried to abduct the bride. Many centaurs were killed in the battle that followed.

Centaurs, good and evil, were central to Hercules' life. Noble Chiron taught the young hero the warrior's arts and a code of honor; but the treacherous Nessus attacked Hercules' wife, Deianeira, and was killed by a poisoned arrow from Hercules' bow. The dying centaur tricked Deianeira into dipping a tunic in his blood, to use as a love potion. Years later Deianeira gave Hercules the tunic, and the poison caused his death.

Highlights: The centaurs fail in their bid to kidnap Penelope, but these marvelous creatures from Kevin O'Neill's special effects team easily steal the episode.

No Centaurs were harmed in the production of this motion picture.

Casting coups: Cliff Curtis, who played Nessus in the TV movie *Hercules in the Underworld*, is conveniently revived as the late centaur's twin brother. Lucy Lawless appears as Lyla, a seductive auburn-haired beauty who first blinds, then helps Hercules.

Kevin's take: They let me do something a little bit different, as Hercules goes blind, and I think it played very well. I really liked that episode, and the director, George Mendeluk, who knows [how to work with] actors. For the first time the series showed the compassionate side of Salmoneus as well: that he really cared for me, and he got past his fears as he tried to lead and help me.

7. Pride Comes Before a Brawl

Writer	Steve Roberts
Director	Peter Ellis
Original Air Date	Feb. 27, 1995

Guest cast

Iolaus	Michael Hurst
Lydia	Lisa Chappell
Nemesis	Karen Witter
Rankor	John Dybvig
Rak	Jeff Gane
Boatman	David Stott
Ugly on Bridge	B. J. Johns
Fisherman	Eric Gruendemann

Story: On their way to the games at Thrace, Hercules and Iolaus come upon a band of thugs. Hercules ignores their taunts but Iolaus, his pride offended, plunges into a brawl. Hercules finally steps in to save his friend's life, but Iolaus afterward angrily protests that he needed no help. They part company at a fork in the road, with Iolaus betting that he will reach Thrace first. Instead he is caught by thieves and dumped into a deep cave, where he escapes with a Thracian prisoner named Lydia. Hercules meanwhile is visited by his childhood sweetheart Nemesis. He is delighted to see his old flame, but shocked to learn that Hera has sent her to kill Iolaus for the sin of pride. On reuniting with Iolaus in Thrace, Hercules tells Lydia he would trust his friend with his life. Brashly testing these words before a crowd, Iolaus places a pomegranate on Hercules' head and aims an arrow—blindfolded. Just then the leader of the thieves fires at Iolaus. But

Nemesis deflects the thief's arrow, and Iolaus shoots the thief, killing him. When Hercules thanks Nemesis for sparing his friend's life, Nemesis reveals that Iolaus never intended to fire at the pomegranate for fear of injuring Hercules, and thereby earned his own reprieve.

Mythic connections: Nemesis is the goddess of vengeance, the daughter of Nyx, or Night.

Highlights: Michael Hurst moves to the foreground with a hero's field day, battling thieves, a giant eel, and a computer-generated Hydra.

> *No Hydras were harmed during the production of this motion picture.*

Kevin's take: They decided they really wanted more "beefcake" with me. And so I played half an episode with my shirt off, rowing the boat, and stuff like that. And all these letters came in—people loved it! So they started writing in the scripts after that: "shirt off" here, "shirt off" here, "shirt off" here. And I started saying, "Look, I work out hard and I think I've got a good body for a guy who's not twenty years old anymore! But I also don't want to take my shirt off for the sake of taking my shirt off. That's just tacky." So I think in [the first] forty-two episodes I've taken my shirt off six times; you know, we try not to overdo it!

Michael's take: I had a fabulous time. I remember the great fight scene in the beginning, and I remember working with Lisa Chappell [as Lydia]. I'd taught her in a few acting classes in poetic drama, and I've known her over the years, so that was great fun. The director, Peter Ellis, was an Englishman, and because I have an English background too, before long we were both being *terribly* English, it was very funny. I also remember wrestling the [giant] "eel" [during Iolaus' escape from the thieves]. I kept diving into that lake and wrestling that monster, it was unbelievably tiring. [A monster?] Well, it was a big rubber dead thing, is what it was. . . . But wrestling it in deep water [take after take] was exhausting!

8. The March to Freedom

Writers	Adam Armus and Nora Kay Foster
Director	Harley Cokeliss
Original Air Date	Mar. 6, 1995

Guest cast

Oi-Lan	Lucy Liu
Iolaus	Michael Hurst
Cyrus	Nathaniel Lees
Belus	Stig Eldred
Alcmene	Elizabeth Hawthorne
Mudo	Terry Batchelor
Peplus	Robin Kora
Admeta	Margaret-Mary Hollins
Gringus	Te Paki Cherrington
Nasty Mother	Maya Dalziel
Beautiful Girl	Joanna Barrett
Lapithus	Christian Hodge
Tmoulus	Peter Sa'ena-Brown
Tapus	David Mercer

Story: Hercules returns to his childhood home to see his mother, Alcmene, and visit the memorial to his late wife and children. On a nearby beach, the slave trader Belus captures a band of travelers, among them a couple named Cyrus and Oi-Lan. At the marketplace, Hercules sees Oi-Lan being dragged to the slave auction block, and he impulsively buys her to set her free. Oi-Lan immediately sets off to find Cyrus, and Hercules goes to help her. The slavers transporting Cyrus taunt him with tales that Hercules has purchased Oi-Lan for his own pleasure. Crazed by jealousy and fear for his beloved, Cyrus escapes into the woods and ambushes Hercules with a deadly catapult. Belus' thugs suddenly appear from all directions, unfurl their nets, and easily recapture the defenseless lovers. But Hercules somehow rises, overtakes the slave party, captures Belus, and frees Oi-Lan and the now remorseful Cyrus. Charmed by the loving couple, Hercules' mother offers to have their wedding at her home. And as a lasting tribute to his fallen family, Hercules invites them to settle on the land he once shared with his wife and children.

Casting coups: Nathaniel Lees has appeared in many different guises on *Hercules* and *Xena*, most notably as the Blue Priest in *Hercules and the Lost City*.

Kevin's take: [Off camera] Lucy Liu was like that great black-and-white photographer Ansel Adams. Now, I'm a novice in shooting scenery but Lucy would take these wonderful black-and-white photos every day. I just loved working with her. And I enjoyed that episode because of the heart and soul in it. We had Hercules come to grips with the reality of losing his family.

Michael's take: This was the second episode we filmed, and we were still finding our feet. I thought Lucy Liu [as Oi-Lan] was marvelous. And I remember [the scene where] Hercules wants to buy Oi-Lan to free her and he asks me to lend him the money. And I was sulking [as Iolaus], because I had been hoping to buy a new forge. That scene just seemed so natural and so right, we laughed about that. Another one we laughed about was when I was introduced to [Oi-Lan]. I like this about Iolaus, he assumed that because she looked vaguely Asian that she could not understand English, and he also did that condescending thing [treating her as though she were] also stupid and half deaf: "Hel-lo. I'm I-o-laus." Sort of blundering into that. And then she flips me! And that was a moment of discovery because I thought, Man, we can do more of this [showing Iolaus' flaws]. And we did, in the very next one we filmed, "Pride Comes Before a Brawl."

9. The Warrior Princess

Writer	John Schulian
Director	Bruce Seth Green
Original Air Date	Mar. 13, 1995

Guest cast

Iolaus	Michael Hurst
Xena	Lucy Lawless
Alcmene	Elizabeth Hawthorne
Petrakus	Bill Johnson
Theodorus	Michael Dwyer
Estragon	Patrick Wilson
Syreena	Rebecca Clark
Villager	Bill Borlase
Drinker #1	Eddie Campbell
Drinker #2	Danny Lineham

Story: A female warlord named Xena sets out to kill Hercules, for only then will she be able to secure full control of the region of Arcadia. With

the help of her love-struck lieutenants, Xena poses as a maiden in distress to lure away Hercules' best friend, Iolaus. Enchanting him and preying on his loneliness, the beautiful warrior uses him as bait for Hercules. When Hercules learns Xena's true identity, he goes to rescue Iolaus, falling into her trap. Blinded by Xena's guile, refusing to believe anything bad about her, Iolaus turns on Hercules and attacks him. This is exactly what Xena wants, for she believes that Hercules will kill Iolaus and then be so horrified and confused over his deed that "he'll be ripe for slaughter." Hercules does indeed defeat Iolaus easily, but he refuses to harm his misguided friend. Her plans thwarted, Xena orders her soldiers to kill both men. Iolaus joins Hercules in fighting against Xena's army. But when Iolaus is beaten, Hercules goes to his rescue rather than pursuing Xena. No matter: Xena vows as she rides away, "Ha! You haven't seen the last of me, Hercules!"

Mythic connections: Arcadia, a mountainous area in the central Peloponnesus, a Greek peninsula, was the site of many deeds by gods and heroes. Any warrior seeking to conquer the region would have first to reckon with mighty Hercules, whose early labors took place there.

Highlights: The character Xena became an immediate fan favorite in this first segment of a three-episode story arc. A warrior of surpassing beauty, cunning, and fighting skills, she makes a worthy foe for Hercules. Best exchange: Iolaus, on hearing that enemy soldiers are nearby: "What do you want to do?" Xena (brandishing her sword and pushing her horse to a full gallop): "I want to kill them all!"

Casting coups: Lucy Lawless first appears as Xena, the Warrior Princess.

Kevin's take: I had a hard time with that episode, because I didn't buy that Iolaus would not believe me. This guy and I have known each other since we were kids. And I'm Hercules, for crying out loud! He knows me as an honest guy. And if I said [to my closest friend], "Look, this woman's a maniac!" you know, I don't care how much you're in love with somebody, at least you'd go, "Okay, let's talk about it." But for us to fight was silly. And the fight got a little too carried away. What I remember the most is Michael Hurst hitting me in the back of the head with his sword and giving me nine stitches and a three-inch gash into my skull. *That's* what I remember the most about that episode!

Michael's take: I really like the *idea* of Hercules and Iolaus fighting each other. But there was never enough time to bring us convincingly around to a point where I actually want to kill Hercules, which in hind-

sight is kind of ridiculous, but at the time seemed a good thing to go with.
. . . But we had to change a lot of scenes to make it half way convincing
that Iolaus would turn this way. I think it only *just* works. And if you look
at the way Iolaus suddenly gets back on side with Hercules, it's like, *bing!*,
wow, how did *that* happen? . . . Working with Lucy [Lawless] in that
episode was neat. We go back a long way. Lucy and I had been in a miniseries together a few years earlier, *Typhon's People*. We weren't close
friends, we just got on well. And we were two Kiwis in this [American pro-
duction], and we were a bit gleeful. We had a really good time with all
that.

10. Gladiator

Writer	Robert Bielak
Director	Garth Maxwell
Original Air Date	Mar. 20, 1995

Guest cast

Iolaus	Michael Hurst
Menas Maxius	Ian Mune
Postera	Alison Bruce
Gladius	Tony Todd
Felicita	Kyrin Hall
Leutis	Stuart Turner
Turkos	Nigel Harbrow
Spagos	Gabriel Prendergast
Deianeira	Tawny Kitaen
Bellicus	Jeffrey Thomas
Rankus	Ray Bishop
Highwayman	Jonathan Bell-Booth
Toll Collector	Ian Miller
Skoros	Mark Nua

Story: Hercules and Iolaus rescue a woman, Felicita, and her baby from highway bandits. She tells them she is on her way to introduce her husband, the slave Gladius, to the son he has never seen. Hercules and Iolaus agree to help her and deliberately get thrown into prison in order to help free her husband. Once inside they

learn that Gladius, along with the other slaves, is routinely forced to battle wild animals for the amusement of Menas Maxius and his wealthy landowner friends. To please his cruel wife, Postera, Menas orders Hercules and Gladius, his most powerful and skilled gladiator, to fight to the death. And to ensure that they obey, he produces Felicita and Iolaus, bound and gagged, vowing to execute them should the warriors refuse to fight. The anguished Gladius attacks Hercules in a desperate bid to save his wife. Although Hercules could easily overcome his foe, he simply defends himself and at last convinces Gladius that they must turn on their oppressors and fight for their freedom. Together they overthrow the guards and bring the evil Menas and his wife to their knees.

Highlights: The gladiators' battles in the arena effectively echo scenes from the classic film about a Roman slave revolt, *Spartacus*.

Casting coups: Tony Todd would go on to play Cecrops the lost mariner on *Xena*.

Kevin's take: Our ode to *Spartacus*. I really want to do more episodes like that. I want Hercules to get more involved in mythology, more involved in dramatic parts. It was probably our biggest episode of that first season. I thought, in terms of scope and drama and just the number of extras we had and the use of CGI [computer-generated imaging], trying to make the arena look like a big stadium. If people watch very closely, they'll notice a scene where people are screaming, "Kill him, kill Hercules." It's actually our executive producer, Rob Tapert, our producer, Eric Grundemann, and his wife, Patricia, all dressed up as extras, doing all the yelling. If people only knew the stuff we do in that show! There's a lot of inside jokes that go right over people's heads, and that's done on purpose.

> ### Legendary Facts
>
> Hercules saves Gladius, a prisoner forced to fight as a gladiator in what appears to be ancient Rome. Public fights between gladiators in Rome began in 264 BC and ended more than five hundred years later.

Michael's take: "Gladiator"'s great! It was the last episode [of the season] that we shot. [On Tony Todd, who plays Gladius:] Tony Todd had this intensity, he did every line of every scene on the edge of tears, it was really quite theatrical and powerful. *Candyman* [starring Tony Todd] was one of the best horror movies I've ever seen. And when he told me, "I

played Worf's brother in *Star Trek*," I nearly fell off my seat. Because I was being all cool, and suddenly I was like a kid [stammering], I was so impressed!

This episode was also directed by a New Zealander whom I know, Garth Maxwell. And my memory of that is watching him dealing with the [production] "machine." He kept walking around with the shot list [sighing and panting]. Because the list is so big, and from the first setup you're running out of time. But I remember seeing Garth conquer [his anxieties] on the third day, he got past it, and suddenly he'd worked it out how to deal with this juggernaut. Seeing that and talking to him about it, we had a really interesting discussion about what translates visually, and when you can compromise.

In one scene a guy had to take the stock of a whip and beat me over the bridge of the nose. I had my hands tied, I think, so there was no way I was going to soften the blow. And afterward they were going right on to do the next shot. And I said to the guys, "Well, what about my nose?" And they said, "What?" And I said, "Well, I've been hit over the bridge of the nose with the stock of a whip. And I'm not half god." "Oh, well, it's too complicated to do a makeup, it will take up too much time." And I said, "This is not a good message to send kids." It would be different if it's Hercules, he's half god, but I think Iolaus needs a broken nose at this point. So they gave me one. I played the rest of the show [here he speaks as if his nose were broken]. And it was a wonderful poignancy. Sure, we have big punch-ups on *Hercules* and [our characters] don't get as injured as we would in real life, but with something so blatant, I just fought for that, and I was very happy to get that. Hercules could say, "Sorry," and I'm there with this big bruised nose. In fact that's one of the darker episodes we ever shot.

11. The Vanishing Dead

Writers	Andrew Dettmann and Daniel Truly
Director	Bruce Campbell
Original Air Date	Apr. 24, 1995

Guest cast

Iolaus	Michael Hurst
Jarton	Reb Brown
Daulin	Erik Thomson
Poena	Amber-Jane Raab
Krytus	Chris McDowall
Aelon	Richard Vette
Mercenary #1	Steve Wright
Mercenary #2	Jon Brazier
Mortis	Lewis Martin
Ogre	Mark Nua
Sentry	Joseph Hassell
Lead Soldier	Stephen Hall
Mother	Jean Hyland

Story: In the city of Tantalus, Hercules and Iolaus find that the bodies of slain warriors have been mysteriously disappearing from the battlefields. The new king, Daulin, tells them that his sister Poena has formed a rival army. Later Poena insists to Hercules that her brother murdered their father in order to assume the throne. When Hercules goes to the site of a recent battle to investigate the vanishing dead, he discovers huge sharp-clawed paw prints belonging to Graegus, Ares' ferocious dog. He realizes that Ares himself killed the king to start a family war, simply to feed the casualties to his bloodthirsty hound. Racing back to stop an impending battle, Hercules spies Graegus menacing Iolaus and rescues him by using a vine as a makeshift lasso to leash the beast. They reach Tantalus just in time to see two armies charge from either side of a riverbank. Suddenly the ghostly figures of the fallen warriors of Tantalus rise up out of the river and stop the battling soldiers. Ares himself then provokes Hercules, who finally realizes that his own rage is giving strength to the god of war. When Hercules stops fighting back, Ares is rendered powerless and disappears, leaving Daulin, Poena, and their armies in peace.

Mythic connections: The Ares of myth was a brash and boastful warrior rather than a schemer. *Hercules* presents Ares more as a warlike devil, a tempter who thrives on human folly and weakness.

Highlights: This episode marks Bruce Campbell's directorial debut.

Casting coups: Erik Thomson, who plays Daulin, later portrayed Hades, god of the Underworld.

Kevin's take: There was a good scene at the end, where I'm in the river getting zapped by Ares with bolts of lightning. They actually built a "river" inside the studio set. I walk into the river and get zapped and go flying. [Unfortunately] the carpenters hadn't flattened out all the nails as they were piecing everything together. And [as I did this stunt] and landed, a nail went right into my hand about an inch. Sideways, luckily. I finished the scene, I don't know why I didn't stop it right then and there. I felt the nail go in, but I just pulled it out and turned around and did two more takes.

12. The Gauntlet

Writer	Robert Bielak
Director	Jack Perez
Original Air Date	May 1, 1995

Guest cast

Xena	Lucy Lawless
Salmoneus	Robert Trebor
Darphus	Matthew Chamberlain
Iloran	Dean O'Gorman
Cretus	David Aston
Spiros	Peter Daube
Young Woman	Vanessa Rare
Ipicles	Anthony Ray Parker
Shepherdess	Sela Brown
Emissary	Nathaniel Lees
Soldier #1	Ross Campbell
Soldier #2	Lawrence Wharerau
Soldier #3	Mario Gaoa
Baby	Fleur and Zana Coric

Story: Hercules learns from his young cousin Iloran that Xena's marauding army is heading for Iloran's native town of Parthis. Xena faces her own crisis after she saves the life of an infant and is denounced as weak by a lieutenant named Darphus. He makes Xena walk a gauntlet, where she is pummeled by her mutinous troops as she struggles forward.

Surviving through sheer will, she staggers alone into the wilderness. Hercules and Iloran are meanwhile joined by Spiros, a man seeking revenge for the murder of his family by Xena's troops, and by Salmoneus, the bumbling salesman, who tells of being Xena's prisoner and claims, "Compared with Darphus she looks like the goddess of love and light." Suddenly Xena steps out to challenge Hercules to a duel. In a spectacular battle, Hercules finally triumphs but, to Xena's amazement, spares her life. At Parthis Hercules battles the invaders but has difficulty protecting the entire village by himself. Just as hope is fading, Xena storms in from the woods, fights side by side with Hercules, and kills Darphus. Afterward, Spiros is overjoyed to find that the baby Xena saved is his son. Hercules and Xena look at each other in a new light: This could be the beginning of a beautiful friendship.

Highlights: This dark episode contains a chilling gauntlet scene and grimly realistic battles. Yet "The Gauntlet" is also a stirring tale of two great warriors, featuring a superbly staged sword fight between Hercules and Xena. The surreal comic encounters between Salmoneus and Xena, coming amid scenes of unrelieved intensity, are all the more amusing.

Casting coups: Lucy Lawless is again riveting as Xena. Robert Trebor as Salmoneus offers some inspired comic improvisations, including a "Xena" theme song.

Kevin's take: I like the story, I like the episode, and it's funny how it all came together. At that time they didn't know *Xena* would be made into a series. I mean, Lucy [Lawless] was a last-minute replacement. They had started casting in the States. [When that fell through] they said, well, we've used Lucy before, in one of the [*Hercules*] movies and in one of the earlier episodes. Let's go with her. And she's perfect for the part—Lucy *is* Xena!

13. Unchained Heart

Writer	John Schulian
Director	Bruce Seth Green
Original Air Date	May 8, 1995

Guest cast

Iolaus	Michael Hurst
Salmoneus	Robert Trebor
Xena	Lucy Lawless
Darphus	Matthew Chamberlain
Pylendor	Stephen Papps
Village Elder	Mervyn Smith
Villager	Robert Pollock
Warrior #1	Shane Dawson
Camp Boss	Ian Harrop
Quintus	Mario Gaoa
Enos	Bruce Allpress
Surviving Warrior	David Mercer
Lieutenant	Gordon Hatfield
Sentry	Campbell Rouselle

Story: Xena's evil lieutenant, Darphus, has been raised from the dead by Ares and is once more slaughtering innocent people. Darphus feeds his victims to Ares' dog Graegus, who grows larger with every sacrifice and soon will become unstoppable. Hercules and Xena set out to stop Darphus and his army once and for all. On their way they meet Iolaus, who is outraged that Hercules treats Xena like a friend. Iolaus reminds him, "She tried to kill us!" He comes along but remains bitterly suspicious of Xena until she saves his life in battle with Darphus' troops. Then Iolaus sees that the warrior princess has truly changed. That night, while Iolaus scouts ahead, the friendship between Hercules and Xena blossoms into romance by a campfire. The next morning, in a final battle, Hercules signals Xena to push Darphus beside a hungry Graegus, who swallows him whole and then bursts into flame and vanishes. "Evil destroyed itself," Hercules explains to an astonished Iolaus and Xena. Despite their love for each other, Xena feels compelled to leave Hercules in order to make amends for her violent past. With mingled sadness and affection, she thanks Hercules for unchaining her heart, and rides on.

> No Vicious Beasts intent on taking over the world were harmed during the production of this motion picture.

Highlights: In contrast to "The Gauntlet," "Unchained Heart" has a notably lighter tone. Xena herself is mellower.

Kevin's take: I thought it was a good beat to have Hercules and Xena sort of fall for each other. And I thought that it was also good *not* to have that continue. It showed her to be a strong-willed woman, that she wants to go out on her own and mend her ways. Also, you can't really have Hercules and Xena together as a team fighting evil, because it hurts both shows. The love scene was done quite well: It was steamy enough but it was definitely passable for TV. It left more to the imagination. Why don't they do more of that? Also, humor started popping into the story. They made Lucy's character a much lighter person by the third episode, which is good. I mean, she's still got a bad side, but now she has a sense of humor about herself, too.

Michael's take: Lucy and I had both been invited to go to the States, and the studio wanted to thank us and tell us we were going to be doing a lot more work. And all this was going on during the filming of "Unchained Heart." And then we all went to a [studio] party in the States, and found out we were going to be doing another twenty-two episodes [of *Hercules*], and that *Xena* was going to be starting. So we were really excited, two excited Kiwis, I'll tell you!

The
Second
Season

14. The King of Thieves

Writer	Doug Lefler
Director	Doug Lefler
Original Air Date	Sept. 11, 1995

Guest cast:

Iolaus	Michael Hurst
Dirce	Lisa Chappell
King Menelaus	Martyn Sanderson
Autolycus	Bruce Campbell

Story: On his way to the kingdom of Scyros to meet Hercules, Iolaus sees a gang beating a man who struggles to hang on to a large wooden box. After driving away the attackers, Iolaus watches in amazement as their "victim" hurls a grappling hook over a tree branch and swings off into the forest. Caught by villagers with the box, which contains jewels from the king's treasury, Iolaus is arrested and sentenced to death. Hercules is taken to Iolaus by the king's daughter, Dirce, who believes that the real culprit is Autolycus, a former carnival escape artist whom the peasants have dubbed "the King of Thieves." Dirce stalls the execution while Iolaus undergoes several trials by ordeal, the last one to see whether he can spend three hours in a pit with a wild boar and emerge unbloodied. Somehow Iolaus survives—then pricks his finger on the edge of the pit and starts to bleed. Meanwhile, Hercules captures Autolycus, whom he cannot help liking for his charm and daring but still brings back to confess his crime. Just before Iolaus can be executed, Autolycus declares that he alone stole the jewels. But while Iolaus is being freed, "the King of Thieves" effects another amazing escape.

Mythic connections:

Autolycus, son of Hermes, the god of thieves, was "honored" as an extraordinary thief and liar. Tutored from childhood by Hermes himself, Autolycus even had the power to alter the appearance of stolen goods. Among his many thefts, Autolycus took the prize mares of Eurytus but went unpunished because the owner suspected Hercules instead.

Highlights:

The slyly appealing Autolycus makes the first of many appearances on *Hercules* and its sister show, *Xena*.

Casting coups:

Bruce Campbell, star of *The Evil Dead*, the first film made by producers Sam Raimi and Rob Tapert, makes Autolycus more a daredevil adventurer than a thief: a thrill seeker for whom a ruby is valued mainly as a trophy of outrageous risk-taking.

Kevin's take:

I loved this one. Autolycus is a great comic foil for Hercules, and I really enjoyed working with Bruce.

No Subterranean Serpents were harmed during the production of this motion picture.

Michael's take:

Bruce Campbell is so funny. And I knew him already because he had directed an episode of *Hercules* ["The Vanishing Dead"]. I love it when directors [like Campbell] have acted. . . . It's like we share a secret code.

15. All That Glitters

Writer	Craig Volk
Director	Garth Maxwell
Original Air Date	Sept. 18, 1995

Guest cast:

Salmoneus	Robert Trebor
Flaxen	Tracy Lindsey
Voluptua	Jennifer Ward-Lealand
King Midas	Noel Trevarthen
Segallus	Terry Batchelor

Story: When Salmoneus leaves for King Midas' new gambling palace, Hercules goes along to see how his royal friend is faring. All is not well: The Touch of Gold Gambling Palace turns out to be a gaudy racket to fleece the poor. Midas explains that the gambling house let his kingdom raise money during a time of bad harvests. But now it is controlled by his sinister partner, Voluptua, who sponsors such gruesome thrills as betting on whether two boys can walk a tightrope over a bed of spikes. When Hercules catches a boy before he is impaled, Voluptua plots to add Hercules to the palace's crowd-pleasing entertainments. Midas at last defies Voluptua, but is beaten senseless by her henchman Segallus. Hercules finds Midas tied to a crossbow aimed at his own head and the trigger tied to his daughter Flaxen. Voluptua tells Hercules that to free them, he must defeat a succession of foes in the boxing arena, all before a burning fuse releases the crossbow's trigger. Hercules quickly knocks out all comers, including Segallus, then inspires the townspeople to revolt against Voluptua and destroy the palace. A grateful Midas vows to rebuild the kingdom, based once more on honest labor in the fields.

Mythic connections: King Midas of Phrygia was at once tragic and pathetic. Offered any wish by the god Dionysus, Midas asked that anything he touched turn into gold. To his horror he found that his food, his drink, even his beloved daughter all changed into gold. He prayed to lose his gift, which he now realized was a curse, and was permitted to wash away his "golden touch" in a nearby river.

Highlights: "All That Glitters" offers a modern spin on the tale of King Midas, who is now the front man for a mob-style gaming house and once more discovers through hard experience the folly of greed.

Casting coups: Jennifer Ward-Lealand, Michael Hurst's wife, appears as Voluptua.

Kevin's take: "Viva Las Vegas!" This episode was fun for me because I got to work with Michael's wife Jennifer [Ward-Lealand, as Voluptua]. And I wish I had more scenes with her. She's very funny and a very good actress. . . . In the boxing scenes we put in an ad-lib: The last guard is doing a Muhammad Ali shuffle, and he says, "Float like a butterfly, sting like a bee!" And I ad-libbed after I hit him once and knocked him out immediately, "So much for insects." Now, the guy I hit is Ray Sefo, who is the second or third top-rated kick boxer in the world, so for him to let his ego sit aside and let me, little ol' me, give him a good wallop and go down with one punch, I thought he was a great sport. It was a kick for me, and I told him so!

16. What's in a Name?

Writer	Michael Marks
Director	Bruce Campbell
Original Air Date	Sept. 25, 1995

Guest cast:

Iolaus	Michael Hurst
Iphicles	Kevin Smith
Rena	Simone Kessell
Gorgus	Kenneth McGregor
Pallaeus	Ross Duncan
Josephus	Paul Glover
Priest	Lewis Martin

Story: A man masquerades as Hercules and allies himself with the cruel warlord Gorgus, whose stepdaughter, Rena, he loves. Hercules arrives with Iolaus and is dismayed to discover that the impostor is his jealous half brother, Iphicles, who angrily refuses to end his charade for fear he will lose Rena. When Gorgus' soldiers seize Iolaus and throw him into the dreaded catacombs, Hercules descends into the labyrinth and faces a series of ingenious death traps, including a trip wire that sends five blades whizzing at him from all directions, a wall that threatens to crush him, and a line of spiked weapons that swing at him from above. He survives to find Iphicles poised to kill him on Gorgus' orders. Hercules refuses to fight, instead urging Iphicles to honor his own good name. While the brothers argue, Rena arrives and is shocked to learn that her fiancé has lied about his identity. Just then Gorgus' soldiers attack Hercules, aided by a special mandrake root supplied by Hera, which changes into a snarling, monstrous lizard. While Hercules destroys Hera's deadly pet, Iolaus subdues Gorgus. And Iphicles, overcoming his own jealousy, fights on the side of his brother, Hercules, rescuing Rena and rekindling her love.

Mythic connections: Iphicles was the mortal twin brother of Hercules. Their mother was Alcmene, but whereas Hercules' father was Zeus, king of the gods, Iphicles was the son of the shepherd Amphitryon, Alcmene's husband. In Greek myth Iphicles was the father of Iolaus, but this relationship is not presented in *Hercules: The Legendary Journeys*, which depicts both men as warriors in their prime.

Highlights: This marks the first of several appearances by Hercules' mortal half brother, Iphicles.

Casting coups: Kevin Smith, who appears insecure as Iphicles, in later episodes conveys supreme confidence and charm as another half brother of Hercules: the god of war, Ares.

Kevin's take: I thought this had some really good scenes with Iphicles. Also, there was an ad-lib in the scene where I'm going through a maze—spears flew at me that I had to duck, a wall came out at me. I finally think I've gotten through the maze, but I trip one more wire and these big logs with spikes come down at me. And the camera comes back to me, and I say, "Who *makes* these things?"

Michael's take: Kevin Smith, who plays Iphicles, is an old friend of mine. We always called him the "low-rent Hercules" in this, because he had to [wear this leather costume] like a walking velour couch. We had a lot of fun on that set. . . .

This was the first time Kevin gave me a delivery that was much more Californian, and it really worked! My line in the script was, "Well, it if came down to a choice between digging ditches and going after ghosts, I guess ghosts are gonna win all the time." Kevin said, "It's too long-winded, you want to do it more Californian." So, as I'm delivering the line, Kevin turns away, and I say, "—*ghosts* are good." It has a California ease about it that I don't necessarily have. Something *I* would never say, something *New Zealanders* would never say.

17. The Siege at Naxos

Writer	Darrell Fetty
Director	Stephen Posey
Original Air Date	Oct. 2, 1995

Guest cast:

Goth	Brian Thompson
Elora	Rebecca Hobbs
Charidon	Patrick Smith
Iolaus	Michael Hurst
Bledar	Ray Woolf
Dax	Robert Harte

Story: Hercules and Iolaus arrive at a country tavern just in time to stop rampaging barbarians and capture their chieftain, Goth. They resolve to bring him to Athens to stand trial, but Goth's brother, Bledar, is determined to rescue him and pursues with reinforcements. The two heroes take shelter inside a fortress, deserted ex-

cept for a woman named Elora and her aged father, Charidon. As barbarians climb over the fortress walls, Hercules and Iolaus repel the first wave of attackers. But they have problems inside the fortress as Elora secretly visits Goth, who was once her lover. Bledar adds to their woes by bringing up a giant catapult called Titantus. Iolaus sneaks out to dismantle the weapon but is caught by Bledar's men. As boulders fly at the fortress walls, Hercules helps free Iolaus while cleverly convincing Bledar that reinforcements have arrived. By the time Bledar discovers the truth and attacks, Charidon and Elora have led Hercules and Iolaus, together with their prisoner, Goth, through an underground tunnel to safety. As Elora renounces Goth, the heroes resume their journey to Athens.

Mythic connections: Naxos is a large island in the Aegean sea. Here Ariadne, daughter of King Minos of Crete, helped the hero Theseus defeat the fearsome Minotaur in his labyrinth and then find his way back again.

Highlights: The series' "Alamo" episode stands out for the battle sequences.

Kevin's take: I remember claustrophobia. It was one of the first shows we shot ninety percent indoors. We had to, because it was during winter, where it rains basically every day. I think we had reached a point where we had shot so many shows in a row that everybody was going a little bit crazy in a way. . . . There was a scene at the very beginning where Michael and I are walking with a bunch of fish and I hit [one of the barbarians] with the fish. On the very first take, I wind up the fish on the end of a pretty heavy-duty stick that I'm holding. Well, they didn't tie the fish on well enough, the fish broke off, and with the momentum I had, the stick swung back, and I came about an inch away from taking my eye out. [Instead] I put a small dent into my forehead and almost knocked myself out! We can laugh about it now, but at the time it wasn't that funny. . . . This was one of our darker episodes, and I like the way it turned out.

18. Outcast

Writer	Robert Bielak
Director	Bruce Seth Green
Original Air Date	Oct. 9, 1995

Guest cast:

Salmoneus	Robert Trebor
Deric	Peter Muller
Jakar	Jon Brazier
Demicles	Kelson Henderson
Lyla	Lucy Lawless
Kefor	James Croft
Leuriphone	Rose Dube
Cletis	Chris Bailey
Sepsus	Andrew Kovacevich
Merkus	Neil Holt
Tersius	Norman Forsey

Story: Lyla, the wife of Deric the centaur, is taunted by bigots because of her marriage to a half human. That evening, while Deric is away, a mob torches his house. Lyla manages to send her young son, Kefor, to safety before dying in the fire. Hercules vows to bring the killers to justice and finds clues that they are Cretans, a racist rabble dedicated to preserving "Athenian purity." At a local tavern, Hercules sees Deric hurl the lifeless body of a mob member in the doorway, warning that others will also die for the murder of his wife. Although Deric had killed only in self-defense, the mob leaders, Merkus and Jakar, spread the lie that Deric has gone berserk. They organize a bloodthirsty posse, but Hercules diverts it and finds Deric himself. He persuades him to leave Kefor with Salmoneus, surrender to a fair magistrate, and clear his name—for his son's sake. To conceal their crime, Merkus and Jakar kidnap Kefor and blackmail Deric into confessing to the murder of his own wife. But Hercules holds off a lynch mob until a youth who had reluctantly joined the mob attack on Deric's house reveals the real murderers. Deric regains his freedom, his son, and, astonishingly, his beloved Lyla, whom Zeus restores to life.

Mythic connections: Hostility between humans
and centaurs continually erupted until the centaurs were finally driven out of their native Thessaly.

No Centaurs were harmed during the production of this motion picture.

Highlights: Salmoneus makes an endearing foster parent for the young centaur, Kefor.

Casting coups: Lucy Lawless reprises her first role in the series as Lyla, a complete contrast to her fury as the warrior Xena.

Kevin's take: I thought there was a great message in this episode about [the evils of] racism, and I think it's good that we send such messages. . . . The studio made the decision to bring Lyla back to life at the end. And I went ballistic! I was on the phone up until two minutes before the cameras rolled on that scene, saying, "This makes no sense to me." But [they] felt it just isn't right to have this kid [Kefor] motherless. And I said, "We have people getting killed all the time! And [restoring Lyla] appears as a total aberration. To me the strong ending is having her show up at the end just as a spirit, the kid sees his mother, nobody else can see her. And he says, 'I love you, Mommy.' And she says, 'I love you too. Whenever you need me, I'll be there.' And she disappears. I think that brings more goose bumps and tears to people watching the show than her popping up [alive] all of a sudden." Instead the way the show ends, she says, "It was Zeus, he brought me back to life. Sorry he couldn't do the same for your family." And I'm thinking, "My father [Zeus] brought *you* back to life? You whom I hardly *know*?!" I met [Lyla and Deric] in a prior episode when she made me go blind! But I don't know them. I don't hang out with them! They're not dear friends of mine. So why does Zeus bring her back to life [and not Deianeira and our children]? Now, I like the moral messages we have. But to bring her back to life, that cheapened it in my book.

19. Under the Broken Sky

Writer	John Schulian
Director	Jim Contner
Original Air Date	Oct. 16, 1995

Guest cast:

Salmoneus	Robert Trebor
Lucina	Maria Therese Rangel
Atticus	Bruce Phillips
Pilot	Carl Bland
Heliotrope	Julie Collis
Mica	Katherine Ransom

Story: Hercules finds Salmoneus working in an unsavory pleasure palace in the tough town of Enola. Soon after his arrival Hercules comes upon a farmer named Atticus, who has been robbed, beaten, and left for dead. Learning that the man was attacked by thugs working for the bandit chieftain Pilot, Hercules battles his way into Pilot's camp and recovers Atticus' purse. Atticus has journeyed to Enola to win back his young wife, Lucina, who sadly has become the main lure at the town's pleasure palace. He begs for Hercules' help, explaining that Lucina was consumed by guilt and ran away after a fever killed their two young sons. Hercules engineers the couple's reunion at Salmoneus' quarters, where Lucina is overcome by emotion. The next day she is accosted by the lecherous Pilot. When Atticus appears and persuades Lucina to give their love another chance, Pilot strikes him with a dagger. Hercules helps Atticus to safety as Pilot gathers eight vicious mercenaries. Brandishing spears, crossbows, chains, and swords, the assassins attack, but Hercules defeats them all. Pilot then turns to flee but runs into a sword held by Lucina. Encouraged by Hercules, Atticus and Lucina gratefully head home to build a new life together.

Highlights: The opening dance by Lucina surely made Salmoneus very glad to be working a regular job.

Kevin's take: Maria Rangel danced in the opening. It was a great opening, a very sensual, sexy dance. And Salmoneus is sort of running a combination hotel-brothel. There are some funny scenes in this episode, including a cute scene where the women grab me and say, "Oh, flex for me!" And I say, "Sorry, ladies, I don't flex." But that's a forgettable episode for me. [One problem is that] it's never really clear that [Lucina] had turned to prostitution. We call that one, "Under the Broken Script."

20. The Mother of All Monsters

Writer	John Schulian
Director	Bruce Seth Green
Original Air Date	Oct. 23, 1995

Guest cast:

Iolaus	Michael Hurst
Alcmene	Liddy Holloway
Echidna	Bridget Hoffman
Demetrius	Martin Kove
Archer #1	Rebecca Clark
Archer #2	Katrina Misa
Leukos	Graham Smith

Story: Hercules is shocked to learn that his mother Alcmene has a suitor, Demetrius. Feeling concern for her welfare and guilt about not spending enough time with her, he returns home with his friend Iolaus. His mother insists that his worries are exaggerated, but in fact the dangers are greater than he suspects. Echidna, the hideous mother of several monsters that Hercules has killed, is using Demetrius in a plan to avenge her offspring by slaying Hercules in front of his mother. At Alcmene's home, Hercules is ambushed by six female archers whose arrows were forged in the fires of Hades. One archer severely wounds Hercules while Demetrius abducts Alcmene. Pulling the arrow out of Hercules' chest, Iolaus pleads with fate to spare his fallen friend. Hours later a weakened Hercules struggles to his feet and sets out to rescue his mother. At the entrance to Echidna's cave, Hercules and Iolaus disarm the archers in a surprise attack. Then Iolaus defeats Demetrius while Hercules musters his fading strength to overcome Echidna. But Alcmene, sensing Echidna's grief for her children, pleads with her son not to kill his foe. Relenting, Hercules creates a rockslide that seals the monster in her lair.

Mythic connections:
Echidna (meaning "snake") was half woman, half serpent. Her children included, among other monsters, the rampaging Nemean lion, which Hercules killed with his bare hands for his first labor; the multiheaded Lernaean Hydra, which Hercules killed by beheading and burning for his second labor; Orthos, the fierce guard dog of the monster Geryon, which Hercules killed with his club during his tenth labor; the eagle that gnawed at Prometheus, which Hercules slew with an arrow in the course of his eleventh labor; and Cerberus, the hound of Hades, which Hercules overwhelmed and brought back to earth for his twelfth labor. Echidna lived in a cave in the Peloponnesus and robbed passersby. The hundred-eyed giant Argus, a favorite of Hera, caught Echidna asleep and killed her.

Highlights:
Echidna is a formidable "performance-based" creature, enhanced by computer-generated swirling tentacles.

Kevin's take:
The bad guy was Marty Kove, from *The Karate Kid*, who was a lot of fun to work with. He was a great bad guy in that movie and he played a great bad guy in this episode! . . . In the fight sequences, Echidna's not even in the shot. They might have the tentacle snap around, but for most of that scene I am fighting nothing! . . . Bridget Hoffman, an old favorite of the Renaissance people, played Echidna. And God bless her, she had to go through about six hours of prosthetic makeup every day. . . . The scene when I'm shot with the arrows and almost died was fun for Michael and me to play, in terms of having more dramatic "beats." My family watched that scene and it affected them. They told me afterward, "God, we thought you were in pain." I thought, Well, good, then I did it right!

Michael's take:
I loved the scene where Hercules is complaining to me about his mother's suitor and I say, "Come on, Hercules, just because she's your mother doesn't mean she can't get married." I thought that was great, with Hercules being petulant, revealing a flaw, which we played on in a later episode when she marries Jason.

21. The Other Side

Writer　　　　　　Robert Bielak
Director　　　　　George Mendeluk
Original Air Date　Nov. 6, 1995

Guest cast:

Deianeira	Tawny Kitaen
Hades	Erik Thomson
Persephone	Andrea Croton
Demeter	Sarah Wilson
Charon	Michael Hurst
Klonus	Simon Lewthwaite
Aeson	Paul McIver
Ilea	Rose McIver

Story: Persephone, daughter of the earth goddess, Demeter, is strolling among the flowers, when she is abducted by Hades, god of the Underworld. Demeter begs Hercules to rescue her daughter, but he tells her that he is powerless to intercede in a battle between gods. Demeter will not be placated. She summons freezing rains to ruin the earth's harvests until Hercules agrees to go after Persephone. On reaching the Underworld, he is overjoyed to see his wife Deianeira and their three children in the paradise known as the Elysian Fields. Hercules then makes his way past Hades' watchdog, Cerberus, to reach Persephone. To his surprise, he learns that she and Hades are in love. Hades offers to restore Hercules' family to life if only he will let Persephone stay. Hercules is powerfully tempted but insists on Persephone's release. The two engage in a thunderous battle until both are near exhaustion. Hercules then has an inspiration: He proposes a compromise that will let Persephone spend six months each year with her mother and six months on the other side. Hades assents, Demeter lets the world bloom again, and Hercules returns with the memory of his beloved wife and children.

Mythic connections:
The story of Persephone (meaning "maiden") explains the origin of the seasons. Persephone was the daughter of Zeus and Demeter. Hades abducted her while she gathered flowers in Sicily. In her anguish and anger, Demeter allowed the crops to fail. Zeus, reluctant to take sides between his brother Hades and the mother of his child Persephone, said that Persephone could return to earth provided she had eaten nothing during her captivity. But Persephone had eaten six pomegranate seeds, and was compelled to spend six months of the year in the Underworld. During that time the grief-stricken Demeter withheld her bounty from the earth; but when Persephone returned, the goddess once more nourished the land and provided good harvests. The episode makes Hercules rather than his father, Zeus, the arbiter of Demeter's strife with Hades. In this retelling, it is not the accident of the pomegranate seeds but rather Hercules' diplomatic wisdom that brings winter and spring each year.

Neither Phil nor Sal nor any of the other Piglet Brethren were harmed during the production of this motion picture.

Highlights:
A beautifully written episode, letting Kevin Sorbo show Hercules' anguish over the loss of his family. Hades, a featured character in the TV movie *Hercules in the Underworld*, makes his first appearance in the series.

Casting coups:
Tawny Kitaen returns as Deianeira. Kitaen and Sorbo exude the same magic they projected together in their TV movies (*Hercules and the Circle of Fire*, *Hercules in the Underworld*, and *Hercules and the Maze of the Minotaur*). Michael Hurst reprises his role as Charon the boatman, from *Hercules in the Underworld*.

Kevin's take:
This was one of my favorites. It was fun from an actor's standpoint to be able to do more emotion and to show a different side of Hercules. We all wonder what our lives would be like if we had taken a different road, who we would have met, what we would say to those who have passed away. And it's just a matter of timing. And so Hercules goes down [to the Underworld] and he has another chance to speak with his wife and children. It was a satisfying episode to do, very touching.

22. The Fire Down Below

Writer	John Schulian
Director	Timothy Bond
Original Air Date	Nov. 13, 1995

Guest cast:

Salmoneus	Robert Trebor
Nemesis	Teresa Hill
Zandar	Andy Anderson
Syreeta	Emma Menzies
Ayora	Stephanie Wilkin
Purces	Stephen Hall

Story: Salmoneus strikes it rich by selling off a treasure trove long sealed in a cave. But things go wrong: The cave entrance collapses, and Salmoneus' partner dies at the hand of Nemesis, the goddess of divine retribution. Hercules arrives to warn a panicky Salmoneus that the treasure is Hera's, and later sees Nemesis aiming an arrow at Salmoneus. Appealing to her sense of justice, Hercules convinces Nemesis to spare Salmoneus and instead investigate a schemer named Zandar, who is behind the excavation of Hera's treasure. Zandar strikes first, capturing Salmoneus and also Nemesis,  who finds that Hera has helped Zandar trap her because of her disobedience. Hera also sends the fiery monster Pyro to kill Hercules.

While the two battle, Nemesis escapes and frees Salmoneus from Zandar, who flees to Pyro for protection but is instead consumed by flames. After barely avoiding Pyro's fiery charges, Hercules lures the creature into a barrel of water and clamps down the lid until Pyro's evil spirit is extinguished. A relieved Salmoneus thanks Hercules and Nemesis for saving his life; and Nemesis, no longer Hera's obedient avenger, kisses Hercules farewell and travels on to discover her new purpose in life.

Mythic connections: Nemesis was never involved with Hercules, but his father, Zeus, did fall in love with her and chased her over the earth. She changed into different animals, including a swan, but could not elude him. According to one tradition, the offspring of their union was the world's most beautiful woman, Helen.

Highlights: Hercules' astounding battle with the creature of fire, Pyro.

Kevin's take: I liked the story and the episode very much. I wish the fight with Pyro had been even longer [in the final cut], be-

> No Completely-Engulfed-in-Flames-Evil-Dudes were harmed during the production of this motion picture.

cause we filmed much more great footage than what they showed. I had put myself in danger for the whole day, I got singed more than once. But the CGI (computer-generated imaging) team just didn't have the time to piece more [effects] together. I understand, that's television, there are time frames. It still came out great, but I'm a perfectionist and I'm telling you what it *could* have been. Because there's footage you'll never see that was just amazing. The fire team [on location] and the lighting and camera work by John Mahaffie and [director] Tim Bond were all great.

Why did they change from Karen [Witter, as Nemesis]? I don't know. I really enjoyed working with Karen, I thought she was good. And they're both equally sexy. But I think they wanted somebody even hotter in terms of what they thought [Nemesis should look like], someone darker, more exotic looking. And she [Teresa Hill] is certainly stunning. And maybe they wanted someone who looked a little [tougher], with a bit more of the Xena appeal because, after all, it's the goddess of retribution.

23. Cast a Giant Shadow

Writer	John Schulian
Director	John T. Kretchmer
Original Air Date	Nov. 20, 1995

Guest cast:

Iolaus	Michael Hurst
Typhon	Glenn Shadix
Echidna	Bridget Hoffman
Maceus	Stig Eldred
Breanna	Fiona Mogridge
Septus	Bruce Allpress
Pylon	Bruce Hopkins

Story: The warrior chieftain Maceus vows revenge against Hercules for killing his brother Demetrius. Hercules meanwhile frees a clumsy but kindly giant named Typhon, who has been held captive by Hera for over a hundred years. They head off to meet Iolaus, but Maceus' soldiers find him first. Despite repeated beatings, Iolaus refuses to reveal his friend's location and escapes to warn Hercules that Maceus is on their trail. Hercules has larger problems: He discovers that Typhon's wife is Echidna, "the mother of all monsters." And when Typhon hears that Echidna was sealed in a cave by Hercules, the giant storms off to rejoin her. Hera hopes to use Echidna against Hercules by freeing the deadly creature to fight for Maceus. Hercules and Iolaus catch up with Typhon and persuade him that his wife is being controlled by Hera, as were his children, whom Hercules was forced to destroy. In a free-for-all battle, Maceus falls accidental victim to Echidna's deadly tentacles. Before Echidna can attack Hercules, Typhon announces cheerfully that he's finally home. He tells Echidna how Hera had kept him imprisoned to provoke her hatred, and she vows to change. As she and her husband embrace, Hercules and Iolaus slip away.

Mythic connections:
Typhon, the husband of Echidna, was not so endearing in the Greek myths as on *Hercules*. The largest of all the giants, taller than any mountain, Typhon had serpent's feet and a hundred serpent's (or dragon's) heads, each spewing fire and speaking in terrifying shrieks and bellows. He attacked the gods on Mount Olympus and they fled in terror to Egypt and disguised themselves as animals. Zeus eventually made a stand at Mount Casius in Syria, but Typhon cut his sinews and left him in a cave guarded by the serpent-woman Delphyne. The Olympians rallied. Hermes, messenger to Zeus, distracted Delphyne and stole the sinews, which he placed once more in Zeus' body. Zeus then returned to Olympus, renewed his supply of thunderbolts, and lit out after Typhon. On a mountain in Thrace, the king of the gods defeated the giant, chased him into the Mediterranean near Italy, and hurled a mountain on him. This became known as Mount Aetna, its volcanic eruptions caused by Typhon's struggles and his fiery breath.

> *Neither Typhon nor Echidna was harmed during the production of this motion picture. They went on to lead long and happy lives with their adopted family. However, attempts to reinflate Pylon were unsuccessful.*

Highlights:
An episode that plays for comedy rather than chills despite featuring two of the most horrific monsters in Greek myth. Typhon's closing kiss with Echidna pays homage to Jackie Gleason as Ralph Kramden, on the series *The Honeymooners*. . . . Michael Hurst had just broken his arm during a fight scene on a crossover episode of *Xena* called "Prometheus." Hurst's mishap was incorporated into the script by having Maceus' goons break Iolaus' arm.

Kevin's take:
Glenn Shadix was a great guy, and this episode also featured one of my all-time-favorite directors, John Kretchmer. John learned from the best. He was the first AD [assistant director] on *Jurassic Park* with [Steven] Spielberg [directing]. And he works well with everyone; he is a lovely man and just a pleasure to work with.

24. Highway to Hades

Writer	Robert Bielak
Director	T. J. Scott
Original Air Date	Nov. 27, 1995

Guest cast:

Iolaus	Michael Hurst
Hades	Erik Thomson
Sisyphus	Ray Henwood
Karis	Leslie Wing
Timuron	Craig Hall
Daphne	Angela Gribben

Story: Hades bids Hercules help the spirit of a young man named Timuron, who was tricked on his wedding night by King Sisyphus of Corinth into taking his place in a dread region of the Underworld. Hades urges Hercules to bring Sisyphus back so that Timuron's spirit can rest in the Elysian Fields, where it belongs. With three days to accomplish his mission, Hercules sets out with Timuron's spirit. At the palace, a contrite man emerges, confessing that he is Sisyphus and offering to go back to atone for his evil deed. Later, though, Hercules learns that the man is an impostor sent to delay him. The real King Sisyphus adds to his deceit by telling Timuron's widow, Daphne, that if she agrees to bear him an heir he will make her queen in place of his childless wife, Karis. Still mourning for Timuron, Daphne runs away in tears. Later she sees Timuron's ghost and, hoping to reunite with him in the Underworld, tries to end her life. Hercules rescues her and, aided by Karis, who discovers her husband's treachery, he captures Sisyphus and returns him to the Underworld. Hercules then convinces Hades to bend the rules and allow Timuron and Daphne to enjoy one night of their honeymoon together before saying good-bye.

Legendary Facts

King Sisyphus boasts of having made Corinth the wealthiest city in the world. In fact, Corinth had become a center of trade, famed for its pottery, by 650 BC.

Mythic connections: Called by Homer "the craftiest of men," Sisyphus founded and ruled the city of Corinth. He outwitted even Death (the Greek Thanatos), binding and holding him prisoner until the god of war, Ares, released him. Sisyphus later escaped from the Underworld through surpassing cunning, resuming his rule over Corinth and living to a ripe old age while Hades fumed. In part because of this defiance, Sisyphus was punished after death by having to roll a boulder forever up a hill. When he had pushed it nearly to the top, the stone would roll down and he had to begin again. Moderns commemorate his sad lot by terming a hopeless effort "Sisyphean."

Kevin's take: This was fun because T. J. [Scott, the director] goes a little more out there than other directors in terms of camera angles and camera movements.

25. The Sword of Veracity

Writer	Steven Baum
Director	Garth Maxwell
Original Air Date	Jan. 15, 1996

Guest cast:

Iolaus	Michael Hurst
Leah	Kim Michalis
Trachis	Paul Minifie
Amphion	Brad Carpenter
Lycus	Danny Lineham
Epius	Kelly Greene

Story: In the town of Pluribus, Hercules and Iolaus find their friend Amphion, once a great warrior but now preaching peaceful resistance to the local tyrant, Trachis. When Ámphion is arrested for the murder of a local couple, Hercules and Iolaus vow to uncover the truth by retrieving the Sword of Veracity, hidden in the Thalian Caves, which renders people incapable of lying. They are joined by Leah, who claims to be a Hestial virgin able to guide them. Iolaus struggles with his strong attraction to this beautiful woman, who leads them to just the right cave

among hundreds. Overcoming three ferocious Minotaurs, Hercules and Iolaus at last find the Sword of Veracity. On their way back to Pluribus, a band of Trachis' soldiers spring an ambush, but Hercules, Iolaus, and a surprisingly skilled Leah fight them off. Then Leah reveals her true identity—she is Amphion's fiancée. The trio returns just in time to point the Sword of Veracity at Trachis, who now cannot deny that he framed Amphion for the murders. Trachis is overthrown and the entire town celebrates the marriage of Amphion and Leah as Hercules and Iolaus set out to return the Sword of Veracity to the Thalian caves.

Mythic connections: The Sword of Veracity is a modern invention but it has ancient cousins, like the Cap of Invisibility that the Cyclopes forged for Hades.

Highlights: A scene in which Hercules, Iolaus, and Leah tell extravagant lies in order to find the real "Sword of Veracity" among dozens of look-alikes is clever and played to the (sword) hilt.

Casting coups: Brad Carpenter, who plays Amphion, also works at Renaissance Pictures.

Kevin's take: "The Sword of Veracity" was not one of my favorites. Maybe it was the story line, though there was some good humor and I thought the villain was pretty good. . . . Kim Michalis was actually in three of the *Hercules* movies. In the first one she plays Hercules' mother, Alcmene, as a young woman. You see her very quickly, nursing a one-year-old Hercules.

Michael's take: The New Zealand director Garth Maxwell wanted it broad, and I *played* quite broadly in that. It was a fun episode.

26. The Enforcer

Writer	Nelson Costello
Director	T. J. Scott
Original Air Date	Jan. 22, 1996

Guest cast:

Iolaus	Michael Hurst
The Enforcer	Karen Sheperd
Nemesis	Teresa Hill
Gnatius	Jed Brophy

Story: Hera creates an inhuman assassin in the shape of a woman known as the Enforcer, who is made of water but hard as stone. After tear-

ing apart several patrons in a local roadhouse, she seizes a chariot and races off to find Hercules, who has arrived with Iolaus at the annual Festival of the Harvest. There Hercules is happily reunited with Nemesis, who tells him that she has broken with Hera and warns him of the Enforcer. Later, at the edge of a cliff, Hercules greets an approaching woman, but her savage kicks and punches signal that he has just met the Enforcer. She charges him, swinging a log, but misses and falls onto the rocks below. Hercules staggers away, unaware that the water in the Enforcer's body has fully re-formed in the ocean. At the festival, Nemesis declares her love for Hercules, and romance blossoms between them. Iolaus has a more trying night, suffering a brutal beating as he vainly tries to hold off the Enforcer. Nemesis next tries to stop Hera's assassin but survives only because Hercules arrives. After a long battle, he flips the Enforcer into a blacksmith's forge, vaporizing her. Hercules then bids farewell to Nemesis, whose divine powers have been removed by the gods but who sets forth hopefully to discover her new, human identity.

Highlights: An exciting homage to the science fiction thriller *The Terminator*, starring Arnold Schwarzenegger. The fight scenes between Hercules and the Enforcer are among the series' best.

Casting coups: In an inspired casting move by producer Rob Tapert, Karen Sheperd, a veteran of Hong Kong martial arts films, is riveting as the Enforcer.

Kevin's take: I loved it. These are the episodes you can really show Hercules as a thinking man's hero, not just as somebody who uses his brawn. Because he's up against a formidable foe, he's not up against these generic guards we have that come in and I throw them into some salad stand! Here you have somebody—and a woman, too—who can hurt Hercules. And I think that makes it interesting for people. Otherwise it becomes too predictable. . . . And it was fun working with Karen. She'd never done television before, and she was so energized about doing the show. So she was a pleasure to work with and she was very professional. And we had a great time doing the fight scenes together. . . . [The choreography was] all Peter Bell. Karen was very cool about, you know, she might have made a suggestion now and then, but she didn't come in with any kind of ego and saying, "I want to do this, I want to do that." You know, the fights were put together completely by Peter and I think she was impressed with Peter, as everybody is.

27. Once a Hero

Teleplay	Robert Bielak and John Schulian
Story	Robert Tapert and Robert Bielak and John Schulian
Director	Robert Tapert
Original Air Date	Feb. 5, 1996

Guest cast:

Iolaus	Michael Hurst
Jason	Jeffrey Thomas
Castor	Peter Feeney
Marcus	Lathan Gaines
Artemus	Edward Campbell
Valerus	Anthony Ray Parker
Archivas	Tim Raby
Domesticles	John Sumner
Phoebe	Willa O'Neill
Otus	Mark Nua

Story: In Corinth for a reunion of Jason and the Argonauts, famed for their voyage to win a fabulous Golden Fleece, Hercules saves a drunk from a robbery. To his astonishment, it is King Jason himself. Hercules learns from the Argonaut Castor that Jason's drinking began after his wife and children were killed.

Their reunion suddenly gives way to a raid by the "Blood-Eyes," a Hera-worshiping cult led by a masked demon, who steals the Golden Fleece. Hercules rallies the Argonauts to recover the Fleece but they insist that Hercules lead them, for they doubt Jason's fitness for command. Hercules reluctantly accepts on condition that Jason navigate. Tracking the Blood-Eyes to an island temple, Hercules reveals the demon to be Castor, who admits that he hates Jason and the other Argonauts for stealing his glory. Castor escapes with the Fleece to Corinth, where a newly resolute Jason challenges him to single combat. But the regent Marcus, who covets Jason's throne, hurls dragon's teeth into a fire, releasing eight sword-wielding skeletons to attack the Argonauts. Hercules, Jason, and his fellow heroes join in an epic battle to retrieve the Golden Fleece, and are once again united in victory.

Mythic connections: The Argonauts traveled with Jason on the ship *Argo* to find the Golden Fleece. Jason, who like Hercules was tutored by the centaur Chiron, was the rightful heir to the throne of Iolcus in Thessaly. A usurper king, Pelias, agreed to give up his crown provided Jason could bring home the Golden Fleece, in the distant land of the Colchides at the edge of the Black Sea. It was a task Pelias confidently believed was virtually impossible. Jason recruited an extraordinary group of fifty adventurers, including the boxer Castor, the minstrel Orpheus, and the great Hercules himself, who saved the Argonauts from the savage giants of Bear Island. But Hercules later left the *Argo* when a young friend became lost, and Hercules remained to search for him. After travels to many lands and battles with armies and monsters, Jason returned with his fellow Argonauts, bearing the Golden Fleece.

The dragon's teeth relate to a myth involving another hero, Cadmus. The son of a Phoenician king, Cadmus stoned to death a dragon and, guided by Athena, sowed the monster's teeth on the ground. A troop of armed men, or "Spartae," sprang up and battled each other till all but five were slain. The survivors helped Cadmus build the city of Thebes.

Jason's drunkenness in "Once a Hero" is a gentler version of the mythic hero's fall from grace. On his travels with the Argonauts he was aided by Medea, a sorceress who fell in love with him. Jason lived with Medea in Corinth for ten years but then left her for a young woman. The furious Medea killed her rival and her own children. Jason survived, a broken man dreaming of past glories, until one day, as he sat in the shade of his old ship, a falling beam fell on him and killed him.

Highlights: The whole episode is a highlight, down to the final toast by the Argonauts: "To heroes!" It features a series of adventures that culminate in a spectacular battle with the warrior skeletons, a tribute to the 1963 movie *Jason and the Argonauts* and the special effects genius Ray Harryhausen. The episode also engagingly depicts the fall and rebirth of the hero Jason, under the nurturing friendship of Hercules.

Casting coups: Jeffrey Thomas first appeared in *Hercules* as the evil Bellicus in the episode "Gladiator."

Kevin's take: Big one. Huge one. That was the one that, of course, our executive producer Rob Tapert directed. "Once a Hero" was overwhelming to try to film. It could have been a two-hour movie. This was always Tapert's pet project. Rob is a huge fan of Ray Harryhausen, and he always wanted to do this. And *I* always wanted to do it, because as a kid I always wanted to fight the skeletons. You know, all those old movies like *Jason and the Argonauts* and [*The Seventh Voyage of*] *Sinbad*. And I *got* to fight the skeletons. It was really a kick. All of us really enjoyed it. And I think it's a great way to end it, when we all toasted each other.

Michael's take: I remember my arm in that one was actually broken. They wanted to put me into a kind of a sling, but instead I went to Ngila [Dickson] in wardrobe and we designed a leather strap that looked more rugged. . . . Our filming got washed out one day. The boat was on the beach, and there was a howling gale wind and rain. We lost a half day. . . . I loved the episode. Rob Tapert was very patient as a director, and he had plenty of time do the postproduction, so it looks wonderful. He paid a lot of attention to detail, a lot of attention to performance.

28. Heedless Hearts

Writer	Robert Bielak
Director	Peter Ellis
Original Air Date	Feb. 12, 1996

Guest cast:

Iolaus	Michael Hurst
Rheanna	Audie England
Jordis	Bruce Hopkins
King Melkos	Michael Keir-Morrissey
Grovelus	Michael Saccente
Syrus	Nigel Godfrey
Clarion	Grant Triplow
Vericles	Robert Horwood
Gnossus	Nigel Corbett
Hephates	Sara Wiseman

Story: A lightning bolt strikes Iolaus, who awakens with the power to predict events. He warns a skeptical Hercules about the appearance of a young woman only moments before Rheanna arrives on horseback. She tells them of the death of her husband, Jordis, during a failed rebellion against the ruthless King Melkos, and pleads for help in saving her village. Iolaus later predicts that his friend will be betrayed by Rheanna, but to no avail: Hercules is falling in love with her. Melkos'

troops ambush the rebels and take everyone prisoner, including Hercules. The real traitor turns out to be Rheanna's sister-in-law Hephates—the woman Iolaus "saw" in his first vision. King Melkos sentences the rebels to death but Hercules and Iolaus lead a daring escape. Now much in love, Hercules and Rheanna take shelter in a farmhouse, where she is amazed to see her husband, Jordis, who was secretly rescued by rebels after a battle. That night, Hercules and Iolaus scale the walls of the king's castle and help the rebels defeat King Melkos, though Iolaus suffers a blow to the head that ends his ability to foretell events. Hercules parts with Rheanna, who has stirred his heart in a way he had not felt since losing his family.

Highlights: The daring escape from the castle walls by Hercules, Iolaus, and Rheanna.

Kevin's take: We went nuts on that one in terms of just having fun with it. Michael started ad-libbing like a fool when he got struck by lightning, talking about seeing planes and buildings and skyscrapers. . . . Audie England [who plays Rheanna], is a beautiful, exotic, very interesting actress. It was an enjoyable episode for her because the writers so rarely have Hercules falling in love, we've only done it really with his family, then with Rheanna, and later Serena the Golden Hind. Other than that, there really haven't been any episodes. Michael is the one who always gets the girl!

29. Let the Games Begin

Writer	John Schulian
Director	Gus Trikonis
Original Air Date	Feb. 19, 1996

Guest cast:

Salmoneus	Robert Trebor
Atalanta	Cory Everson
Damon	Matthew Humphrey
Brontus	Paul Glover
Tarkon	Chris Bailey
Taphius	John Watson

Story: Hercules breaks up a battle and tends a Spartan named Damon, who has been struck from behind by Brontus the Elean. At Damon's village, Hercules finds that the young man's aunt is his friend Atalanta. She reveals that Damon's father was killed in battle and that Damon has become obsessed with war. During a walk around the village, Hercules watches two boys settle a dispute by racing each other rather than arguing. The sight inspires him to organize a series of athletic tests of speed and strength, as an alternative to combat. Atalanta wins Damon's promise of cooperation by besting him

in an arm-wrestling match, and Salmoneus signs on as well, hoping to make money and become closer to the beautiful Atalanta. Meanwhile the Elean leader Tarkon prays to Ares, who transforms his soldiers into monstrous killers, known as Mesomorphs. A huge crowd turns out for the events, and cheers as Atalanta wins the javelin contest. Just as the hundred-meter dash begins, Tarkon's warriors attack the Spartan competitors. As Hercules leaps into the battle, the competing Spartans and Eleans, including Damon and Brontus, join forces. Tarkon's men are defeated, and the world's first Olympic games proceed in peace.

Mythic connections: Hercules founded the Olympic games, held every four years at Olympia, in honor of Zeus.

Highlights: "It's *Herculean*!" Salmoneus proclaims of the majestic games Hercules is planning against the background of Mount Olympus. "I prefer to think of it as—*Olympian*," Hercules modestly replies. This clever episode gives an idealistic spin to Hercules' founding of the Olympics (make sports, not war), and also brings back the character Atalanta, a woman famed for her athletic prowess.

Kevin's take: A fun episode to do. Gus Trikonis directed and he did a great job making that script work. And who better than to have Hercules kick off the Olympics? It just made total sense. I also had fun working with Cory and Bob Trebor (as Salmoneus). Cory is a great sport! . . . It was also one of more enjoyable fights, against the Mesomorphs [the transformed Elean soldiers]. Really nasty-looking creatures, and now they actually have their own doll [in stores]! Just as Cory's got her own doll out there, and so does Salmoneus.

Legendary Facts

The first official record of the Olympics dates to 776 BC. The first Olympic Games were confined to running events, and Coroebus was the first winner of the foot race in 776 BC.

30. The Apple

Writer	Steven Baum
Director	Kevin Sorbo
Original Air Date	Feb. 26, 1996

Guest cast:

Iolaus	Michael Hurst
Thera	Claire Yarlett
Aphrodite	Alexandra Tydings
Epius	Jonathan Blick
Sidon	Ian Mune
King Diadorus	Stephen Tozer
Artemis	Rhonda McHardy
Athena	Amanda Lister

Story: A day on the beach was never like this for Iolaus, who reels in a giant clamshell that opens to reveal the goddess of love, Aphrodite. She and her sisters, Athena and Artemis, ask Iolaus to choose who is the most beautiful. The three goddesses compete for his favor with gifts that most mortals can only dream of. Artemis promises to make Iolaus the world's greatest  hunter. Athena promises matchless wisdom. But no one can sway men like Aphrodite: She offers Iolaus a golden apple that will make any woman he wants fall in love with him, and he names her the most beautiful. Iolaus tests his prize on a woman named Thera, not realizing she is a princess who is about to marry Prince Epius in a ceremony that promises to end a feud between their cities. Hercules finds Thera in Iolaus' arms and tells his sheepish friend who the woman is. Iolaus brings Thera back to the two royal families but cannot stop her from embracing him, an outrage that threatens to trigger a new war. Just as the rival armies clash, Hercules grabs the hands of both kings and thrusts the apple into their joint grasp, causing them to become soul mates for life. Thera regains her love for Epius, and Aphrodite mischievously departs.

Mythic connections:

The contest between three goddesses foreshadowed the Trojan War. When Eris (Greek for "strife") tossed a golden apple bearing the inscription "For the Fairest," Hera (rather than Artemis), Athena, and Aphrodite all claimed it. They asked a shepherd named Paris to judge the fairest, and each goddess promised a fabulous prize if he chose her. Hera offered power, Athena a warrior's glory, and Aphrodite the most beautiful woman in the world. Paris awarded the apple to Aphrodite, who in turn helped him elope to Troy with Helen, the wife of King Menelaus of Sparta. Menelaus and the combined forces of many Greek kingdoms sailed to Troy and fought for ten years to take Helen back.

Highlights:

Kevin Sorbo's directorial debut makes for a wonderfully funny episode. Self-consciously campy (the goddess of wisdom, Athena, briefly appears in high-fashion glasses, and Aphrodite surfs in her clamshell), it also features two sly dream sequences in which Iolaus envisions how his life will change if he chooses Artemis, Athena, or Aphrodite as the most beautiful. Aphrodite's manipulation of Iolaus and her sibling squabbles with her half brother Hercules are written and acted with great comic flair.

Casting coups:

"The Apple" marks Alexandra Tydings' first appearance as Aphrodite, a sly, sensual, and thoroughly modern goddess of love.

Kevin's take:

You know what? A total ball, a total kick, a total blast. It introduced a new goddess, Aphrodite. This was my first time directing, but I had a few things in my favor. Number one, I know the show. Number two, I know the characters. Number three, the crew is great and they know me and they were there to protect me and work with me. And number four, I had a three-week Christmas break, so that gave me the time that most directors get to prep for a show. I was able to read the script a thousand times, to break the scenes down, and get to the locations. I took photos of everywhere we would film. I talked to the heads of wardrobe and makeup and locations. And it was summertime [Christmas in New Zealand coming at the peak of summer]. It was sunny in January, and beautiful. And everybody was glad to be back. We had a great episode. We put three beautiful women in scanty outfits, so the crew loved me. Everybody was happy. And it was just a fun episode to do. The other two actresses were really models. . . .

In one of Iolaus' dreams, where I'm getting beaten up and he saves me, I added a bit: During our lunch breaks the crew always plays Hacky Sack. And I said, "Why don't we make a human Hacky Sack of Hercules? These guys are kicking him and we'll send me up in the air and we'll do slow-motion shots of me just falling around and screaming out, 'Iolaus, save me!'" In another dream scene [where Hercules appears a foolish foil to Iolaus' wise man] Rob Tapert had a problem with that because he said, "God, you know, you are the hero, and you are making fun of yourself." I said, "But Rob, it's a dream. Who cares?"

We made this an over-the-top episode. I put in [words like] "tubular," the whole idea about Iolaus surfing in on a board, and Aphrodite's wind-surfing. And we made up things [as we went along]. For example, having Michael and the fisherman he's with on the beach drop their poles as soon as they see Aphrodite.

Michael's take: The script was already pretty far out. And both Kevin and I went, "Are you kidding, this is really what they want us to do?" And then we thought, what the hell! And Kevin had the sensible notion to go with it, not just a hundred percent but a million percent. And he said, "Whatever we can make up, [do it]." So we went for it. Man, did we go for it! . . . Yes, he did make fun of himself [and Hercules], but didn't it actually intensify the truth, which is that he is amazing? The ability to be mocked and to mock oneself makes one bigger. I think any actor worth their salt knows that if you can take the custard pie, the figurative custard pie, that's great!

31. Promises

Writer	Michael Marks
Director	Stewart Main
Original Air Date	Mar. 4, 1996

Guest cast:

Iolaus	Michael Hurst
Tarlus	Marton Csokas
Ramina	Josephine Davison
Beraeus	Joel Tobeck
Natros	Calvin Tutaeo

Story: King Beraeus laments to Hercules that Ramina, his bride-to-be, has been kidnapped by the warrior Tarlus. Hercules remembers Tarlus as a good man and convinces the king to let him and Iolaus rescue Ramina. Iolaus, though, later relates bitterly that Tarlus had been his friend but abandoned him in battle. Hercules and Iolaus surprise Tarlus' men and make off with Ramina, but she soon disappears again. Beraeus, losing patience, gathers his troops to hunt for her himself. After driving off a group of Primords, hairy half men, half beasts, Hercules and Iolaus slip into Tarlus' camp and are amazed to see Ramina kissing him. Though confused, they grab Ramina and fight their way out. Ramina explains that Beraeus is actually a merciless king who is forcing her to marry him. When Hercules and Iolaus later see Ramina bound and led away by Beraeus, they join with

Tarlus' soldiers to rescue her. A furious Beraeus, his plans thwarted, raises his sword to strike Ramina down, and Hercules must kill him. Tarlus then reveals that he had left Iolaus' side in battle years before in order to save Beraeus' father, who swore him to secrecy. He and Ramina then welcome Hercules and Iolaus to attend their joyful wedding.

Kevin's take: Probably my least-favorite episode. I like that we go for moral messages, but this one hit [viewers] over the head way too many times. Every scene ends with Hercules saying, "I promise." It just didn't work, and I think [Rob] Tapert, [Eric] Gruendemann, and Michael [Hurst] would all agree with me.

Michael's take: Marton Csokas (Tarlus) and Jo Davison (Ramina) are household names here [in New Zealand], and it was great working with them. I have actually cast Josephine as Desdemona in my production of *Othello*. She's a real do-anything, ready-for-anything actress, so it was good to work with her. . . . I hated those "Primords." It was reminiscent of [creatures from the old] *Flash Gordon* episodes.

32. King for a Day

Writer	Patricia Manney
Director	Anson Williams
Original Air Date	Mar. 18, 1996

Guest cast:

Iolaus/Orestes	Michael Hurst
Princess Niobe	Lisa Ann Hadley
Archias	Will Kempe
Minos	Robert Pollock
Hector	Derek Payne
Linus	Ross McKellar
Pylon	Brendan Lovegrove

Story: Iolaus discovers he is a look-alike for Prince Orestes of Attica, whose coronation and marriage to Princess Niobe are scheduled for the next day. When General Archias has Orestes drugged in order to put the prince's jealous brother Minos on the throne, Orestes' loyal aide, Hector, begs Iolaus to become "king for a day." Iolaus reluctantly stands in for Orestes at the coronation and the wedding, then learns that Orestes has been kidnapped by Archias. Trapped by duty, Iolaus accedes to Hector's pleas to serve as King until Orestes is freed. Iolaus' fair and generous rule wins the hearts of the people, and, to his surprise, that of Princess Niobe. The ne'er-do-well Prince Orestes meanwhile finds that a dungeon, for all its perils, is not a bad place to grow up: He refuses demands to yield the throne, insisting that he will at least die

like a king. Before Archias can oblige him, Iolaus scales his fortress by climbing a ladder of spears and arrows thrown at the walls by Hector, the reformed Prince Minos, and Niobe. He defeats Archias in a hard-fought duel and frees Orestes, who vows he will try to rule with the wisdom Iolaus has shown. And Niobe, trapped by her duty as queen, bids farewell to Iolaus, the man she thought she married.

> No slightly soused kings-to-be who finally pull themselves up by their bootstraps and realize the true meaning of leadership were harmed during the production of this motion picture.

Highlights: Michael Hurst shines in a double
role in this clever homage to the swashbuckling film *The Prisoner of Zenda*, with ancient Attica standing in for the mythical European kingdom of Ruritania. The final, furious duel between Iolaus and master swordsman Archias is brilliantly choreographed by Peter Bell, and Michael Hurst, a veteran stage fencer and fight choreographer, is clearly in his element.

Michael's take: "King for a Day" was great, great fun. It was fan-
tastic meeting [director] Anson Williams and working with him. . . . No, I didn't [try to draw on memories of *The Prisoner of Zenda*], I just stayed within the moment, because that's the only way to do it. You don't go to *see Hamlet* if you're going to *play* Hamlet. You don't go watch someone else do the role if you're going to play it. Absolutely not!

33. Protean Challenge

Writer	Brian Herskowitz
Director	Oley Sassone
Original Air Date	Apr. 22, 1996

Guest cast:

Iolaus	Michael Hurst
Daniella	Ashley Laurence
Thanis	Paul Gittins
Trilos	Stephen Papps
Magistrate	John O'Leary
Bornus	James O'Farrell
Proteus	Jane Cresswell

Story: The sculptor Thanis is sentenced to lose both his hands for an act of theft. Thanis insists he is innocent, yet Iolaus himself witnessed the crime. When Hercules later reassures Thanis' daughter Daniella, she innocently kisses him just as Iolaus rounds the corner. When Iolaus later questions Hercules about kissing Daniella, he denies to his shocked friend that he did so. Later Iolaus astounds Hercules by leaping at him with a sword. Forced into battle, Hercules is surprised again when the real Iolaus approaches from another direction. Then Hercules realizes that Pro-

teus, the deformed god who can change his shape at will, is wreaking havoc. Daniella confirms that Proteus is punishing the village because she fled from him after seeing his real reflection in the water. Proteus tries to elude capture by changing into Daniella and then into Hercules himself. But when the real Hercules holds up a shiny shield so that Proteus can see his real reflection, the god loses his will to fight. He confesses that he only wanted to win Daniella's heart. Hercules convinces Proteus to face the townspeople. Proteus admits publicly that Thanis is innocent and wins the gratitude of the villagers, including Daniella.

Mythic connections: Proteus, an ancient sea god, was not known as a shape-shifter but many other gods, including Zeus, often disguised themselves as mortals and animals.

Highlights: Hercules battling Hercules—there's a sight you don't see every day.

Kevin's take: [on playing the evil Hercules] It was a kick to do that. I think we borrow from *Star Trek* a lot [in the episode "The Enemy Within," Captain Kirk battles his savage half]. But that's what TV is: Everybody borrows from everybody. But that was just a fun episode because I got to play an evil guy. You know, any time I get to do something a little different than the heroic Hercules, it just infuses new blood into me. . . . No, the producers had no problem about [the false] Hercules showing an evil side. The whole idea now is to get a little darker and do more interesting things. So I don't think anybody was nervous about that at all.

No Slightly Discolored and Impish Gods who vaguely resemble any Candidate in the 1996 presidential elections were harmed during the production of this motion picture.

Michael's take: It was a lovely show. The woman playing Proteus, Jane Creswell, is actually an art director now. And she's also done some acting: there's a kids' television series in New Zealand called *The Boy from Andromeda*, and she was the boy, who is another alien. Jane went through a long makeup process [for this episode], quite distressing for her, I think. . . . And I got to attack Hercules and growl. So, yeah, it was fun.

34. The Wedding of Alcmene

Writer	John Schulian
Director	Timothy Bond
Original Air Date	Apr. 29, 1996

Guest cast:

Iolaus	Michael Hurst
Alcmene	Liddy Holloway
Jason	Jeffrey Thomas
Iphicles	Kevin Smith
Rena	Simone Kessell
Sera	Sabine Karsenti
Amphion	Brad Carpenter
Leah	Kim Michalis
Dirce	Lisa Chappell
Patronius	Simon Prast
Blue Priest	Nathaniel Lees
Phoebe	Willa O'Neill
Falafel	Paul Norell
Archivus	Tim Raby
Domesticles	John Sumner
Salmoneus	Robert Trebor

Story: Alcmene, Hercules' mother, shocks her son by revealing that she's planning to marry Jason. Alcmene apologizes for keeping her romance a secret, and Hercules is moved to forgive her when he sees how happy she is. Jason reigns in Corinth, but the arrogant regent, Patronius, reminds him that if he marries a commoner he will lose his crown. Jason replies that the law allows him to name his successor, thereby foiling Patronius' own ambitions. He asks Hercules to succeed him, but, although honored, he declines. Jason's wedding plans appear to have the gods' favor, however, when a woman named Sera offers to host the ceremony at her magnificent seaside

estate. Patronius meanwhile conspires with Hera's Blue Priest—and Sera—to kill Hercules, Jason, and his chosen successor—Hercules' brother Iphicles. Before the wedding can take place, the servants, allied with Petronius, attack the guests while Hera sends a sea serpent that swallows Jason. Hercules dives into the serpent's mouth, kills the monster from inside, and emerges with Jason in time to see the wedding guests, a formidable group of heroes, triumph over Hera's killers. Then, with the noble King Amphion presiding, Jason and Alcmene marry at last.

Highlights:
A remarkable cast reunion from many episodes features the Argonauts, King Amphion and his bride, Leah, and other heroes and friends of Hercules and Iolaus.

Kevin's take:
Yes, a cast reunion is exactly what it was. That was fun for me because my parents were in town, watching us shoot that over Valentine's Day.

35. The Power

Writer	Nelson Costello
Director	Charlie Haskell
Original Air Date	May 6, 1996

Guest cast:

Salmoneus	Robert Trebor
Jacobus	Bruce Phillips
Karis	Grant Bridger
Deon	David Drew Gallagher
Sirene	Greer Robson
Big Titus	Patrick Wilson
Little Titus	Liam Vincent

Story: After overpowering a band of thieves who charge at him in strange land-based Windsurfers, Hercules witnesses an inexplicable sight: As a youth named Deon pleads with bandits, they simply drop their weapons and depart. Villagers jeer at Deon's story until he orders one to dance like a chicken and, to everyone's amazement, the man obeys. So, too, does Salmoneus, who is in Deon's line of vision. Afterward Salmoneus boasts to Hercules that he has been summoned by the Titus brothers for his "marketing genius," but is appalled when they force him to sell manure. Jacobus meanwhile confides to Deon that his strange power comes from his real mother, the goddess Aphrodite. Hercules reluctantly conveys another discovery: The bandit chief is Deon's uncle Karis, whom the boy idolizes. Deon spurns his father's warnings against joining Karis and, to keep Hercules away, he orders Salmoneus to attack him. After Hercules sends his sword-wielding friend into a trough, he and Jacobus overtake Deon. Karis attacks Jacobus, and when Deon interferes he turns on the boy, but Jacobus saves his son with a skilled knife throw. Deon reconciles with his father and promises Hercules that he will use his god-given power only to help others.

Highlights: The opening battle between Hercules and the windsurfing bandits is inventive and visually striking.

Kevin's take: David Drew Gallagher was good to work with. . . . And of course, any time we're at the beach shooting, I'm happy.

36. Centaur Mentor Journey

Writer	Robert Bielak
Director	Stephen L. Posey
Original Air Date	May 13, 1996

Guest cast:

Salmoneus	Robert Trebor
Ceridian	Tony Blackett
Cassius	Julian Arahanga
Theseus	James Townsend
Myrra	Marcia Cameron
Gredor	John McKee
Perdidis	Edward Newborn
Locus	Robert McMullen

Story: Hercules is summoned by his dying mentor, the centaur Ceridian, to prevent a war between centaurs and humans. Ceridian's student

Cassius, seething over discrimination by the bigoted magistrate Gredor, spurs his fellow centaurs to demand equal rights by any means necessary, including bloodshed. Hercules tells Cassius that there may be a better way, but the centaur is too suspicious to listen. Nor are the humans in a mood to compromise. Even the tolerant Perdidas, whose daughter Myrra loves Cassius, vows that if the centaurs ride armed across his land, he will repel them by force. Relishing the prospect of a war to annihilate the centaurs, Gredor orders his spy Locus to assassinate Perdidas and blame Cassius. But Hercules saves Perdidas, who then joins the centaurs in a march to the town fountain, where only humans may drink. Angry citizens pelt them with stones, but are won over when the marchers remain nonviolent even after Cassius is wounded by an arrow. Hercules presses Locus to expose Gredor's treachery, and the townsfolk now see that the centaurs are not their enemies, only prejudice. Humans and centaurs drink from the fountain in peace, Hercules' final gift to his beloved mentor.

> No Centaurs were harmed or discriminated against during the production of this motion picture.

Mythic connections: Just as Hercules and Cassius in this episode are linked by reverence for their tutor, the ancient myths portray a centaur, Chiron, as mentor to Hercules and other heroes, including Jason and Achilles.

Highlights: A wonderfully written episode that plays on themes from the American civil rights movement. Cassius speaks in the cadences of black militants from the 1960s ("Centaur Power!" replacing "Black Power!"), Perdidas is the story's sympathetic white liberal, and the march to the fountain reenacts the decade's protests by blacks and their white allies, who endured violence without striking back in order to overcome injustice.

Kevin's take: Yes, it was a civil rights episode. I know they were trying to get a message across there—and violence certainly isn't the answer—but the ending just didn't work for me. People are throwing rocks and I'm saying, "Just keep walking, just keep walking to the fountain." And I didn't totally buy into it, to be honest with you. . . . What *was* good about that episode, is that they [the producers and special effects team] really went for it with the centaurs. People *love* these centaurs, and they didn't show just one or two, they showed about nine. And some of the shots turned out really, really well.

I had a good scene with Rob Trebor [as Salmoneus] that was cut out [for reasons of time]. It was a raging emotional scene, when I really snap at Salmoneus. [My character has] never done that before. Because while everything else is going on, I'm dealing with my own emotions over my mentor dying.

37. The Cave of Echoes

Writers	John Schulian and Robert Bielak
Director	Gus Trikonis
Original Air Date	June 24, 1996

Guest cast:

Iolaus	Michael Hurst
Parentheses	Owen Black
Elopius	Mark Perry
Melina	Mandy Gillette

Story: A writer named Parentheses, awestruck on meeting the great Hercules, insists on tagging along after him and Iolaus to the Cave of Echoes. They arrive to find an old man, Elopius, despairing over the disappearance of his daughter, Melina, inside the cave. As Elopius warns that no one has ever come out of this cave alive, they hear a monstrous roar. Parentheses follows Hercules and Iolaus into the dark cavern, eager to witness "real heroes" in action. With each bloodcurdling roar, however, the writer trembles, and it is only Hercules' and Iolaus' tales of monsters they have fought in the past that begin to calm him. When the trio find Melina clinging to the edge of a pit, Hercules sees that the "monster" clutching her foot is in fact an ancient tree root, and he sends an unsuspecting Parentheses down to save her. The writer is overjoyed to discover that there is no horrible beast to fight after all, and pulls the girl out. Melina then leads them into an adjoining cavern toward another deafening roar, which turns out to be the cry of her tiny kitten, Zeus, magnified a thousandfold by the Cave of Echoes. Parentheses and a grateful Melina walk off arm in arm as Hercules and Iolaus are called to another adventure.

Highlights: In this "clips" episode showcasing scenes from earlier stories, the highlights are action-packed "flashbacks" related by Hercules and Iolaus to the eager writer.

> No Vicious Tabby Cats were harmed during the production of this motion picture. However, the Pre-Hellenic Litter Box is in dire need of a change.

The
Third
Season

38. Mercenary

Writer	Robert Bielak
Director	Michael Hurst
Original Air Date	Oct. 7, 1996

Guest cast:

Derk	Jeremy Roberts
Sordis	Neill Duncan
Trayus	Philip Jones
Kara	Sarah Smuts-Kennedy
Older Boy	Owain Pennington
Sister	Charlotte Pennington
Marcus the Magistrate	Paul Willis

Story: While Hercules is transporting the ruthless mercenary Derk to Sparta to stand trial, he and his prisoner are shipwrecked on a desert island. In spite of a fractured arm, Hercules leads Derk across an expanse of

scrubby trees in search of fresh water while a band of pirates hunts for gold they believe was aboard the shipwrecked boat. The pirates are not the only hunters: When Derk attacks Hercules in an attempt to escape, a huge wormlike creature springs out of the sand and grabs Derk's leg. Hercules saves Derk, and the two men find tempo-

rary refuge in an outcropping of rocks. As more of the underground creatures close in on them, they reach an uneasy truce, and Hercules even
agrees to let Derk see his family one last time before standing trial. The
bargain is sealed when Derk agrees to reset Hercules' broken arm, which
has become badly infected. Meanwhile the pirates track the two men to the
desert but are soon caught and killed by the sand creatures. Hercules tricks
these predators into colliding with each other and sails with Derk in the pirates' boat, bringing him first to see his family and then to face judgment
in Sparta. But when Hercules learns that the trial will not be fair, he helps
Derk escape in exchange for his vow to leave the mercenary life behind.

Kevin's take: Loved "Mercenary"! Michael Hurst directed that
one. One of my top five favorites, because it was gritty and it was dirty.
And because of the scenes I had with Jeremy Roberts, the wonderful actor who played Derk. I would like to work with more actors like him, and
more story lines like this. I think that the humor in the show is fun, and
we're doing a lot of comedy this [fourth] season, which I think people are
going to enjoy. But, man, do I like something to sink my teeth into! And
Michael is a great director. We know each other well, so it was very comfortable working with him.

Michael's take: This was the first episode that I directed. I re-
member feeling confident about the drama but nervous about the special
effects, which were a considerable aspect to it. But Kevin O'Neill [the FX
supervisor] came down and helped me greatly.

This episode was grueling to shoot. We had to create a desert environment [on Bethells Beach] where there is no desert. I decided to keep
the camera angles low to the ground so you didn't see just beyond the sand
dune to all the lovely green trees and the houses! And when you see Kevin
and Jeremy Roberts sitting on the rooftop there, right behind the camera
is a farm and sheds and tractors. When I did have to shoot panoramas, the
computer guys [at Flat Earth] got rid of the valley and the green, and put
in sand dunes instead!

I thought, The scary creature is under the ground. Therefore, if you
shoot low to the ground, you're constantly feeling slightly terrorized. And
when Herc and Derk are sitting on the rocks, I decided to put ruins there,
as if there had been some kind of town or city years and years ago that
these creatures had slowly invaded and taken over, and the whole city is
now silted up.

It was a dream directing Kevin. An actor talking to actors about how to act is really good. I said to Kevin right at the beginning, I don't want the usual flip tone. I want to get some really gutsy stuff happening. And those guys all worked hard. I was in their faces a lot, you know, and Kevin loved it, and responded really well. And it's a different look for *Hercules*. You know, it isn't done that often, that kind of heavy drama. . . .

Yes, it was gritty. Literally! The sand got everywhere. Quite often at the end of the day, I'd be exhausted, though more from dealing with my stress than from actually dealing with the situation. Because the stress was huge— you know, you have to get these things shot quickly!

Legendary Facts

Michael Hurst directed and appeared in this episode, sort of. He explains: The fellow who played the bald-headed pirate . . . had to be completely revoiced. So in the end, I said, Oh, well, look, I wanted to be in the episode myself, the way Hitchcock appeared in each of his films, but I never had the time. So I just revoiced the lines myself, so when the pirate speaks you're really hearing my voice.

39. Doomsday

Writer	Brian Herskowitz
Director	Michael Lange
Original Air Date	Oct. 14, 1996

Guest cast:

Daedalus	Derek Payne
Katrina	Rebecca Hobbs
Nikolos	Frankie Stevens
Icarus	Ryan Lowell
Perdix	Frankie Stevens
Falafel	Paul Norell

Story: Hercules travels to Euboea to see his old friend Daedalus, a brilliant scientist mourning the death of his son. On the way, he stops a group of soldiers who are attacking a village using a giant crossbow built by Daedalus for King Nikolos. Hercules gets his friend Daedalus to see that the king is using his inventions to terrorize defenseless women and children. He then confronts one of those deadly inventions, a giant contraption of stone fists and feet called a Megalith that he defeats by hurling it to the ground. When Daedalus learns that Nikolos has used the Megalith against Hercules, he tries to blow up his lab. However, the guards rush in and save the equipment, including a more advanced version of the Megalith. Nikolos himself climbs into the stone-and-steel body of the new Megalith, which uses a crystal to convert beams of sunlight into fireballs shooting out of the helmet's mouth. After barely dodging the flames, Hercules manages to block the mouth of the Mega-

> ## Legendary Facts
>
> Works named for Daedalus have been found in Crete from the time of the Minoan kings, between 2200 and 1400 BC.

lith, which blows up with Nikolos trapped inside. Daedalus burns the last of his blueprints and vows to devote his life to peaceful inventions.

Mythic connections:
Daedalus was a sculptor, architect, carpenter, and inventor without peer. His greatest creation was also his most tragic. Daedalus and his son escaped from a prison in Crete using wings he had fashioned of wax and feathers. But Icarus, disregarding his father's instructions, flew too close to the sun, and as the wax melted he fell into the sea and drowned.

Highlights:
Hercules uses another of Daedalus' creations, an ancient version of Silly Putty, to defeat the fire-breathing Megalith.

> No Silly Nutty was harmed during the production of this motion picture. However, quite a few filberts and cashews sacrificed their lives in the name of progress.

Kevin's take:
There's a scene with the actress Rebecca Hobbs at the very beginning, where she wants to do an autobiography of Hercules. I'm walking back and forth, loading up sand in order to dike a river. And she's talking and talking, and I'm telling her, "People don't care about my life." And she's saying, "Oh, yeah?" And I say, "Wait a minute, you write about people's lives and you get *paid* for it?" And she says, "Yeah!" And I look at her totally amazed. It was actually one of my favorite scenes because I like the way it was written and acted by both of us.

I also liked that we talked about Daedalus' son flying too close to the sun, because I missed the mythology of Hercules and whenever we can go into those stories, I enjoy it. And the director Michael Lange just filmed it wonderfully and [the director of photography] John MaHaffie lit it just beautifully.

40. Love Takes a Holiday

Writers	Gene O'Neill and Noreen Tobin
Director	Charlie Haskell
Original Air Date	Oct. 21, 1996

Guest cast:

Aphrodite	Alexandra Tydings
Hephaestus	Julian Garner
Leandra	Sarah Smuts-Kennedy
Iagos	Mervyn Smith

Story: "I quit!" says Aphrodite as she walks off her job as the goddess of love. Unfortunately, her decision to "shift career gears" causes upheavals on earth, as women everywhere lose interest in love and leave men pining. The god Hephaestus, who makes the world's strongest weapons in his underground forge, has long been pining for Aphrodite. Taking advantage of his loneliness, his assistant, Iagos, persuades the god to propose to Leandra, a mortal woman who rejected him fifty years earlier. As revenge, Hephaestus cursed her village, leaving it in a state of suspended animation. Hephaestus agrees to let Iagos approach the girl on his behalf so long as he lets her choose freely. But Iagos, who wants to please Hephaestus in order to obtain a shield of invisibility made by the god, is determined to bring the girl back by any means.

Legendary Facts

Iolaus learns that his grandfather died fighting in the Punic Wars. The three Punic Wars between Rome and the North African city of Carthage took place between 264 BC and 146 BC, when Carthage was destroyed.

Iolaus rescues Leandra from Iagos, then learns that she is his grand-mother. When Iagos deceives Leandra into coming with him by warning that otherwise Hephaestus will curse her village forever, Iolaus sets out to save her. He is joined by an unlikely hero—Aphrodite, who now fancies herself a warrior like Hercules. Iolaus defeats Iagos while Aphrodite finds herself attracted to Hephaestus, who willingly releases Leandra. Suddenly more interested in Hephaestus than in grand adventure, Aphrodite happily resumes her reign as the goddess of love.

Mythic connections: Hephaestus, the smith
god, was born lame. His appearance so displeased his mother Hera that she threw him down from Mount Olympus. But Hephaestus made such magnificent metal objects in his underground forge that Hera called him back and even let him marry Aphrodite. Their marriage was troubled, however, by her affairs with other gods and mortals.

> No Metal Panthers were tarnished during the production of this motion picture. When polishing your metal animals, remember to use salt and lemon.

Highlights: Aphrodite finds it's not easy to be a mighty warrior, and
Iolaus finds it's just as difficult to make Aphrodite behave.

Michael's take: It's always a challenge for me when Kevin is not
in an episode. And it wasn't simply a case of Kevin's not being available so they give Iolaus what were Hercules' lines. That episode was actually written with me in mind. . . . I love working with Alexandra Tydings. She is a generous, fabulous actor. She's so different on-screen from what she is in real life. She has the "It" factor, you know, she holds the camera. We had a lot of fun. It was a cheeky episode, and I loved playing the comedy.

41. Mummy Dearest

Writer	Melissa Rosenberg
Director	Anson Williams
Original Air Date	Oct. 28, 1996

Guest cast:

Salmoneus	Robert Trebor
Anuket	Galyn Gorg
Sokar	John Watson
Phineus	Alan de Malmanche
Keb	Henry Vaeoso
Mummy	Mark Newnham

Story: The Egyptian princess Anuket commands Hercules to help her find a stolen mummy. Angered by her arrogance and her ownership of slaves, Hercules refuses. However, when he learns that the mummy has awakened and is hungry for human life, he changes his mind. Also on the mummy's trail is the renegade priest Sokar, who hopes to unleash its powers and use them to become Pharaoh of Egypt. But the merchant Salmoneus, unaware of the mummy's powers, is planning to exhibit it in his new House of Horrors.

Sokar seizes the mummy from Salmoneus, along with a pendant known as an ankh that gives him control of the creature. Knowing the mummy will become unstoppable once it consumes the life force of a human, Sokar turns it loose on Hercules. The son of Zeus traps the mummy in a tomb and riddles it with spikes, but this proves only a temporary setback to a creature already dead. After Hercules rescues Anuket from Sokar, the mummy reappears, kills Sokar, and absorbs the priest's life force. It now threatens to become all-powerful, but Hercules literally unravels this scheme as he grabs one end of the mummy's wrappings and gives a mighty yank, causing the creature to spin furiously before tumbling into a vat of boiling wax. Anuket, grateful to Hercules and to a slave who gave his life for hers, promises that on returning to Egypt she will work to free all slaves.

Highlights: Salmoneus shamelessly hawks his "House of Horrors" until finding that his prize exhibit wants to devour him. The fights between Hercules and the mummy are cleverly staged, and the mummy's final spin cycle is eye-catching.

> Any similarity between our Mummy and the foot-dragging classic we all know and love is purely intentional.

Kevin's take: I still think that was one of the best jobs that the boys from WETA, that's the special effects company down in Wellington, did with the mummy. I mean, it looked great on TV, but in person I think it scared the hell out of me! With a lot of the "monsters" in person, unless they've got the lighting and they put some slime and some special coloring on it, it doesn't look that impressive or that scary. But this thing was spooky-looking. Also, fighting with the mummy was just hilarious. There were a lot of one-liners thrown in. The episode was just perfect for Halloween.

42. Not Fade Away

Writer	John Schulian
Director	T. J. Scott
Original Air Date	Nov. 4, 1996

Guest cast:

Enforcer	Karen Sheperd
Enforcer II	Cynthia Rothrock
Alcmene	Liddy Holloway
Jason	Jeffrey Thomas
Hades	Erik Thomson
Persephone	Andrea Croton
Skouros	Bruce Allpress

Story: Iolaus is mortally wounded battling Hera's new Enforcer, an assassin whose essence is fire and whose only desire is to kill Hercules. Refusing to accept the death of his friend, Hercules carries Iolaus to the other side to seek Hades' intervention. The god of the Underworld tells them that to return Iolaus to life, Hercules must defeat Hera's new Enforcer. Hades also instructs Hercules to team up with  original Enforcer, whose final resting place has not been determined.

Freed of Hera's evil influence, the original Enforcer becomes increasingly sympathetic, even saving Hercules' mother, Alcmene. She also battles the new Enforcer with amazing skill, but perishes as the water that is her life's essence is vaporized by the new Enforcer's searing flames. Hercules tracks Hera's assassin to a forge and dodges her flames, then uses a bellows to blow one of her own fireballs back down her throat, incinerating her. Iolaus, who has finally made peace with his estranged father, Skouros, in the Underworld, is now free to return to the land of the living. Skouros, in turn, is able to enter the Elysian Fields, accompanied by the original Enforcer, who has earned the right to an honorable resting place.

Casting coups:

Rob Tapert, a fan of Hong Kong martial arts movies, outdid himself by casting two legends of the genre, Karen Sheperd and Cynthia Rothrock, as the rival Enforcers. Sheperd reprises her role as the Terminator-like creature from the second-season episode "The Enforcer," and infuses her reformed character with surprising poignance as she becomes ever more human and caring. Rothrock and Sheperd had last battled nearly ten years earlier in the Hong Kong flick *Above the Law*. Rothrock now improves to 2 and 0 lifetime against Sheperd.

Kevin's take:

This is the second episode where we killed Iolaus and brought him back to life. Geez! That's a story line that I get tired of because we've taken the danger of death away from people. I think that's something we should never have touched. If you die on a show, you die! If I can go down there and get Iolaus anytime, then why don't we bring back my family? If you do this at all you do it one time and one time only. And we've already done it at least three or four times on the show.

T. J. Scott directed it and he created some great visuals. And I think people enjoyed watching Cynthia and Karen go at each other! I mean, these two women, between the two of them, must have about seven or eight world titles.

Michael's take:

I enjoyed doing the [stumbling] across the sand, dying, like something out of *Lawrence of Arabia*. I like playing death scenes. And I remember Iolaus' waking up dead and feeling pretty funky about it as opposed to tragic—I played it as a comic beat. . . . Karen Sheperd is a wonderful woman, and we got on well. She would take photographs and then sign them [for us], so that was really cool.

43. Monster Child in the Promised Land

Writer	John Schulian
Director	John T. Kretchmer
Original Air Date	Nov. 11, 1996

Guest cast:

Echidna	Bridget Hoffman
Typhon	Glenn Shadix
Klepto	Grant Heslov
Bluth	Tony Wood
Head Archer	Rebecca Clark
Henchman	Grant Boucher

Story: Typhon and Echidna welcome a new monster to their family: baby Obie. But the thief Klepto, posing as a baby-sitter, kidnaps Obie in order to impress the warlord Bluth. Iolaus comforts the grieving Echidna while Typhon and Hercules set out to find the baby. They want not only to save Obie but to keep him from tasting blood, an act that turned all Echidna's other children into vicious predators.

After Obie nearly falls over a cliff, Klepto rescues him and finds he has begun to like the little monster. By the time Hercules and Typhon catch up to him, Klepto tearfully admits that Bluth now has Obie, and he volunteers to help get the baby back. When they find Bluth's hideout, the warlord attacks Hercules but is impaled on his own sword during the fight. Echidna is overjoyed when Obie arrives home safely and she even forgives Klepto, whose affection for the baby has become obvious.

Kevin's take: Ah, the introduction of Obie—one of the best possible Christmas toys they could have come up with. There are certain episodes I like that have "Muppets," and that are really funny and entertaining. But this episode just didn't work for me because that little five-year-old cute kid Obie just doesn't work as a monster. I did have fun working on this, though, as I always do when Glen Shadix [as Typhon] is in town. He's a great guy.

Michael's take: It was like acting with Muppets. I felt it was so corny. And I felt I was there as wallpaper. I often get asked, "What is your least favorite episode?" And I'm afraid that is it.

44. The Green-Eyed Monster

Writer	Steven Baum
Director	Chuck Braverman
Original Air Date	Nov. 18, 1996

Guest cast:

Aphrodite	Alexandra Tydings
Salmoneus	Robert Trebor
Psyche	Susan Ward
Cupid	Karl Urban
Holidus	Martin Baynton

Story: Aphrodite is jealous of a mortal woman, Psyche. She orders her son, Cupid, to shoot the girl with one of his arrows to pair her off with someone. Cupid, however, is in love with the girl and refuses. Aphrodite implores Hercules to talk to her son, but he guesses her real motives and refuses. So the goddess devises a plot: She sends Salmoneus to Psyche's home and orders Cupid to shoot Psyche so that she'll fall in love with Salmoneus. But Cupid accidentally shoots Hercules, who falls in love with Psyche.

Cupid's jealousy causes him to sprout claws and wings and transform into a green-eyed monster. He grabs Psyche in his talons and carries her away. Hercules finds Aphrodite and learns the truth behind his

sudden love for Psyche, and Cupid's transformation: Hera placed a curse on Cupid following a fight with Aphrodite. Cupid will turn into a monster every time he feels unrequited love. Eventually, the horrible transformation will become permanent.

On his way to rescue Psyche, Hercules begins to think of his late wife and the spell is broken. Meanwhile, Cupid and Psyche are falling in love. But when Hercules appears, Cupid is again transformed, and the two fight. They stop when Aphrodite feeds Psyche a potion causing her to turn into an old woman. When Cupid declares that he still loves Psyche, Hercules suggests a happy ending. Taking his advice, Aphrodite restores Psyche's youth on condition that she become immortal and live with Cupid on Mount Olympus.

Mythic connections:
Psyche was a princess so beautiful that people began worshiping her instead of Aphrodite, who angrily ordered her son, Cupid, to make Psyche fall in love with the ugliest man on earth. But the handsome Cupid fell in love with Psyche himself, and brought her to his palace.

Psyche's own love for Cupid caused her much suffering, including humiliation by Aphrodite. But after Cupid brought Psyche to Olympus to be his wife, Aphrodite forgave her and consented to have Zeus grant Psyche immortality.

Kevin's take:
The transformations of Karl [Urban, as Cupid] into the monster were cool. So was the idea behind them, and Herc's getting all goofy-eyed after getting Cupid's arrow in his rear. I thought it was cute and fun. And Salmoneus was funny because he's always looking for a deal. He's thinking he can make money [selling maps to Psyche's home]. I don't like how Hercules comes out of the spell cast by Cupid's arrow, though. You know, I get tired of these mirror images of Hercules' dead wife popping into his mind and breaking the spell that way. I really think there are better ways we could have come up with. But as a whole, I enjoyed that episode.

45. Prince Hercules

Teleplay:	Robert Bielak
Story	Brad Carpenter
Director	Charles Siebert
Original Air Date	Nov. 25, 1996

Guest cast:

Kirin	Sam Jenkins
Parnassa	Jane Thomas
Lonius	Paul Gittins
Styros	Tom Agee
Lahti	Kate Harcourt
Scarred Man	Steve Wright
Protos	Sean Marshall
Macreus	Nicko Vella
Garas	David Press

Story: Queen Parnassa, the ruler of Kastus, conspires with Hera to make Hercules the leader of her army. Hera has Hercules knocked unconscious while trying to save an elderly couple. Although the blow would have killed any other man, Hercules regains his senses—but not his memory. Just outside Kastus, Parnassa's soldiers stop the travelers and greet Hercules as  their long-lost prince, Milius. Hercules is taken to the palace and introduced to his "wife," Kirin, a princess who is being forced to cooperate in Parnassa's scheme. Hercules also meets Kirin's children, who cannot remember their real father and are told that he has returned at last. Parnassa hopes that by deceiving Hercules into believing he is Milius, he will pledge his loyalty to Hera on Equinox Day.

Iolaus arrives in Kastus and tries to jog Hercules' memory, but the guards arrest him, telling Hercules that the man is an assassin. Hercules meanwhile begins falling in love with Kirin, who finds the courage to defy Parnassa and helps free Iolaus. Disguised as priests, Iolaus and Kirin slip into the Equinox Day ceremony where Hercules is about to pledge his loyalty to Hera forever. They urge Hercules to remember who he really is, and when Iolaus mentions Deianeira's name, Hercules' memory suddenly returns. The two heroes quickly defeat Parnassa's forces, Kirin assumes the throne of Kastus, and Hercules bids a sad farewell to the new family he has come to love.

Highlights:
Iolaus is thrown into a vat of grapes and spends much of the episode purple, a mischance that does not go unnoticed by the overly solicitous Kirin and Hercules.

Kevin's take:
I had a great time on that one. Herc gets amnesia. Every drama show does that! I loved it for a number of reasons. Number one, I got to wear something different! And Ngila [Dickson], our wardrobe woman, did a fantastic job with the costuming. The writers were also great in the [exchanges] with Iolaus, which were very funny. And Herc gets to play a prince who meets his princess. That's really nice!

> Iolaus was not harmed or permanently stained in the production of this motion picture. In fact, thanks to the miracle of sandblasting, his skin was restored to its original color and lustrous sheen.

Michael's take:
We enjoyed that a lot. The whole purple thing. In fact, my fans—there's a hard-core group of Iolaus fans called the "Iolautians" who went to a convention wearing purple T-shirts with the words "Purple because I like it!" printed on the back, because I say that in the show. Now I made that up myself, because the gag was, "Why are you purple? Why are you purple?" And finally I explode, "Because I like it!" because I'm sick of being asked about it, and it was a good moment. . . . It was also good to see Kevin get to play a slightly different side.

46. A Star to Guide Them

Writers	John Schulian and Brian Herskowitz
Director	Michael Levine
Original Air Date	Dec. 16, 1996

Guest cast:

Trinculos	Jon Brazier
Uris	Brent Barrett
King Polonius	Edward Newborn
Queen Maliphone	Denise O'Connell
Captain	Latham Gaines
Loralei	Kirstie O'Sullivan

Story: The Delphic Oracle warns King Polonius that he will be succeeded on the throne by a child outside his own family. Determined to prevent that, Polonius' wife orders him to round up every male child in the province and bring them to the palace. Meanwhile, Hercules and Iolaus are camping on their way to the winter solstice festival. Iolaus has a dream in which he travels down a twisted path, passing a distinctive rock formation and a gnarled old oak tree as two glowing red eyes swoop down at him. Then he is struck by a blinding ray of light, which sunburns his palms. Waking up, Iolaus tells Hercules about his dream and an-

nounces that he must travel north, but can't explain why. Hercules decides to go with him. They meet Trinculos, a thief who also has sunburned palms, and agree to let him travel with them.

The next day, Uris and Loralei flee the king's soldiers with their newborn son, and are rescued by Hercules and Iolaus. The two heroes agree they must stop the king. However, Uris, who also has sunburned palms, wants to continue on his journey north. As the four men travel north, Polonius prays to Hera for help. She sends six members of her Death Squad. Unaware that Loralei has been captured, the men continue to travel north. Iolaus, Uris, and Trinculos share their dream and realize that the answer lies in the king's palace. On arriving they are attacked by Hera's Death Squad, but Hercules overcomes them. The king is killed in battle, the queen exiled, and Uris and Loralei reunite. Looking up at the night sky, the three dreamers see a single star shining on a stable. They follow the light and find a man and woman bent over a tiny cradle as shepherds and their flocks look on.

Mythic connections: Greek myth enters the world of the Bible in this Christmas episode, as Iolaus is portrayed as one of the three wise men traveling to Bethlehem to witness the birth of Jesus.

Highlights: Hercules overcomes the Death Squad enforcers by hurling them into each other so that they explode in a fireball.

Legendary Facts

Hercules accompanies Iolaus to Bethlehem, where Iolaus apparently witnesses the birth of Jesus. Jesus was born around 4 BC (after adjustment of the calendar).

Kevin's take: I thought it was a potentially touching episode, because I love Christmas and the whole holiday season, but it just didn't come off. . . . I think it's fine to break a rule and do a biblical episode on *Hercules*, though I personally would like to get back to more of the [Greek] myths.

Michael's take: I said to Rob Tapert, "Rob, do you realize [we're making Iolaus one of the wise men]?!" And his answer was, "Sir, it's Christmas!" That episode starts out really well, Kevin and I do some kind of funny and funky things at the beginning and near the end, but it just becomes a little bit sappy and predictable. But then again, there's nothing wrong with having an uplifting sort of episode, as this one tried to be.

47. The Lady and the Dragon

Writer	Eric Estrin and Michael Berlin
Director	Oley Sassone
Original Air Date	Jan. 20, 1997

Guest cast:

Cynea	Catherine Bell
Adamis	Rene Naufahu
Orenth	Geoff Dolan
Toth	Grant Tilly
Lemnos	Charles Pierard
Leandra	Phaedra Hurst
Gyger	Alexander Gandar
Zachariah	Buzz Moller

Story: Hercules heads for Laurentia after learning that many comrades who helped overthrow the warlord Adamis have mysteriously disappeared there. Passing through a burned-out village, Hercules encounters old friends who tell him that Adamis has returned from exile and is attacking villages. Iolaus also heads for Laurentia with Cynea, a young woman he defended from thugs in a tavern. She confides that her fiancé was killed by the dragon Braxis in Laurentia, and Iolaus offers to fight the beast. But Braxis is not the evil monster everyone fears. Instead he is a lonely baby dragon who has been tricked by Adamis into believing that humans want to kill him and that Hercules and Iolaus are responsible for his mother's death.

Iolaus sets out to kill the dragon, bearing one of Cynea's purple scarves tied to his sword for luck. When Hercules arrives, Cynea tells him of Iolaus' plan, and Hercules rushes off to save him. But, like Braxis, Cynea is not what she seems: She is Adamis' sister, and wants nothing more than to see Hercules destroyed and her brother once more in power.

At the dragon's lair, Iolaus finds it no easy task to defeat a flying dragon, especially when it breathes fire. Hercules tries to reason with Braxis, then captures him in a chain mail net. Before Iolaus can kill the dragon, Hercules shows him a pit filled with a half dozen swords with purple scarves tied to them. Iolaus realizes that Cynea was behind their friends' deaths. Adamis, Cynea, and their troops appear, and in the battle that follows, Adamis accidentally stabs Cynea. Adamis then tries to kill Braxis and boasts that he also killed Braxis' mother. But Hercules frees the enraged beast, who engulfs Adamis in a fireball. No longer controlled by Adamis' lies, Braxis flies off toward home, rejoicing in his freedom.

Highlights: In about four eye-catching minutes of screen time, the dragon talks, flies, fights, breathes fire, and rescues a child.

Kevin's take: I thought there was huge potential there, but as a whole I was a little disappointed with the story line. And I wasn't crazy about the voice of the dragon—it was such an obvious, comical beat to use this little kid's voice, but I wish we had done something more majestic with it. Some parts of [the episode] worked and I thought there were some good humorous beats in there between Michael and me. . . . Working with Catherine Bell, who is on the series *Jag* now, was a pleasure.

Michael's take: I thought it was groovy to have a dragon, but it was underwritten. It didn't feel like we were adults in that, but more like kids. And the show doesn't work for me when Iolaus and Hercules feel like children themselves. I'm not saying we can't have childish behavior, but not this foolish. It was cool doing the special effects with the dragon. There was a claw which was operated over a guy's hand like a glove, a *giant* glove. And there was a dragon's head that was solid, with no mouth moving, which we used in a lot of reverse high-angle shots. But apart from that, we were acting to a pole off camera with a cape stuck to it! And we were just miming the jumping and running.

[On Iolaus' scenes with Cynea:] I was tired of Iolaus always flirting with the girls, and I was trying to play a little more [seriously]. He needed to be really struck by this woman so that when he was betrayed it was painful.

48. Long Live the King

Teleplay	Sonny Gordon
Story	Patricia Manney
Director	Timothy Bond
Original Air Date	Jan. 27, 1997

Guest cast:

Niobe	Lisa Ann Hadley
Hector	Derek Payne
Linus	Ross McKellar
Xenon	Roger Oakley
Boron	Peter Ford
Arcarious	Crawford Thomson
Phaedron	Walter Brown
Euriana	Ilona Rodgers
Cleitus	Ranald Hendriks
Choleus	David Downs

Story: Iolaus sets out to help his cousin King Orestes, who is trying to form a peaceful League of Kingdoms. The treacherous King Xenon pretends to consider the idea but then has Orestes murdered. Iolaus promises his dying cousin that he will take his place and make the peace plan work.

Disguised as the king, Iolaus travels with Queen Niobe to meet with

Xenon, who agrees to support the peace plan provided that he can accompany them as they present their plan to the other kings. In Marathon, King Phaedron invites them all to a feast that night. Iolaus and Niobe, who have struggled against their feelings for each other, acknowledge their love but are interrupted by Phaedron's guards, who accuse Iolaus of trying to kill their king.

Iolaus' accuser turns out to be Xenon, who has framed him by having Phaedron wounded with one of Orestes' distinctive arrows. Xenon plans to have Phaedron murdered after Iolaus' execution, and invites three other kings to the palace, planning to kill them as well and take over their lands.

Niobe convinces Phaedron's wife to help her prove Iolaus' innocence. And with the help of Niobe and the king's aide, Hector, Iolaus saves the visiting kings by defeating Xenon and his soldiers in battle. Iolaus then leaves Niobe to continue her quest to make the League of Kingdoms a reality.

Michael's take: I enjoyed that immensely. Playing two characters is always great. It was a good challenge for me, and I actually think there's a third story in there somewhere. I enjoyed the killing of [my character] Orestes, even though the fans went bananas over it. And Lisa Ann [Hadley, as Niobe] and I had already established [a rapport] that we were really able to capitalize on.

49. Surprise

Writer	Alex Kurtzman
Director	Oley Sassone
Original Air Date	Feb. 3, 1997

Guest cast:

Callisto	Hudson Leick
Alcmene	Liddy Holloway
Jason	Jeffrey Thomas
Iphicles	Kevin Smith
Falafel	Paul Norell

Story: Hera promises Callisto, now suffering in Tartarus, one more day of life and a chance at immortality if she agrees to kill Hercules. Callisto eagerly accepts and shows up at the home of Hercules' mother, Alcmene, who is preparing a surprise birthday party for her son. Callisto offers a surprise of her own, drugging Alcmene and her family and friends. When Hercules arrives, they are lying on the floor unconscious. Callisto beams a greeting: "Surprise!" She explains she has used a drug that attacks the mind, rendering its victims mad before killing them. If Hercules wants to save them, he must get her safe passage through the Labyrinth of the Gods to the Tree of Life, for the fruit of the Tree will cure their madness—and make her immortal. Hercules reluctantly agrees, and follows Callisto toward the Labyrinth.

Hercules' friends and family awake, but their nightmares are just beginning. Alcmene's son Iphicles explodes with jealousy at his mother for favoring his half brother Hercules. Alcmene sees an apparition of Hercules, who tells her he's crossed over to the other side and beckons her to follow. Iolaus sees himself as an old man, still clinging to his youthful ways.

Hercules saves Callisto from the Labyrinth's snakelike vines and other traps, but she tricks him into taking a wrong turn and watches the large metal Gates of Hephaestus begin to close behind him. As Callisto eats from the Tree of Life, she gains her prize of immortality just as Hercules escapes from between the metal gates. Callisto viciously attacks him, but he confines her in the Labyrinth: an immortal with nowhere to go. Hercules then rescues his mother and friends by feeding them fruit from the Tree of Life.

Highlights: First-time writer Alex Kurtzman delivers the goods: "Surprise" features action galore, sharp exchanges between Hercules and Callisto about good and evil, and hallucinations by Hercules' friends and family that reveal their darkest fears.

> Hercules' Party Pants were not harmed during the production of this motion picture.

Casting coups: Hudson Leick is riveting as Callisto, a recurring villainess on *Xena* who makes her first appearance on *Hercules*.

Kevin's take: "Surprise" was a lot of fun. It gave all of us a different personality to play with. It's good to give Hercules a foe who is not simply a mortal: a creature or, in this case, Callisto when she's possessed by Hera [and after she becomes immortal]. Hercules should be able to defeat any mortal easily, so it makes sense to have Hercules battle mythological creatures and gods, who are stronger than he is.

Michael's take: I thought it was a good, spooky episode. In my drugged condition I see myself as a lecherous old man. I enjoyed that, though it took an hour and a half of makeup, mostly latex and tissue paper—sort of a poor man's aging technique. But that was fine because we thought it should be pretty grotesque. And I loved working with Hudson Leick. I think she's got a real quality to her that is mesmerizing.

50. Encounter

Writer	Jerry Patrick Brown
Director	Charlie Haskell
Original Air Date	Feb. 10, 1997

Guest cast:

Serena/Hind	Sam Jenkins
Ares	Kevin Smith
Strife	Joel Tobeck
Nestor	Steve Hall
Hemnor	David Mackie

Story: Hercules and Iolaus set off to rescue the Golden Hind, a half woman, half deer belonging to Ares who is being hunted by a local prince named Nestor. While searching for the Hind, Hercules pauses to help a wounded boy. The Hind appears to him as a beautiful woman, Serena, who kneels beside the child, traces her hands over his body, and heals him. Moved by her beauty and kindness, Hercules begins to fall in love with her, not realizing she is the Golden Hind.

When Nestor asks Ares for the Hind's blood, Ares' impudent nephew Strife urges his uncle to cooperate, knowing that the blood of the hind can kill a god—or the son of a god, like Hercules. Meanwhile, the Hind mistakes Iolaus for one of Nestor's hunters and wounds him with a poisoned arrow. Hercules finds Serena and desperately urges her to come back with him to heal his friend. At first she hesitates for fear of being

cornered by bigoted humans, but after Hercules defends the Hind against Nestor's troops, she reappears as Serena to save Iolaus.

Hoping to use Serena to destroy Hercules, Ares traps her in a pit of thorns, claiming it is for her own protection. Hercules helps her escape but drops of her blood remain on the thorns, which Ares gives to Nestor as poison for his arrows. Nestor fires an arrow at Hercules, but he seizes it in midflight. As Nestor flees in panic, he blunders into one of his own traps and is killed. Now Hercules and Serena face a thorny problem of another sort, as they seek to live together despite Ares' schemes and their different worlds.

Mythic connections: For his third labor, Hercules had to bring back the golden-horned deer of Cerynia, which was sacred to Artemis, goddess of the hunt. Hercules pursued the animal for a full year before capturing it and carrying it on his shoulders. Artemis angrily scolded Hercules, but when he explained that he had to obey King Eurystheus, she allowed him to take the deer to the king and then set the animal free. One tale relates that the deer was once a nymph named Taygete, a daughter of the Titan Atlas. When Zeus fell in love with Taygete, Artemis changed her into a doe in a vain effort to guard her from Zeus' advances.

> The Golden Hind was not harmed during the production of this motion picture. To order a Hind of your own call 1-800-555-HIND.

Highlights: A wonderfully written episode and the first by the series' new head writer, Jerry Brown. The amusing exchanges between Ares and his oh-so-hip nephew Strife reveal that even the Olympians must contend with generation gaps.

Casting coups: Kevin Smith as Ares, a recurring character on *Xena*, brings his charming villainy to *Hercules* for the first time. Joel Tobeck's Strife is a villian with attitude who tests Ares' patience more than Hercules and Xena combined.

Kevin's take: I liked that trilogy, and there were some wonderful exchanges. I loved the scene where the man is trying to explain to Iolaus and me that his village is being terrorized by a creature: "A doe." "A deer?" "A female deer?" That was very funny. Some of the [computer-generated] effects could have been better; I thought the Hind looked kind of goofy. And cheap, you know. I don't know if they were rushed, but these

FX guys are so incredibly talented and do some really great things, but I wince when I look at the Hind.

Michael's take: This was a powerful story arc, to have Herc get married and then again to lose his wife. Very powerful stuff to play with. Sam Jenkins, who plays Serena, brought a really special quality to that role. . . . Yes, exactly, offscreen chemistry carries over. Kevin and Sam had met on the set of "Prince Hercules." And I remember the night when they were talking. Kevin was thunderstruck by Sam and he turned to me and said, "Michael!" And I just said, "I can't help you, Kevin!" He was really quite struck by her. So I remember that moment. I was saying, Wow, watch this develop. And I was right.

51. When a Man Loves a Woman

Writers	Gene O'Neill and Noreen Tobin
Director	Charlie Haskell
Original Air Date	Feb. 17, 1997

Guest cast:

Serena/Hind	Sam Jenkins
Joxer	Ted Raimi
Deianeira	Tawny Kitaen
Ares	Kevin Smith
Strife	Joel Tobeck
Klonus	Simon Lethwaite
Aeson	Paul McIver
Ilea	Rose McIver

Story: Having fallen deeply in love with Serena, Hercules asks her to marry him. She hesitates, saying that she belongs to Ares and cannot survive in the mortal world. But she finds the courage to ask Ares for her freedom. Ares pretends to grant her wish, but vows to destroy her relationship with Hercules.

Serena is already finding it difficult to live among humans. A group of villagers tries to kill her, and she is saved only by Hercules' intervention. Convinced that his friend is headed for disaster, Iolaus refuses to be best man at the wedding. But Hercules moves ahead with his plans. He goes to the Underworld to visit Deianeira, hoping to receive her blessing, but she is grief-stricken at the thought of his remarrying. Hercules reassures her that his love for her and their children will never change.

Hercules then confronts Ares and demands that he stop interfering. Ares tells him that the gods will agree to the marriage if Hercules will surrender his strength and if Serena will give up her existence as the Golden Hind and become mortal. Valuing their love for each other above all else, Hercules and Serena each agree to Ares' conditions.

Just as Hercules and Serena begin their private marriage ceremony, Iolaus shows up to serve as best man, explaining that he could never miss such a momentous occasion in his best friend's life. And from the Elysian Fields Deianeira conveys to Hercules her happiness and her blessing.

Highlights: In one of the series' most eventful episodes, Hercules proposes to Serena, battles Ares, confronts Deianeira in the Underworld, loses and regains his friend Iolaus, and remarries.

Kevin's take: I fought and fought and fought, and lost the battle against having Iolaus act like such a jerk. Now, he simply would not walk away from Hercules if he knew there was any danger at all. Even if he didn't want Hercules to marry this deer-woman, he would still come to the wedding! Yes, he shows up at the end, but they're trying to create some kind of dramatic tension between Hercules and Iolaus that never worked. Apart from that, I liked the episode and the larger story.

Michael's take: Why would Iolaus not be Hercules' best man? We wrestled with it but we couldn't change it. You know, these two guys have been friends for life, they support each other. If something bad is going to happen to Hercules, Iolaus isn't going to run away, but [in this episode] he does walk away. And Kevin and I had such a difficult time making that work. I tried to play it that it was really agony for Iolaus to make this decision but that if his friend was so set on marrying, he couldn't really stay away.

52. Judgment Day

Writer	Robert Bielak
Director	Gus Trikonis
Original Air Date	Feb. 24, 1997

Guest cast:

Serena/Hind	Sam Jenkins
Ares	Kevin Smith
Strife	Joel Tobeck
Xena	Lucy Lawless
Gabrielle	Renee O'Connor
Zeus	Peter Vere-Jones
Veklos	Bill Johnson
Elder	Huntly Eliot
Ares	Kevin Smith
Atropos	Elizabeth Pendergrass

Story: While Hercules and Serena are enjoying their honeymoon, Xena and Gabrielle learn of the marriage—and Hercules' loss of his strength—from two drunks in a bar, who turn out to be Ares and Strife. Ares hopes to drive Xena to kill Hercules, which would both rid him of his heroic half brother and perhaps renew Xena's devotion to the god of war. Ares has already succeeded in greatly weakening Hercules, who tries to defend Serena against a group of thugs but is severely beaten until Iolaus and Serena herself intervene. Instead of being grateful for their help, he lashes out at them, his mind clouded by Strife, the god of discord.

That night, Strife visits Hercules with a terrible dream in which Serena taunts him. When Hercules awakens, he is covered in blood and Serena is dead. A lynch mob hunts Hercules but Xena appears to help Iolaus and a badly wounded Hercules scatter the attackers. Although at first Hercules believes he may be responsible for Serena's death, Xena helps him realize that Ares is behind the tragedy. With the help of his friends, Hercules tricks Strife into boasting that he murdered Serena. Hercules attacks Strife but has trouble fighting against the young god until Zeus suddenly appears and restores his son's power. Hercules defeats Strife, who barely escapes with Ares. Then, as Xena chants a funeral dirge, Hercules bids an anguished farewell to his wife Serena.

Mythic connections:
Hercules was happily married to his first wife, Megara. But Hera drove him mad, so that he killed his children and, some sources say, Megara as well. "Judgment Day" softens this gruesome theme, showing that Hercules was tormented by the god Strife, then framed by Ares for killing his wife though he was in no way responsible. Iolaus confides to Xena his fear that this lie might sully Hercules' reputation forever. They set about clearing Hercules so that future generations will remember him as he truly was—a hero.

Highlights:
Hercules discovers his wife has been murdered; suffers his first real beatings by mortals; regains his strength in time to pummel the god Strife; and encounters his father, Zeus, for the first time in the series.

Casting coups:
Lucy Lawless return as Xena and Renee O'Connor makes her first appearance on *Hercules* as Gabrielle.

Kevin's take:
Of the three episodes in this story arc, I liked this one best because of the emotional value. I liked playing the scenes when Serena dies, the exchanges I had with Iolaus, the fight scene with Ares and Strife, and the final scene, saying good-bye to her at the grave site. I thought it was a strong, emotional episode and I had fun as an actor doing it. I thought it was a good chance for me to bite my acting chops into something different than the normal *Hercules* show.

I have to say I had a problem with Xena's coming in and saving the day. Here's the inconsistency: Xena and Iolaus are mortals but they beat people up pretty easily—five, six guys at a time. Now, even if you take away Herc's strength, he's still six three. He's still over two hundred pounds. He still is a big, bruising guy. But now, suddenly he's helpless [because the gods have taken away his special powers]? It was really a sticky plot point that nobody wanted to answer. Let's face it, Hercules is the strongest man in the world. Otherwise, let's rename the guy, because then we've left the mythology.

53. Lost City

Teleplay	Robert Bielak
Story	Robert Bielak and Liz Friedman
Director	Charlie Haskell
Original Air Date	Mar. 3, 1997

Guest cast:

Salmoneus	Robert Trebor
Moira	Fiona Mogridge
Kamaros	Matthew Chamberlain
Aurora	Marama Jackson
Regina	Amber Sainsbury
Lorel	Hannah Malloch

Story: Salmoneus finds a pile of gold bullion, but before he can take it he falls down an unseen shaft and disappears. Iolaus and Moira later seek shelter in the same temple while searching for Iolaus' missing cousin. Iolaus tumbles down the same shaft that claimed Salmoneus, and Moira follows him. At the bottom they find a city inhabited by members of a  religious cult. Salmoneus approaches them but does not recognize Iolaus. He gives the pair a tour of this utopian community. Iolaus and Moira soon find out that the ruler, Kamaros, is a master at mind control who laces his followers' food with drugs. Kamaros has even convinced his people that Lorel, a ten-year-old girl, is their supreme god.

Iolaus and Moira run into Iolaus' cousin, but she cannot remember him any more than Salmoneus. Moira meets Lorel's sister and with Iolaus they plot to rescue the girl. But Iolaus is caught by Kamaros' guards and sent for "reeducation" through drugs, hypnosis, and other tortures. Iolaus emerges sounding like the a perfectly programmed cult member, but he has secretly used his knowledge of meditation to resist the brainwashing. When Kamaros tries to reprogram Moira, Iolaus springs at him. As they battle, Iolaus recognizes Kamaros as the warlord Karkis, the Butcher of Thessaly. His identity exposed, Karkis rigs the lost city to self-destruct. But Iolaus kills Karkis and leads the former cult followers to safety before the lost city collapses.

Highlights: The episode parodies both the hippie movement of the sixties and the many cults whose leaders have grown rich and powerful preaching the joys of giving up wealth and power.

Michael's take: I had an absolute ball doing that. And that is an episode which Kevin was originally supposed to be in. If you listen to some of what I say, you can tell it's Hercules' lines. I loved that sixties send-up, and I was trying to be a gritty sort of hero when I was being brainwashed. It was just highly charged action, and Bruce Willis–type acting. We were always looking for the one-liners—you know, the hero in extreme circumstances who comes up with gritty sayings. And Robert Trebor [as Salmoneus] was just great to work with on that episode. He went over the top, and so all I had to do was pull back. This episode was directed by Charlie Haskell, a New Zealander, who encouraged us to have fun with it.

54. Les Contemptibles

Writer	Brian Herskowitz
Director	Charlie Haskell
Original Air Date	Apr. 14, 1997

Guest cast:

Robert	Kevin Sorbo
Jean-Pierre	Michael Hurst
François Demarigny	Robert Trebor
Marie DeValle	Danielle Cormack
Captain Gerard	Patrick Wilson

Story: The year is 1789 in Troyes, France. Count François Demarigny produces a yellow rose and convinces the Lady Marie DeValle that he is the daring revolutionary the Chartreuse Fox. DeValle asks why he would risk his life for peasants, and he tells her that he believes there is good in every man. When their carriage is attacked by the bandits Robert and Jean-Pierre, François gets the upper hand. However, at Marie's suggestion he agrees to try to turn the men into heroes.

Holding their attention with promises of money, François begins to tell Robert and Jean-Pierre about Hercules, the champion of the common man. They are moved, and urge Marie to prove her own commitment to the revolution by giving them money. When she leaves, the three men drop their act and reveal themselves as con men out to get Marie's wealth. When Marie returns, they are suddenly surprised by the police. Marie hides the three men but disappears with their money, leaving a single yellow rose—she is the Chartreuse Fox.

After Marie is captured by Captain Gerard's guards and sentenced to die at the guillotine, Robert is moved to save her, just as Hercules would do. He and his reluctant friends battle Gerard's men, and inspire the peasants to join in the battle. Marie herself impressively defeats Gerard in a duel, then joins her new allies Robert, Jean-Pierre, and François in the fight for justice.

Legendary Facts

French look-alikes of Hercules, Iolaus, and Salmoneus fight for "liberty, equality, and fraternity," the principles behind the French Revolution. The French Revolution succeeded in 1789. Records of Hercules' participation remain sketchy.

Highlights:
This clever parody of the series allows Kevin Sorbo and Michael Hurst to give splendid comic turns to their usual characters.

Kevin's take:
I absolutely adored this episode! I would love to do more like that. Michael and I had a blast, and [Robert] Trebor was wonderful in it. Danielle Cormack, who played the fair lady, was fantastic! She is a sexy lady and a wonderful actress. One scene that was cut for reasons of time had my character, Robert, always quoting people, and it drives my companions nuts. There's a scene where they're both coming up behind me together, ready to strangle me, and of course I don't even know it. I saw the dailies of that scene, and it's very funny. Another scene cut for time had us giving a big group hug when we think that we've fooled her, and we improvised quite a bit!

Michael's take:
There was a reluctance by the writers and the producers to let us do French accents. And we just kept saying, Guys, we understand that you're worried that people may not be able to understand us, but this is just so funny! It's such a wild idea. So finally they let us do the accent. We played this episode in the manner of grand farce. And I loved being that sort of scruffy, dirty individual. We would send up [the characters] as much as we could, and [the director] Charlie Haskell let us go for it.

The French accents depicted in this motion picture are entirely fictitious. Any similarity to actual accents, living or dead, is purely coincidental. Vive La Révolution!

55. The Reign of Terror

Writer	John Kirk
Director	Rodney Charters
Original Air Date	Apr. 21, 1997

Guest cast:

Salmoneus	Robert Trebor
Palamedes	Bruce Phillips
Melanippe	Rainer Grant
Augeas	Grant Bridger
Aphrodite	Alexandra Tydings
Machus	Laurie Dee
Stichius	Brett Stewart
Silicles	Alex Moffat
Minteus	Albert Belz

Story: King Augeas has gone mad and believes he is Zeus, king of the gods. He orders his subjects to have a temple of Aphrodite rededicated to his "wife," Hera, an act that leaves the goddess of love fuming. Aphrodite comes to earth to save her temple but learns from the king's stable master, Palamedes, that the people want her to worry more about protecting her worshipers from the mad king. She is impressed by his honesty and devotion, and decides to help.

Hera alone is pleased by Augeas' madness, granting the king superhuman powers and telling him he can keep them if he kills Hercules. Augeas eagerly tries out his lightning bolts, causing a roof to collapse and killing Palamedes. To Hercules' surprise, Aphrodite shows her compassion for Palamedes by surrounding his body with an aura that will prevent his spirit from departing until nightfall. The goddess then tries to stop Augeus from doing any more damage, but Hera has her imprisoned. Hercules confronts the king, who hurls his lightning bolts at him. Using a shield-size square of copper, Hercules deflects one of Augeas' blasts toward Palamedes, who convulses back to life. When Augeas unleashes another blast, Hercules deflects it back at the king, who is jolted back to his senses—at least until he announces that he is Ulysses. For Aphrodite, the happy ending lasts longer, for her kindness toward Palamedes and her courage toward Augeas have shown Hercules a side to her character that he had never before seen.

Mythic connections: Augeas owned vast

herds of cattle on the isle of Elis but his stables had not been cleaned for many years. For his fifth labor, Hercules was commanded to clean the stables in a single day, which seemed an impossible task. But Hercules showed he had cunning as well as

> The Sheep's political and cultural independence was restored after the production of this motion picture. Run Free Ewe Wildebeast!

strength, diverting a river to wash out the stables, then returning the river to its course. "Augean stables" symbolizes a condition of extreme, almost hopeless dirt and disorder.

Highlights: In a comical cameo, Salmoneus makes a bid for the ma-

nure cleanup concession of King Augeas' famous stables. Hercules and Aphrodite have their first heart-to-heart sibling talks. And the lightning bolts take on as many functions as a Swiss Army knife, serving as weapons for Augeus, a resuscitator for Palamedes, and therapy for the hallucinating king.

Kevin's take: I thought Grant [Bridger, as Augeus] did a great job.

I enjoyed working with [the director] Rodney Charters, who is a friend of mine and was the director of photography on *Kull*. I remember there were a lot of fight scenes and some good humor in that one. And I always like working with Alex [Alexandra Tydings, as Aphrodite].

56. The End of the Beginning

Writer	Paul Robert Coyle
Director	James Whitmore, Jr.
Original Air Date	Apr. 28, 1997

Guest cast:

Autolycus	Bruce Campbell
Serena/Hind	Kara Zediker
Ares	Kevin Smith
Strife	Joel Tobeck
Falafel	Paul Norell
King Quallus	Ian Watkin
Hemnor	David Mackie

Story: Hercules is in the village of Cerynia, where he and Serena were so happy, when he leaps to defend Falafel from a group of bullies. During the ensuing brawl, everyone except Hercules suddenly freezes. Someone, he realizes, has stopped time. The culprit turns out to be Autolycus, who has stolen the Chronos gemstone. When Hercules tries to grab the stone from him, he and Autolycus vanish, then reappear in Cerynia five years earlier.

The stone is crushed under the wheels of a wagon, but Hercules reminds Autolycus that it still exists in this earlier time. Autolycus tries to steal the Chronos stone, only to meet himself, the Autolycus of five years before. The two thieves join forces while arguing incessantly over which is the handsomer, cleverer, and braver.

Seeing a firestorm, Hercules sets off to investigate. He finds several dead Golden Hinds, all killed by Zeus. But one has escaped, and as Hercules watches, Ares transforms her into Serena. Knowing of the tragic fate that awaits her, Hercules begs Ares to leave Serena alone. But Ares sees in Serena a chance to kill his half brother, and he has Strife shoot Hercules with an arrow dipped in her blood. Hercules almost dies, but Serena heals him. Ares then tries to kill Serena but Hercules defeats him in battle and forces him to spare her human half. "What is she to you, anyway?" Ares complains. "She was my wife!" Hercules roars. Ares obeys him, and although the Hind perishes, Serena is left alive.

Autolycus manages to steal the Chronos stone, enabling him and Hercules to return to their own time. Suddenly Hercules sees Serena, now a happy wife and mother. In changing the course of history, Hercules has wiped out everything they would have shared together, but he has spared her life.

Highlights: The squabbling of Autolycus with his younger self is memorable.

Kevin's take: I liked the episode, and I always have a blast working with Bruce [Campbell]. . . . [On why Sam Jenkins did not reprise the role of Serena:] Here's the deal on that. Sam was busy shooting something back in America, so they cast a woman who's a good seven inches shorter. That's taking nothing away from the new actress, who is very sweet, but when you run Sam's episodes and this one so close together, fans are going to notice! They can see the difference. . . . But beyond the look, you know, the chemistry wasn't there that I had with Sam. And fans did like her character.

57. War Bride

Writers	Adam Armus and Nora Kay Foster
Director	Kevin Sorbo
Original Air Date	May 5, 1997

Guest cast:

Melissa	Lisa Chappell
Alexa	Josephine Davison
Tolas	Chic Littlewood
Gordius	Ross McKellar
Acteon	Mark Raffety
Hargus	Marcle Kalma

Story: Princess Melissa of Alcina is appalled at the prospect of her impending marriage to Prince Gordius of Lathia, whom she has never seen. Then her problems worsen as she is kidnapped by two thugs secretly hired by her younger sister, Alexa, who is plotting to become queen.

Strolling through a village, Hercules recognizes Melissa chained with a group of slave girls. He frees her and agrees to escort her home. Back in Alcina, Alexa suffocates her father and seizes the throne. She orders her army to prepare for war against the Lathians, and tests her father's greatest weapon, a catapult called the Fist of Tolas, against an innocent village. Hercules encounters the wounded Gordius, who has been searching for Melissa, and brings the two together. Their attraction is instant. As Alexa's troops attack the remaining villagers, Hercules turns the tide of battle by breaking the Fist of Tolas. Alexa flees but is bowled over by a punch thrown by her sister. Melissa then happily announces to Hercules that the idea of spending her life with Gordius sounds better and better.

Highlights: Iolaus does not take kindly to Melissa's spoiled ways, and makes that clear while carrying her across a stream. Hercules makes a rare godlike leap of several hundred feet to snap the deadly catapult.

Kevin's take: This was the second time I directed. I got wonderful help from John Mahaffie, our director of photography, and the rest of the crew. They always come to my aid, and they really helped me on this episode a lot. I liked the episode, but the story was schizophrenic [swinging from comic to tragic]. There are scenes in there I really liked. When we first pick up Melissa, there are some funny moments between Iolaus and her while crossing the river. And at the beginning Iolaus and I take a mud bath, in order to relax.

Michael's take: I feel it was an episode that didn't quite know what it was. It started out as a really humorous premise and then it sort of turned in the middle. But a lot of fun to do. Working with Lisa Chappell was great, and so was being directed by Kevin.

58. A Rock and a Hard Place

Writers	Roberto Orci and Alex Kurtzman
Director	Robert Trebor
Original Air Date	May 12, 1997

Guest cast:

Cassus	Lindsey Ginter
Perius	Tony Ward
Lyna	Lee-Jane Foreman
Geryon	Sterling Cathman
Nico	Caleb Ross
Villager #1	Graeme Moran
Little girl	Hannah Collins

Story: Accused of murdering a family, a man named Cassus flees an angry mob until he is cornered by Hercules and Iolaus. The desperate man takes a girl hostage, but the threat does not keep a villager named Perius from firing his crossbow at Cassus, nearly killing the child. Tossing the terrified girl aside, Cassus takes refuge in an abandoned mine. When Hercules follows him inside, Cassus attacks him with a knife and accidentally triggers a rockslide that pins him under a boulder. Hercules tells Cassus that he will bleed to death immediately if the stone is lifted. The cynical Cassus, realizing he is doomed, begins to tell Hercules his story. He relates how he arrived in the village looking for work when a scream drew him to the house of the murdered family. By the time he entered, everyone was dead and he was mistaken for the actual killer. Hercules is skeptical but refuses to let Cassus be lynched by Perius and the other villagers. As Cassus grows weaker he confides that he has a son, Nico, whom he describes as a runaway. Iolaus finds the boy living among delinquents on the streets, but learns that Nico never ran away—his father abandoned him. Nico returns to confront Cassus, who, desperate to keep his son from repeating his own terrible mistakes, finally confesses that he murdered the family when he was caught stealing. These are Cassus' dying words and, Nico realizes, his first real act of courage and caring.

Highlights:
A gripping episode, well written and directed, that features intense performances by Kevin Sorbo and Michael Hurst. Action is an afterthought in this dark drama, but Iolaus displays some flamboyant moves with a staff in beating up two rowdy drunks.

> *No Convicts were squished like a bug during the production of this motion picture.*

Kevin's take:
Robert Trebor directed this and he did a wonderful job. He should be proud of his work, because eighty-five percent of the episode is set in a cave and yet he did original things with the camera that make it really interesting to watch. I like episodes like this that feature a little more drama. Lindsay Ginter, who played the bad guy under the rock, did some amazing work. He kept his emotional level during the scene where he dies. We had to shoot so many different angles, and this guy just had tears coming out of his face all day long!

Michael's take:
This was Robert Trebor's directing debut. He wanted it to be quite gritty, and it was. He would say, "Guys, don't send this up, this is very serious." He actually had me go away with the young guy who played the son, and we had to do an improvisational exercise to get the right level to the scene. Which was great, I'm all for that. And Lindsay Ginter, who played the bad guy, was great to work with and a real "Method actor." He knew how to get the tears!

59. Atlantis

Writers	Alex Kurtzman and Roberto Orci
Director	Gus Trikonis
Original Air Date	May 19, 1997

Guest cast:

Cassandra	Claudia Black
Skirner	William Davis
Demitrius	Ross Harper
Panthius	James Beaumont
Aurelius	Norman Fairley

Story: Hercules is shipwrecked on the island of Atlantis after a bolt of lightning tears through the hull of his vessel. He is helped by a woman named Cassandra, who tells him of her dreams that Atlantis will be destroyed. Her visions always come true, she says, but she fears to tell the citizens because they shun her as a nonconformist, living on the fringes of

their advanced society. Hercules urges her to tell the council and goes with her to the city. Sleek gliders soar overhead, powered by crystals and used by the king to guard the island. Cassandra warns the council of the island's impending doom, but they mock her. The king, Panthius, is furious and orders Cassandra and her friend arrested for spreading unrest. The king reveals his secret weapon, a giant crystal cannon, which Hercules realizes caused his shipwreck. Hercules escapes and discovers a cavern where slaves toil, mining the crystals. There he finds that the foundation of the island has been undermined and is dangerously unstable. Hercules rescues Cassandra just as an earthquake strikes the island. The king is crushed by his falling cannon, but Hercules and Cassandra soar to safety in one of the gliders.

Legendary Facts

Writing in the fourth century BC, the philosopher Plato described the island of Atlantis as having vanished long before.

Mythic connections:

The lost continent of Atlantis was an island larger than all Asia. It lay beyond the Pillars of Hercules, which stood at the western edge of the Mediterranean Sea. Plato described how the citizens of Atlantis prospered under the rule of good kings. But each generation of kings became more tyrannical until they tried to conquer the world and were at last defeated by the Athenians. A flood later destroyed Atlantis and it sank forever.

Other myths tell of Cassandra, the daughter of the King of Troy. She received the gift of prophecy from the god Apollo, but when she spurned him he cursed her, so that no one would ever believe her predictions. When the Greek armies left a wooden horse outside of Troy, Cassandra warned her countrymen not to bring it within their gates, but they laughed at her and dragged the horse inside. That night Greek soldiers emerged from the horse and sacked Troy, and Cassandra became a captive of the Greek king Agamemnon.

Highlights: Hercules experiences culture shock on

seeing the futuristic inventions that are everyday machines in Atlantis.

Kevin's take: Probably one of our most expen-

sive episodes, and heavy in CGI [computer-generated imaging] effects. . . . I enjoyed working with Claudia Black, an actress from Australia. There was a great re-

WARNING: Crystal-waves were used during the production of this motion picture. Pregnant women should leave the room immediately.

sponse from fans who urged that Claudia return, not necessarily as a love interest but as someone who should team up with Hercules again.

PRODUCTION CREDITS

Starring:

Kevin Sorbo as Hercules

Michael Hurst as Iolaus

Produced by:

RENAISSANCE PICTURES
IN ASSOCIATION WITH
UNIVERSAL TELEVISION ENTERPRISES

Executive Producer: Rob Tapert

Executive Producer: Sam Raimi

Co-Executive Producer: Jerry Patrick Brown

Co-Executive Producer: Robert Bielak

Co-Executive Producer: Eric Gruendemann

Producer: Liz Friedman

Co-Producers: David Eick, Paul Robert Coyle

New Zealand Producer: Chloe Smith

Coordinating Producer: Bernadette Joyce

Music by Joseph Lo Duca

Bibliography

Readings on the Greek Myths

Among many sources that helped me in preparing this book, I found the following of special value: Robert Graves, *The Greek Myths*, complete and unabridged edition (Wakefield, Rhode Island: Moyer and Bell, 1988); Michael Grant and John Hazel, *Who's Who in Classical Mythology* (New York: Oxford, 1993); Edward Tripp, *The Meridian Handbook of Classical Mythology* (New York: New American Library, 1974); J. E. Zimmerman, *Dictionary of Classical Mythology* (New York: Bantam, 1964); and *The Chiron Dictionary of Greek and Roman Mythology: Gods and Goddesses, Heroes, Places, and Events of Antiquity*, translated by Elizabeth Burr (Wilmette, Illinois: Chiron Publications, 1994).

Young readers may enjoy learning more about the Greek myths from Ingri and Edgar P. D'Aulaire's *D'Aulaire's Book of Greek Myths* (New York: Doubleday, 1962); Cheryl Evans, *Greek Myths and Legends*, illustrated by Rodney Matthews (London: Urborne House, 1985); Aliki, *The Gods and Goddesses of Olympus* (New York: HarperCollins, 1994); and Bernard Evslin, Dorothy Evslin, and Ned Hoopes, *The Greek Gods*, illustrated by William Hunter (New York: Scholastic, 1966).